The  Body in the

Ditch

Phillip Strang

BOOKS BY PHILLIP STRANG

DCI Isaac Cook Series

MURDER IS A TRICKY BUSINESS
MURDER HOUSE
MURDER IS ONLY A NUMBER
MURDER IN LITTLE VENICE
MURDER IS THE ONLY OPTION
MURDER IN NOTTING HILL
MURDER IN ROOM 346
MURDER OF A SILENT MAN
MURDER HAS NO GUILT
MURDER IN HYDE PARK
SIX YEARS TOO LATE
MURDER WITHOUT REASON

DI Keith Tremayne Series

DEATH UNHOLY
DEATH AND THE ASSASSIN'S BLADE
DEATH AND THE LUCKY MAN
DEATH AT COOMBE FARM
DEATH BY A DEAD MAN'S HAND
DEATH IN THE VILLAGE
BURIAL MOUND
THE BODY IN THE DITCH

Steve Case Series

HOSTAGE OF ISLAM
THE HABERMAN VIRUS
PRELUDE TO WAR

Standalone Books

MALIKA'S REVENGE

Copyright Page

Dedication

For Elli and Tais who both had the perseverance to make me sit down and write.

Chapter 1

Ring a ring o' roses
A pocketful of posies
atishoo, atishoo
We all fall down.

The four girls seemed oblivious to those around them as they stood in a circle holding hands and dancing, dropping to the ground at the end of each verse. Sergeant Clare Yarwood – she had retained her maiden name in the police force after her marriage even though she had been married to Clive Grantley for four months – looked over at them. The scene troubled her.

Inspector Tremayne took no notice, not out of disinterest, but to him, seeing young children playing games was part of his generation, not Clare's. Nowadays, they were more interested in messaging each other, playing with their iPads and smartphones.

'If you could go somewhere else to play,' Clare said to the group. 'This is not a place for you to be.'

The four girls took no notice, just kept on with their song.

1

The King has sent his daughter
To fetch a pail of water
atishoo, atishoo
We all fall down.

Clare left them and walked to the other side of the farmyard. A rusting tractor stood over in the distance, its wheels sunken into the mud, and a couple of dogs lazed to one side of an old barn, catching the sun's rays.

Apart from the four girls, the immediate area was empty apart from Clare and the curmudgeonly Tremayne, a man who had guided her career, helped her through the difficult period when her then-fiancé Harry Holchester had died saving her life.

Her mother had been viperous when Clare had first told her that she was marrying Clive Grantley, a man nearly twenty years older than her. Accusations such as being a rich man's bit of fluff, getting a few months more out of his waning libido with her, were not wanted, untrue and insensitive.

However, her father had made an excellent speech at the wedding, welcoming Clive into the family; her mother not saying much, a blessing in disguise.

'It'd help if you got rid of those children,' Tremayne said, finally tired of their repetitive singing. He was looking into a ditch.

'I've tried,' Clare replied.

An old woman stood alongside Tremayne. She was dressed in overalls, a peaked cap on her head.

Clare didn't need an introduction as Bess Carmichael was a well-known local character in the small village near to the farm due to her unusual lifestyle, living as she did in an old and decrepit caravan that was

2

permanently parked down a narrow lane not far from the farm.

'You did the right thing, calling us,' Tremayne said.

'I came over to see if I could help out at the farm,' the old woman said. Clare knew that Bess Carmichael's 'help' referred to taking anything discarded that could be useful.

Tremayne had to admit to a soft spot for the woman; harmless eccentrics were fine by him.

'They're blind to the world, those four,' Bess said.

'You've seen them before?'

'Sometimes, not that they cause me any trouble.'

In the ditch, the body of a woman, her age unclear as she was covered by a plastic sheet, the top of her head just visible.

'This is how you found her?' Tremayne asked.

'I was coming across the field from my place,' Bess said. 'I tripped, not so young anymore, and fell down there with her. When I got out, I could see that the plastic had moved. It gave me the fright of my life. That's why I phoned you.'

'It's a good job you did. Has anyone else been near?'

'No one else, not since I've been here. I phoned you, Inspector. I knew you and your sergeant wouldn't give me trouble, an old woman like me, not in good health.'

'You'll outlive us all,' Clare said.

Over the other side of the farmyard, the four girls continued to play.

> *The bird upon the steeple*
> *Sits high above the people*

3

> *atishoo, atishoo*
> *We all fall down.*

'What's up with those girls?' Tremayne said.

It's that leader of theirs, feeds them all sorts of nonsense,' Bess said scathingly.

'Have you seen anything in particular?' Tremayne had heard the rumours, local gossip mainly, but a body in a ditch pointed to something sinister.

'The authorities have given this place a clean bill of health,' Clare said. 'If they want to live communally, there's not much anyone can do. The children attend school, and there's no sign of abuse.'

'Still, it's odd,' Tremayne said. 'Those four girls, they don't stop.'

Clare walked over to the girls. This time she didn't just speak, she took hold of the shoulder of one of them, a dark-haired girl, her hair tied in ponytails.

'You've seen us here, aren't you curious?' Clare said. 'There's a body in the ditch over there. Do you know who it is?'

'That's Charlotte.'

'Aren't you upset?'

'Why would we be?' the young girl said.

As Clare walked away, the four girls continued with their nursery rhyme.

> *The cows are in the meadow*
> *Lying fast asleep*
> *atishoo, atishoo*
> We all get up again.

***

Jim Hughes, the senior crime scene investigator, was the first person to fully pull back the plastic sheeting that covered the body. He, like Tremayne, did not grimace at the sight of the dead woman.

'What can you tell us?' Tremayne said. He was standing away from the ditch, ostensibly to maintain an air of authority. The truth, if he had been honest, was that he was concerned that the slippery muddy sides of the ditch might have proved too much for him to navigate, his knees giving him more trouble than he cared to admit to.

Hughes, a younger man than the inspector, only five years older than Clare's thirty-eight, had got the measure of Tremayne. Don't give him an inch, hold your ground, and sarcasm came in handy.

'I've been here two minutes, and you want a full report, is that it?' he said as he handed the plastic to one of his team.

'Just enough for us to be going on with.'

'Female.'

'That much we've got already. What else?'

'Eighteen to twenty-five, caucasian, no visible cause of death,' Hughes said. 'Natural causes don't seem to be an option.'

'They're a bunch of weirdos in that farm,' Bess Carmichael said.

Which to Clare was the pot calling the kettle black. A woman in her eighties who went in for petty thieving, haranguing anyone who came near to her caravan, and regarded overalls and a baseball cap as appropriate wear would easily have qualified for the title herself.

The group that occupied the farm were known to be unusual, even if the consensus view was that they were harmless, and they had endeared themselves to the local community by their acts of benevolence and their willingness to help out others in need, and the children were well balanced and doing well at school.

On the other side of the farmyard, several uniforms were attempting to bring the inhabitants of the farm together. The four girls who had been playing were now sitting in the porch of the farmhouse. Clare looked over, wondered what to make of them.

Tremayne's focus still rested with the body. Jim Hughes looked perplexed.

'What is it?' Tremayne asked.

'No weapon, no sign of force, no obvious signs of violence or maltreatment. It's as if the woman just laid down there and died. Almost as if she had willed her death.'

Tremayne had seen enough dead bodies to know that it was murder. His wife, Jean, two nights ago had told him that he was a cynic, always seeing the worst in people, the negativity of society. He knew that she was right, but nobody lasts for more than three decades in Homicide without acquiring a jaundiced outlook on life in general and people in particular.

'Most of those who live here are present,' Clare said after she had walked back to where Tremayne was standing.

'Who's in charge?' Tremayne's reply when he returned with her, not that he needed to ask as Professor Eustace Hampton was known to him.

'She was a good person', the professor, a man in his seventies, said. His long white hair was tied, his balding head only too visible.

To Tremayne, he was a comical figure with his attempts at dressing as though he was in his teens.

Hampton, who had a weekly programme on television, and was in demand as a public speaker, believed that death was a result of a negative attitude, and the secret to a long and fulfilling life was an inquiring mind and a resistance to the ageing process both mentally and physically, which explained why every day, rain or shine, the man could be seen running through the fields in the area and up through the village.

Hampton was an anachronism, the type of person that was admired by many, scorned by a few, but also loved devotedly by others, the reason he had attracted a disparate group of people to join him; some of them former drug addicts, others, professional people. The group of twenty-four who regarded the farm as home, although now more correctly twenty-three as one of his group was dead, were people who had been lost and had found solace in listening to and being guided by a charismatic man.

'Her name?' Tremayne asked.

'Charlotte Merton.'

'We need to inform her next of kin.'

'There are none that I know of.'

'Is that because once they join with you, they renounce their past, hand over their worldly goods?'

Hampton, unflappable under provocation, stood firm. 'Charlotte had been orphaned as a child and raised by a succession of foster parents. A troubled individual until she had come here. And as for those here, they are not required to hand over their worldly goods, only to pay their costs and to help with looking after the place. You, Inspector Tremayne, know this. This is not the first time we've spoken, is it?'

Tremayne realised he had been harsh with the man. It was just that he knew that when there was a dead

7

body, it was essential to rachet up the tempo, to make people sweat, to get them to react.

'Okay, Hampton, I'll grant that we know each other, not sure than I ever understood where you're coming from, or even half of what you say, but we've got a dead woman. You knew her, and she was one of yours, which places you and your people front and centre as the primary suspects. What's the truth?'

'The truth, my dear Inspector,' Hampton said, Tremayne wincing at the 'dear' appellation, 'is that I don't know how she died, and as to finding her in that ditch, if it hadn't been for Bess, it would have been one of us who would have phoned the police.'

Tremayne didn't feel comfortable with the answer, as Jim Hughes had estimated that the woman's body had been under the plastic for at least two hours.

Tremayne and Clare walked with the professor over to the main house, Bess Carmichael not far behind.

'Ladies and gentlemen,' Tremayne said to the gathering in the front room of the house, a blazing log fire in the hearth behind him. Outside it had been cold; inside it was hotter than Tremayne would have liked. He took off his heavy overcoat and hung it on a hook on the back of one of the doors. 'A woman has died here today. One of your group, I am informed.'

'That's correct,' Hampton said. He was standing beside Tremayne, attempting to exert his authority, to show a willingness to help the police in their investigation. Whatever it was, Tremayne knew it wasn't going to work. Professor Eustace Hampton, regardless of his record of academia, his agreeable manner, his willingness to drink a pint of beer with Tremayne occasionally, was, as Bess Carmichael had put it, a weirdo.

But then, Keith Tremayne, not that anyone ever called him Keith, not even his wife, saw the world as black and white, not as shades of grey, and certainly not whatever colour Hampton and his followers saw.

'If you don't mind,' Tremayne said to Hampton, 'I'd appreciate it if you take a seat with the others.'

Hampton meekly obliged and sat down. An academic specialising in the history of alternative cultures, ancient history and primitive religions, he had rejected university life and formed a collective in Wiltshire dedicated to advancing the mind.

'Charlotte was a good person,' Hampton's wife said. She was sitting next to her husband, her arm around his waist. The one-time model, even a centrefold in Playboy in her more rebellious years, and the mother of Hampton's only son, Todd, was as well known as her husband. She'd had a troubled upbringing in the north of England, the daughter of a wealthy businessman and his mistress, although the man had done his duty and ensured that she and her mother had had a comfortable existence, a small cottage, a good education for the child.

Miranda, although models were not given the pre-nomenclature of 'super' back then, had indeed been that. As an adult, her outbursts of antisocial behaviour, drug-taking, even being escorted off a plane at Heathrow once, had deemed her fodder for the newspapers and the scurrilous magazines.

The woman's life changed when at the age of thirty-seven she had married the professor, a man ten years older than her. Todd, the couple's progeny, was not present.

Tremayne looked around the room, counted twenty-one people. 'I thought there were twenty-three.'

'Two are not here today,' Hampton said.

'Your son?'

'He doesn't live here with us.'

'We'll need everyone's name,' Clare said.

'Charlotte is not the victim of foul play,' Hampton said as he looked around at those behind him. The others nodded their heads as one.

'That's for Pathology, but what we have here, murder or no murder warrants a full investigation. You don't cover a dead body with plastic sheeting, leave it for a few hours and then tell us that you intended to contact us as soon as possible. The woman was young. How old was she, by the way?'

'Twenty-four,' a voice from the rear of the room.

'Granted that she may have been adopted and she may not have known her birth parents, but someone somewhere out there is related to her. We need to find them, find out about her background.'

'You make out that we're involved,' Hampton said.

'It's your farm, your ditch. Someone's not telling us the full story, and until we understand why and who, nobody's going anywhere.'

Tremayne was frustrated. A woman was dead, yet no one expressed any sorrow. There should be remorse; it was a natural human reaction, yet none seemed capable.

Chapter 2

Stuart Collins, the pathologist, commenced the autopsy on Charlotte Merton's body within two hours of it arriving at Pathology, an unusually prompt response from him.

Jim Hughes hadn't seen it, as the body had been covered in mud in the ditch, but once cleaned and prepared for the examination, a small puncture mark in the woman's neck had been only too apparent.

'I can't give you any details at this time,' Collins said to Tremayne who was still at the farm, wading through the blank expressions, trying to get some reaction, to get someone to say something other than Charlotte had been a good person.

Bess Carmichael sat on a hard wooden chair, observing all that was happening, and even though she was eighty-five, going on eighty-six – she was keen to emphasise that point – she was alert and keeping a close watch on everyone.

'What do you reckon?' Tremayne said to Collins. 'I've got a group here who say her death was natural, and that they intended to contact us, but nothing more.'

'You know I'm not going to commit that the injection killed her, not yet, not without further checks.'

'Give me something.'

'From where the needle entered, she couldn't have done it herself.'

'This is murder, plain and simple, and I've got a murderer here. One of these starry-eyed fools.'

'The autopsy will reveal more.'

11

'Any idea what she could have been injected with?'

'A fast-acting barbiturate, muscle relaxant, and if the woman had been a heroin addict, then an embolism if the syringe had contained air, but that's unlikely, although she may have had a weakened heart, a deficient immune system. Don't hold me to this. I'm just giving you something to go on.'

'Thanks for your help.'

'Don't thank me, and don't ask me again. You'll have my report tomorrow.'

Tremayne knew that he had pushed his luck, asking for an opinion, but neither he nor Clare was making any headway at the farm.

'So, let me get this straight, you're telling me there is nothing suspicious,' Clare said to one of the women. As with the others at the farm, she was slim, probably due to them embracing veganism, fine in itself, as Clare rarely ate meat, fish only occasionally.

The four girls had been spoken to, although they had given little more than when they had been outside in the farmyard. They all attended school, were doing well academically, as the principal at the school had said when she had been visited by a constable from Bemerton Road. Clare wasn't sure whether the principal had realised the implication of the question, or if she was giving the standard reply.

'I can't say that I know Charlotte that well,' the woman said. 'She arrived here last year, October or November, but I can't remember the exact date.'

'Tell me about her.'

'She was troubled when she arrived, but with time, she settled down.'

'Troubled?'

'Drugs, probably. We don't judge a person's past, only what they are here.'

'It helps to know, though.'

'I wouldn't agree with that.'

'You wouldn't, or are you mouthing Eustace Hampton?'

'Eustace guides us, that's all.'

'In what?'

'In life.'

'Why are you willing to speak when the others aren't?'

'My life was troubled, abusive relationships. Here I am safe and comforted.'

'Not even if Charlotte Merton had been murdered.'

'No one here is capable,' the woman replied indignantly.

'Let us be clear, you do not hold any religious views?'

'We believe in nature, that's all.'

'Any activities that would be regarded as unusual?'

'If you mean wild orgies, demonic voices. I know that's what some people think happens here.'

'Are there?' Clare said.

'We live a contemplative life, and apart from the communal lifestyle, each and every person taking their turn to clean and cook and to help around the place, we keep to ourselves. Those that are married with children have their own space, and no, there is no wife-swapping, nor is there any abuse of the children.'

'Money?'

'We contribute, nothing more. No one has sold their property to come here, handed it over to Eustace. That's not how we live. Eustace believes in a higher plane of consciousness, although what form that takes, we don't always understand; intellectually he is far in advance of any of us.'

'Do you agree with his view?'

'I'm open to the possibility. But it's not of importance, is it?'

'It's all-important. Each piece of knowledge that we acquire helps us to form an understanding as to why Charlotte died.'

'As I said, it wasn't one of us.'

'The four girls when we arrived? Their reaction to her body was not expected.'

'They would not fear death.'

'Indoctrinated?'

'Enlightened,' the woman said. To Clare, it made no sense.

***

Tremayne preferred plain speakers, someone who'd get angry, start to swear, lash out with their feet or fists. But at the farm, four miles from the cathedral city of Salisbury, a ninety-minute train ride from London, an air of serenity prevailed.

Tremayne had interviewed some residents. One of them, Ben Wellesley, had spent a few years in Maidstone Prison, courtesy of Her Majesty, for grievous bodily harm, and the man, as tall as Tremayne, said little, other than to praise Eustace Hampton.

Tremayne persevered, convinced that something was amiss, although according to those who had checked out the small community, there was no sign of drug use.

Frustrated, Tremayne walked over to where Hampton was standing outside the house. 'I can't make sense of this,' he said.

'What is there to make sense of? We live a contemplative life, helping each other as we can, making no demands.'

'That's it. Wellesley had been violent, but here he's semicomatose; the man's got no spark in him.'

'We do not judge a person by his past.'

To Tremayne, once a villain, always a villain, and even if the person never commits another crime, the possibility remains. Scratch the surface, and not too deep, and there is the real person. But he had tried that with Ben Wellesley, and he hadn't got any reaction to indicate that lurking under the surface was a man who had almost killed another outside a pub not far from Salisbury.

'We're convinced that Charlotte Merton was murdered,' Tremayne said to Hampton. One of them was taking deep breaths, savouring the fresh air; the other was desperate to light up a cigarette. But it was Tremayne who was to be disappointed as his cigarette smoking days were behind him now.

It still didn't seem right to him – a seasoned police officer should be down the pub for a drink, and he should definitely smoke. The modern police officer, exemplified by his sergeant, although he made allowances for her, was too gentle on the villains, too politically correct.

Tremayne, if he had been honest, wanted to take Hampton's community and place them all in the cells at Bemerton Road Police Station, and to wait it out till the conditioning they had been subjected to had been broken. Hampton, to him, was not all that he appeared to be. He hadn't given it much thought before, as the man had always been agreeable company.

'The problem is, Hampton,' Tremayne continued, 'you and I are at odds here. You seem to show no interest that the woman died.'

'Inspector, if you spent time with us, you'd understand. I am very much concerned that Charlotte is no longer here.'

'What would I understand?'

'That Charlotte is at peace.'

'She's dead, murdered, not at peace, not in Heaven, or communing with mystical beings. Someone killed her for a reason, and it's for me to find out. Hampton, you're a clever man, much cleverer than I am, that's for sure. How can you act as if nothing has happened? And what about the four girls that were playing a game in the farmyard when we arrived. Are you going to tell me that their behaviour was normal?'

'Before the advent of the television, modern communications, the internet, young people occupied their time more productively.'

'They do go to school, don't they?'

'You know they do. We can't ignore the modern world, but we choose to maintain it at a distance as much as we can. Here, in our small corner of the universe, technology does not control our lives. Sure, we have cars, and those that need to make an income have computers and mobile phones, but it's moderated.'

'By you?'

'By consensus. Don't portray me as a mystic, nor as a religious figure. I'm neither. Just a believer in a simpler, more caring world. Out there, we must go,' Hampton said, pointing to the world beyond the farm, 'but we come back here to reflect and to remove the negativity.'

'The world's complex, full of good and bad.'

'In here, the good outweighs the bad.'

'The bad has entered, taken control. Don't you understand that?'

'Even if I conceded to you on this, don't expect us to react as you would expect. We will, when appropriate, express our feelings to Charlotte, but not here, not now. I'm afraid, Tremayne, that what you want from us, you can't have.'

'Yet one of your group is, unless I'm mistaken, and I rarely am, a murderer.'

'If, as you say, it is one of us, standing here worrying will do no good.'

'It was Bess Carmichael who said you were a bunch of weirdos,' Tremayne said. 'It appears she was right.'

'We are, don't you see. The best kind, the kind that leaves well alone, gains from each other.'

***

Jim Hughes and his team checked over where the dead woman had lived, a room in one of the more substantial barns. The area had been partitioned, the room sizes according to the numbers of inhabitants. The families had small apartments on the upper level, the single people on the ground floor. Hughes could see that the conversions had been professionally done. Later it would be found out that the work had been a community effort, and that Ben Wellesley, a skilled tradesman, had taken overall control. A structural engineer had prepared a detailed plan of the work needed to convert the barn into accommodation, and from Hughes' limited knowledge of the subject, the work had been done correctly. It did not, however, obviate the fact that planning permission had never been given because the necessary paperwork hadn't been submitted.

Hampton and officialdom did not go arm in arm. Quite the opposite in fact and his agreeable demeanour belied a wish for the police and their entourage of experts and vehicles, especially the floodlights at night, to be gone as soon as possible.

He knew he had to deal with the situation, but it was contrary to what he was trying to achieve. Officialdom, university procedures, unnecessary rules and regulations were anathema to him, especially after he had been found cavorting with one of his female students; neither was underage, but it was deemed in bad taste.

She was the daughter of a man of the church; he, an older man who had seduced her. It was the girl's father, a brash and devout Yorkshireman, who had demanded action, as his daughter, although academically gifted, suffered from schizophrenia, and Hampton and his pursuit of her, after years of her father berating her for any indiscretion, breathing fire and brimstone about morality and fornication and the wanton ways of the modern generation, had left the woman confused as to what was right and what was wrong.

The father had threatened the university, not that it got him far, other than a letter of apology for the indiscretion of a well-respected professor, but then the young woman, after a thirty-minute lecture back at home, had, in a moment of weakness, walked out onto the Yorkshire Moors in the middle of winter, a blinding snowstorm. The next day she was found huddled in the lee of a rock, dead and frozen stiff.

After that, the university had no option but to let Hampton go, and for the father, once his anger had subsided, to be given a cash payment not to discuss the matter.

Clare sat with the four girls, found them to be bright, but not inquisitive about what had happened. The two youngest were the children of Gavin and Belinda Fitzwilliam. Gavin was the type of man who'd be lost in a crowd of three. It was his wife, Belinda, who ruled the roost in their family.

The two girls, Gwyneth and Matilda, lived with their parents, yet discipline and responsibilities were shared amongst all that resided there, and they, as well as the other two children, one twelve, the other thirteen, saw themselves as part of a larger family.

To Clare, children should be allowed to err, to make mischief, to make wrong decisions about life in general, men in particular, as they grew older. She had, she knew that, and she had turned out alright.

'We knew Charlotte,' Gwyneth said.

'Why didn't you do something when you saw her lying there?' Clare asked.

'We knew she was dead,' the twelve-year-old said.

'Weren't you sorry?'

'Eustace told us that life is transient. We should cherish the living, allow the dead to go.'

'Go where?'

'Just go, nowhere in particular,' Matilda said.

'Where do you think she went?' Clare asked. She was sitting on the floor with the four girls. It was surreal, as when she had been their age, back in Norfolk, friends had been all-important, more so than parents. But not for the four she sat with.

Chapter 3

In the village of Brockenstoke, three hundred yards down the road, even less if a person walked across the fields, conspiracy theories abounded.

'I always knew something was strange about them,' one comment. 'Mad as hatters, the lot of them,' another.

Clare, tired from the long hours and from the frustration of banging her head against a brick wall, met up with Tremayne at the Bell Inn in the village. The gossipmongers were out in force, and the small bar was full. Tremayne looked at the clock and at the publican.

'You can't begrudge me staying open past normal, can you?' he said. It was also the pub where Tremayne and Hampton shared a drink occasionally, and Tremayne wasn't about to complain.

The English pub, one of the two mainstays of British life, along with the church, was being threatened by the modern age. A quiet pint of a night, a convivial atmosphere, had held people together for centuries, forming a sense of community, but now with the car, cheap alcohol from supermarkets, streaming videos and cinema complexes, the pub was endangered, and many had already closed. The Bell Inn, apart from this one night of drama, was heading for closure. The publican had admitted that to Tremayne on more than one occasion. 'I paid a lot of money, but what's it worth now?' he had said.

Not that it stopped him downing the profits as he matched Tremayne two to one, and the former heavy imbiber had never been a slouch in downing beer.

'What's the gossip?' Tremayne said. 'Any chance of something to eat?' There was no need to answer the publican's question about still being open; he knew Tremayne well enough to know that he wouldn't be too concerned.

'There are some who are willing to grant that they've caused no harm,' the publican said. 'Others believe Hampton's the devil incarnate, dancing naked around an oak tree, orgies every night, and some of the theories, you don't want to know about.'

'The children?' Clare said.

'That's about it.'

'What do you reckon, and I'll have what you're getting the inspector.'

'A meat pie, then. It'll be hot.'

Clare looked at where the meat pies were kept, a glass cabinet to one side of the bar. The pies looked good, but not the publican with his beer belly, his bulbous red nose, his unshaven face. On the walls of the pub, the ubiquitous horseshoes, an oil painting of a country scene: undulating hills, a solitary house in the distance. Clare, no expert, knew that the picture had little value, and it did not enhance the general rundown look of the pub.

After a short time in the microwave the pies appeared, two sachets of tomato sauce as condiments. Tremayne held a pint of beer in his hand; Clare, a red wine.

'You never answered the question,' Tremayne said as he bit into his pie.

'Hampton's an oddball, but there's no one there that I wouldn't invite into my house. One or two must

21

have a record, but if they have, there's never been any trouble, and they spend their money in the local shop.'

'In here?'

'Only Hampton. The others don't drink, one of the rules, I suppose.'

'Then why does he drink if he forbids others?'

'You'd have to ask him,' the publican said as he pulled another pint for one of the patrons who was also breaking the law by purchasing a drink after hours.

Outside, a police car pulled up.

Clare went and had a word with the two incumbents of the vehicle before they left.

'Thanks for that,' the publican said.

'Not the first time, is it?' Tremayne said as he put down his empty glass. The publican took it to fill.

Clare looked over at Tremayne.

'Don't worry. It's my last for the evening, and you don't need to phone Jean, not tonight.'

'Ball and chain,' the publican joked.

'I've got my own conspiracy, and it's not a theory. At home, my wife in my ear to moderate my ways, and at work, my sergeant. Thick as thieves, the two of them.'

'It's only because we love you,' Clare said, enjoying the momentary respite from the doom and gloom of another murder investigation.

Tremayne wanted to offer a pithy comment, but he couldn't think of an appropriate one, and besides, he liked being fussed over. One of the benefits of his advancing years, his declining health, he'd have to admit.

'Did anybody here know the dead woman?' Tremayne asked as he took the first drink from his freshly pulled pint.

'A few of us would have. I knew her, not well, but sometimes she'd come up, have a chat, bring me a few eggs, and I'd give her a few vegetables from my garden. I liked her, not that I can tell you a lot about her. She wasn't the sort of person to speak about her past, although she seemed happy to be with Hampton and the others.'

'Boyfriends?'

'One of the lads in the village asked her out a couple of times, but she wasn't interested. Strange, really, as the two of them would have made a good pair.'

'A difficult past?' Clare said.

'As I said, I wouldn't know. But then, most of them down there would have a story to tell. We all do, don't we? I know I have, but I'm not reluctant to talk about it.'

Tremayne knew the man was correct. Everybody had something they regretted, something they wanted to forget. Hiding away on a farm in the countryside hardly seemed the solution, but then, he was like the publican – an open book, what you see is what you get.

Clare said nothing. Her past was not forgotten; for her, it no longer existed as long as she had Clive and her career as a police officer and Tremayne as her inspector. She was sublimely content.

***

Due to the number of people to be interviewed, the questioning continued the following day. On the first day, key persons had been spoken to, preliminary statements taken from others.

Bess Carmichael remained at the farm, finding herself a warm spot in one of the barns, helping herself to the food that was always available in the farmhouse, not that she was partial to salads and lentils, but she wasn't a fussy eater, and raiding the bins outside the fast food outlets in Salisbury had provided her with sustenance on many an occasion.

As it was a school day, the four girls and a boy of nine had gone to school. Clare had watched them leave. They were smartly turned out, and they were getting a rounded education, although to Clare and Tremayne, what sort of education they were getting at the farmhouse was open to speculation.

Hampton reasoned with Tremayne that other members of his group had employment to go to, businesses to run, chores to do, and that the continued police presence was contrary to the harmonious running of the small community.

Tremayne had had to tell Hampton that an inconvenience was the least of his concerns and if the man wanted the police to leave them alone, then it was up to him as their leader to start giving answers to questions and not to prolong the inevitable by insisting that Charlotte Merton had moved to a better place. Not that he had much success as Hampton continued to smile meekly, to answer when spoken to, but nothing more.

And as to where the woman had gone, Hampton was not forthcoming. Tremayne had seen her after Stuart Collins had conducted his autopsy, and she was not in a fit condition to put on her best dress and makeup to go anywhere.

Collins had revealed more facts about the woman. Firstly, judging by the needle marks on her arm, she had still been injecting herself with heroin, contrary to Hampton's insistence that she hadn't. Secondly, she was underweight, verging on malnutrition. Not an unusual condition given her addiction, and the food at the farm, whereas it satisfied hunger, was lacking in vital proteins. For a healthy person, that would have been fine, but not to a drug-addicted female. The third point that Collins revealed was that she was pregnant, eight weeks, possibly longer.

Collins was clear that the woman's lifestyle, her pregnancy, her drug addiction and her lack of the supplements that she would have needed, would not only have placed the unborn child under severe stress but also would have endangered the woman's life.

Tremayne knew he had been right about the group at the farmhouse: they were all deluded and oblivious to life's realities. Also, who else knew she was pregnant? Who was responsible for her delicate condition? Who killed her, and why? Was the pregnancy a factor, or was it unknown by everyone except the woman herself? How could her drug-taking not be noticed, and how had she obtained the drugs? Drugs needed money and a drug dealer, and the village of Brockenstoke hadn't any criminals that were known, apart from Tony Frampton, but the extent of his crimes was stealing chickens, the occasional suckling pig from a local farm. But then everyone knew that the forty-two-year-old Frampton had the intellectual capacity of a child of eight.

'Our Tony, not too bright. Harmless, though,' appeared to be the most frequent comment when anyone was asked in the village.

***

If Charlotte Merton had negatives against her, then who else at the farm who professed good thoughts, ate poorly and wore a perpetual smile of bemusement hid secrets from the others, from the police, Tremayne wondered.

Something seemed out of kilter to the police inspector. Too many years in the force, he knew, had made him cynical. Give him an old-fashioned villain, he could understand them, but those who were smart could be manipulators of the truth, even capable of deceiving themselves.

'Hampton, Pathology has given us a report on Charlotte Merton,' Tremayne said. He could see that the group's leader was tiring of the police presence.

Hampton said nothing, just looked up at the sky. The two men were standing outside the farmhouse. It was a clear night.

'I'm talking to you.' Tremayne grabbed the man by his right arm and shook it.

'It's beautiful, isn't it?'

'What? Charlotte Merton's death?'

'No, of course not.'

'Hampton, you're starting to get on my nerves. What's so beautiful that you can't deal with reality?'

'The infinity of the universe.'

Tremayne looked up. He couldn't find anything to comment about.

'The statistical probability of intelligent life elsewhere,' Hampton continued.

'Coming back to Planet Earth, the village is having a field day with you,' Tremayne said in exasperation. 'Charlotte Merton was not only injecting herself with heroin, but she was also pregnant. How does that tally with your belief that every one of your group has renounced their sins and chosen a life of contemplation?'

'Once again, Tremayne, we're not religious, we're not mad.'

'Charlotte Merton! Pregnant!' Tremayne emphasised the two statements.

A bland look from Hampton, a condescending smile. 'I knew,' he said.

'Your child?'

'I'm too old to be bringing another child into the world, and besides, I've got Miranda. What would I want with another woman?'

'Would Charlotte have been available if you had?'

'Undoubtedly.'

'Your charisma?'

'People here see me as someone special, but I'm not. Sure, I'm more academic than they are, the reason they listen to me. I can converse about subjects that they barely understand. I'm here to guide them to a better lifestyle, more self-sufficient. A rejection of the more corrosive elements of modern society. I am not here to brainwash the gullible, seduce the available.'

'But you said she would have been.' Tremayne fumbled in his pocket for a cigarette, only found a piece of chewing gum. He removed the wrapper and put it in his mouth.

'Charlotte had led a troubled life, but we've already spoken about that. She was a free spirit and easily led astray. We used to speak about it, the men she had known, the men who had slept with her, either tossing her away or else stringing her along for a few weeks, only to dump her eventually.'

'She was attractive. She could have found someone decent.'

'Her neuroses would have driven them away. She was subject to mood swings; whether they were medical or emotional on account of her past history, I don't know. All I know is that here amongst us she was content.'

'Happy?'

27

'Happiness is a construct of childhood. As adults, there are too many issues to deal with. Contentment is what we can hope for, although not many attain it. Are you a contented man, Tremayne?'

'I'm not the issue here.'

'But are you?'

'I'd say so. I've got Jean and a good life.'

'Before?'

'There have been times when it's not been so good.'

'Here on the farm, we talk through those times, ease the pain.'

'It didn't stop the woman getting pregnant.'

'Your next question will be, who's the father?'

'Psychic?' Tremayne said scathingly.

'It's an obvious question.'

'What's the answer?'

'I don't know.'

'Someone here?'

A resigned look on Hampton's face. 'I hope not, but I can't be sure.'

'The drugs?'

'Charlotte helped out around the place, but she spent time in the village. I'd ask there.'

'Did she go anywhere else?'

'It's possible, but I don't believe so. She was comfortable to be here with us.'

'Who else knew she was pregnant?'

'No one. Charlotte confided in me. I've not told anyone, not even my wife.'

'And when it had become obvious?'

'We would have protected her and the child.'

'Who do you suspect in the village?' Tremayne asked. He felt he was making headway, albeit haltingly.

'She was friendly with the publican.'

'He's not a young man, not her sort.'

'Charlotte would have had no issue, a small cost to pay.'

'Is that how she obtained the drugs?'

'Probably.'

'Did she tell you that she was still injecting?'

'She didn't have to. I could see the signs, the needle marks, her behaviour. I never mentioned it to her. Preaching would not have served any purpose. In time, she would have come to me, to all of us, and we would have rallied around, helped her through the difficult times.'

'Did you like her?'

'Very much. Kindred spirit. I was rebellious in my youth, drug-taking, plenty of women. She would have matured eventually.'

***

Clare had ordered a pub lunch for her and Tremayne after he had phoned her. In the pub, on his arrival, a pint of beer and a shepherd's pie.

Tremayne liked the look of the beer and the pie, not so much the publican who stood behind the bar.

'What is it?' Clare asked after her senior had downed half of his glass, looked over at the barman for a refill, thinking twice about it, before planting the glass on the table. It wasn't only his sergeant who'd be reporting to his wife if he strayed and drank too much, it was him as well, knowing only too well that what we like isn't always good for us.

'Hampton's fingered the publican as a probable lover of Charlotte Merton.'

'It hardly seems likely,' Clare said as she looked over at the man. Clive, her husband, seventeen years her senior, was probably the same age as the publican, but the difference between the two men was startling. Clive was upright, the mayor of Salisbury; the publican was in bad health, his skin pock-marked, his ruddy complexion proof of his unhealthy lifestyle. She tried to imagine the woman in the ditch and the pub owner entwined. It was not a pleasant thought, and she turned back to her meal and to Tremayne.

'All sorts to make a world,' Tremayne said. 'There's still life in us old dogs,' he jested, although it was not a joke in good taste.

Clare ignored his attempt at levity, sometimes necessary with a homicide. 'Why would she have chosen him?' she said.

'According to Hampton, she was friendly with him. The woman was pregnant, so that's one against the man.'

Clare looked over at the publican and raised her glass of wine and nodded over at Tremayne. Tremayne was on a roll, and an extra pint would be needed.

'He's already said that he used to speak to her, exchange eggs for vegetables.'

'We can accept that, but she was getting drugs from somewhere.'

'Another exchange?'

'Hampton reckoned the woman was easy, so you'd better check that. See where she was before she arrived at the farm. How did she know about it? Had she seen the man on the television, attended one of his speeches?'

'Or slept with him?'

'That's it, Yarwood. Get down in the dirt, explore what's in the gutter. Hampton's not Mr Perfect, no matter what his disciples think of him.'

'You said he wasn't religious.'

'That's what he said, but what possesses sane people to join a group such as his? I spend all my time trying to get away from them.'

'But you, Inspector, are an anachronism. A pint in your hand and you're everyone's friend. Sober and you're taciturn, barely willing to give a person the time of day.'

'Yarwood, you're treading on thin ice,' Tremayne said. 'Mayoress or not, you're still a serving police officer, subject to reprimand.'

'Yes, sir,' Clare said, knowing full well it was just the harmless banter of two people who respected each other. It was why she enjoyed working with the man; why she was concerned about his health. She looked at his second pint of beer, half-empty. 'That's your lot for today. We've got work to do, and you've not finished what you were telling me.'

'According to Hampton, he knew about the pregnancy, as the woman had told him. The drug-taking he knew, but he had deduced that from the marks on her skin, the way she acted.'

'He was open with you or spinning tales to make you go away, to chase a red herring?'

'Probably the latter, but let's go with what we've got. The woman was injecting herself, so an air embolism is a possibility. Which means someone knew that and that someone had to have been in the area when she died.'

'Which means that person was visible.'

'Exactly. Someone at the farm could be covering up for someone else. Why, we don't know, other than

Hampton would protect the sanctity of the place at all costs.'

'So would his wife. I checked her out,' Clare said. She took a drink from her glass of wine. Over at the bar, the publican looked across, anxious to see if they wanted refills. After the hubbub of the night before, when the villagers had been out in force, the pub was empty apart from an old man, his walking frame to one side as he drank his beer.

Clare nodded at the publican, shortening the space between her outstretched hands to half. The publican, used to cryptic signs, understood that Tremayne was to get a half-pint.

'What about his wife?'

'She had led a wild life, probably no different to Charlotte Merton, but she had had money, a successful career, a jet-setting lifestyle. Also, she came from a stable family situation, and in time, she found Hampton and settled down.'

'Former lovers?'

'Some famous, one infamous.'

'The infamous one interests me more.'

'A conman, swindled plenty of people in his time. He swindled one too many people; an inside job at the prison and the man had an unfortunate accident in the metalworking shop with a nail gun.'

'Anything else?'

'As her career stalled and the photoshoots became less exotic, she ended up in a couple of magazines devoted to the female form. Nothing too risqué, although not something you'd want to show your staid and narrow-minded aunt.'

'My aunt would have loved it,' Tremayne said. 'She was always up for a few drinks and a dirty joke.'

32

'Like aunt, like nephew.'

'Yarwood, that sarcastic tongue of yours again.'

'Do we suspect that our publican friend was trading drugs for favours?' Clare said, not reacting to Tremayne's comment.

'Anyone else in the village with anything to say?'

'I'm still working my way through them. Some don't want to open the door, some have got too much to say, and others have an opinion, but either doesn't tell us the truth or just waffle.'

'No different to anywhere else,' Tremayne said as he finished off his half-pint.

Chapter 4

The children of Hampton's followers as well as the village children all got onto the bus of a morning and headed into Salisbury. Clare had observed them from a distance. The farm children filed on quietly, the village children and those from a small housing development at one end of the village, the only new buildings of any substance in fifty years, did not. It was jostling from the boys, chattering from the girls. The subdued behaviour of Gwyneth and Matilda Fitzwilliam, and of Sally and Bronwyn Reece, was incongruous; only the nine-year-old boy, identified as Tommy Yardley, the child of John and Eva, acted as he should have, and he had elbowed one of the village boys as they clambered up the steps onto the bus.

Clare knew that Hampton's insistence that it was a harmonious community of like-minded people didn't hold true. She was determined to dig deeper, to ingratiate herself, to act as though she understood them.

Clive, her husband, a logical and self-contained man, had advised her to be careful.

Life was good with Clive, she knew that. It wasn't only love that had drawn them together; it was a melding of two personalities, each complementing the other, each taking the edge off the negatives that everyone has.

Clare had been absorbed by Harry Holchester when he had been alive, not seeing past her love for him, his love for her. She and Tremayne had been investigating a series of seemingly unconnected murders, culminating in a confrontation where the two of them had almost lost their lives. And there was Harry, the love of her life, the man she had pledged herself to, right there in front of her, and not once had she suspected that he was one of the most malevolent of the killers. It had been his selfless action that had saved her, and she had forgiven him. One day she thought that she would revisit his grave, but she would take Clive with her.

Clare watched the bus leave, noticing a laptop in Sally Reece's backpack, the shape of a phone. She then drove down to the farm. The crime scene investigators had departed, and it looked idyllic. But apart from idyllic, nothing else seemed right – nobody was to be seen.

Clare, aware of the need for caution, phoned Tremayne, told him where she was and what she was up to. His advice had been to wait for him. She had said that time was of the essence, and she needed to find out why the place was so quiet. Tremayne knew she was right, and besides, it was what he would have done, but he asked her to leave her phone on, so that he could listen in, and record it as well.

Clare peered through a window of the farmhouse; nobody could be seen. On the cooker in the kitchen, a meal was partly prepared.

Deciding that the farmhouse offered nothing more, Clare headed for the barn that had been converted into accommodation, still disturbed by the silence. It wasn't as if they had all disappeared, as the children had just left for school, and two of the three cars that had been parked there the day before were still there.

At the rear of the barn, no one could be seen. Looking further, advising Tremayne as she moved – he was in his car and on the way out to the farm – she turned another corner. In front of her: Hampton and his wife, Gavin and Belinda Fitzwilliam, Ben and the other members of the community.

Hampton looked around at Clare. Had they known all along that she was at the farm, she wondered. 'We just found her,' he said.

Clare spoke first to Tremayne. 'Get Jim Hughes and his team down here.'

Tremayne needed no more information. He'd be at the farm within fifteen minutes. He phoned Hughes who acted immediately, and then he called for a couple of uniforms to get out the farm ASAP to establish a crime scene.

Clare's next words: 'Please move away and leave this to the police.'

She had learnt to detach emotion from a murder scene – a necessity to act professionally. So had Tremayne, although he was better than her at it. But even so, Bess Carmichael's body hanging from a protruding beam of the barn, a rope around her neck, was not what she had expected to find.

'We've no idea how she came to be there,' Miranda Hampton said.

Clare looked up at the woman, and at the pulley above her. It was clear that it would have required someone on the ground to pull on the rope to yank her up. Whether she was dead before she had been lifted, or whether she had died up high, struggling to free herself, wouldn't be known until the crime scene investigators had completed their work; until the pathologist had conducted his autopsy.

The scene at the bus stop, the second dead woman. Clare knew that the harmless community of like-minded contemplates was looking increasingly fractured. She feared for the children.

***

Not only did the second death bring renewed focus from the police, but it also alerted social services in Salisbury. The children would not be allowed to remain at the farm any longer, although it would require a court order. Clare would assist, and she hoped that Hampton and the others would realise that it was in the best interests of the children. However, her focus was on murder.

The day stretched into night, interspersed with a lunch at the pub, a stack of sandwiches and soft drinks brought to the site by a patrol car in the evening. Jim Hughes and his team spent time with Bess Carmichael, eventually releasing the rope that held her aloft and lowering her to the ground.

'We'll not gain much from the area,' Hughes said. 'Your bunch of crazy hippies have seen to that.'

'They're not mine,' Clare said. 'And as to whether they're crazy or not, that's for others to determine.'

'I don't need a second opinion, that's two murders.'

'Not open to dispute.'

'Who was she?'

'Bess Carmichael, local character. Lived in a caravan not far from here.'

'We've got our people over there. It's a mess, but apart from that?'

'We're trying to find out her history, next of kin, but that's about it, so far.'

'Any idea why she was killed?'

'Not yet. They know something,' Clare said, lifting her head in the direction of the farmhouse.

'She was old,' Hughes said. 'She probably wouldn't have made much noise, and there wasn't much to her, skin and bones. A woman could have managed it.'

'Except that most of them here are starving themselves on dandelion leaves and what else.'

'Not such a charmed life then?'

'I never thought it was, not really. One murder is circumstantial. It could have been someone not from here, but two…'

'One of them inside?'

'It looks that way,' Clare said.

***

Just after nine in the evening, a BMW arrived at the farmhouse. Clare received a phone call from a uniform stationed at the entrance to the farm. 'He says his name is Todd Hampton.'

The prodigal son, Clare thought. She leant over to Tremayne, who was struggling with the long hours. 'The son is here.'

'If he says more than this lot, it'll be a miracle,' Tremayne said, making sure that Eustace and Miranda Hampton heard his scathing comment.

And that was what the day and the night had been, devoid of emotion. No theatrics, no sadness, no regret that a harmless old woman had died. Nothing could break what held the group as one. Not even the removal of the children from the farm – it hadn't taken a court order, it had been acquiesced to by the parents – and the suggestion by the authorities that the mothers and their children would be put into a hotel in Salisbury for the next three days.

The children had spent the day at school, oblivious to what was happening at the farm, and when they arrived back in the village, the mothers were there to welcome them, two police officers in attendance, told not to intrude but to ensure that the adults didn't coach the children on what to say.

Clothes had been packed for them: a small suitcase each for the children, a larger one for each of the mothers. A small bus had transported the five children and the three mothers to their hotel. Preliminary statements from the children had revealed nothing new, but then they hadn't said much when Charlotte had died.

Clare would give the children a day away from the farm, and then talk to them again, see if they were more communicative. She didn't hold out much hope.

It was Ben, the former man of violence, who had found Bess Carmichael. 'I looked up, and there she was,' he said. A strong man, his contribution to the farm as he had no money, apart from casual labouring, was to deal with the more demanding maintenance. The previous summer he had replaced the roof on one of the barns, changed the engine in one of the cars, and repaved the driveway leading up to the farmyard. Tremayne had to give the man his due: he'd done an excellent job from what he could see.

'Is that it, Ben?'

'I don't know how she got up there if that's what you mean?'

'Not entirely,' Tremayne said.

'What do you mean? Okay, I've got a criminal record, but I've done my time.'

Tremayne was determined to continue.

'You're a competent tradesman, I'll grant you that. How did that pulley get up there?'

'I put it there.'

'When?'

'Over a year ago, closer to two. I fitted out the upper level of the barn. It was easier to lift whatever I needed than to struggle up a ladder.'

'Makes sense.' Tremayne could only agree. 'You left the pulley up there.'

'No reason to take it down. It wasn't doing any harm, and if I needed it, I knew where it was.'

'Let's go back to when you fitted out the barn. It would have taken more than one person.'

'Stupid Tony helped me to hump and dump; not much good for anything else.'

'He used the pulley?'

'I was on the rope, he was upstairs pulling whatever was on the end of the rope into the building. You couldn't trust Tony, not with much. One minute he'd be pulling, and then his phone rings, and he'd let go of the rope. They don't call him 'stupid' for nothing.

'They don't call him that from what I've heard.'

'Maybe it's me. But he's stupid, as stupid as they come. Now, I'm not too bright, although Eustace says I'm brighter than I think. He says I need to challenge my energies, to use mind over matter, but I've tried. I can see how to fix things, but don't ask me to explain and don't ask me to write it down.'

'Do you like it here?'

'I never want to leave.'

'Because you're safe?'

'Here, I don't want to hit anyone, and no one's asking me to commit a crime.'

'That's the problem, isn't it, Ben?' Tremayne said. 'Crimes have been committed here. Two of them, murder, the worst kind there is. This place might not be here for much longer, and you'll be out on the street.'

'I'd not want that.'

'Then help me. The others here, they're strange. But you seem to be normal.' Tremayne saw an ally; a former criminal who didn't want to be subjected to temptation again.

'Eustace tries to guide me, so do the others, but I don't understand the metaphysical, the chanting. If he tries to explain, I end up with a headache. Nowadays, he leaves me alone, and sometimes I join in, sometimes I don't. It depends.'

'Depends on what?'

'Depends on me. There's nothing going on here if that's what you're getting at. Not that I mind, and Charlotte, she was a good sort. I fancied her, and sometimes…'

'Sometimes you and she slept together?'

'Charlotte was open to that, not that it happened often.'

'Who else did she sleep with? We don't know much about her, other than she was a heroin addict.'

'She didn't speak to me, not that much. Sometimes, she'd come up to me of a nighttime, tell me she needed a man.'

'Was she easy?'

'She slept around, but I wasn't judging. Easy come, easy go, that's my motto. If she wanted me, I was there, but I never forced her, never asked. It was always Charlotte who made the first move.'

'Who else did she sleep with? You never answered the question.'

'She was friendly with the publican, and she told me that she had been with him once. No idea why as he's fat and ugly. She even tried it on with Stupid Tony once, but he ran a mile.'

'She told you about Tony?'

'It was Tony who told me. We were working on the barn upstairs. I'm holding the hammer, he's holding the wood in place. He starts talking, not unusual as he blabbers on all the time about this and that. Nonsense most of the time, but there he is telling me about Charlotte grabbing his crotch, attempting to get the zip down. The poor fool hadn't a clue what was going on, only that he had run away.'

'We were told that Charlotte was popular.'

'She was, but she'd have these turns. Maybe it was the drugs, maybe it wasn't, but it sure scared Tony. I laughed so much that I dropped the hammer on my foot. I was hobbling around for a couple of days after that, but it was worth it. You don't laugh much around here.'

Tremayne had to agree with Ben. Laughter and the farm didn't go hand in hand. Even on the occasions when he'd shared a pint of beer with Hampton at the pub, the man had not made a joke, yet he had smiled in response to a witticism from Tremayne, more out of politeness than anything else.

'How about the others here?' Tremayne asked.

'Charlotte and me, we're the only two who could be rebellious. The others do what they're told.'

'Told? I was led to believe that people were here of their own free will.'

'People come and go if they want. No one's forced to stay. Not that many leave, certainly not me, but with Charlotte, you couldn't be sure. I used to go around with a rough crowd when I was younger. No doubt you've checked my record.'

'I have,' Tremayne replied. 'Handy with your fists.'

'It was the drink, the reason you'll never see me in the pub.'

'It's not forbidden, other than for Hampton?'

'It's not forbidden for anyone, nothing is. We have these group sessions, where everyone gets a chance to speak, to exorcise the demons.'

'Religious? Hampton always insists the place is not religious.'

'I wouldn't know about that. I don't go to church. Back when I was in prison, we had a chaplain who was keen on converting us to the one true path, not sure what he meant though.'

Tremayne continued to have his suspicions about the community, although he couldn't see anyone stopping Ben from doing what he wanted; the labouring at the farm had developed his muscles, and they bulged. He would have been a formidable street brawler back when he had spent time in the prison cells for being drunk and disorderly. His record was on the police database, and Tremayne had checked it, as he had for the other people at the farm.

Clare was checking on Hampton's reason for his leaving the university where he had lectured. So far, she had found out that there had been a scandal.

Clare had to admit that the thought of children interested her, although Clive, with one daughter of twenty-two, now living with her boyfriend, wasn't sure about a disruption to the lifestyle they enjoyed. Clare knew he'd acquiesce if she pressed the point, but promotion was in the offing, the chance to take over as the senior investigating officer in Homicide when Tremayne retired, if he ever did.

She was convinced they'd drag the man out boots first if he had his way, hers too. And, as for children, she wasn't sure. Her mother had been a nag; she was sure she wouldn't be, but there was a doubt. Years of conditioning from her mother had left its mark.

Ben continued to work as Tremayne stood at his side, handing him tools as required. In the end, Ben tired of speaking and refocussed on his work.

Tremayne discounted Ben as a primary suspect for the time being. He couldn't have killed Charlotte, that had required subtlety, although Bess Carmichael had only needed brute force, and with that, Ben had no difficulty.

Tremayne walked away, wiser than before, but still a long way from uncovering the truth.

***

Outside of the farmhouse, Tremayne came across Todd Hampton. He had been back at his parents' home for three hours, and Tremayne hadn't had a chance to talk to him. The young man was on strict instructions not to leave until he had been interviewed, and a uniform was stationed up at the road.

'Not much of a homecoming,' the young and slightly overweight Hampton said. Tremayne's initial impression, not often wrong, was that the man was not of the ilk of his father.

The two men, one old and feeling it, the other young and clearly enjoying his life away from the farm, walked out into the field behind the farmhouse. A stream flowed through the field, and a bench had been placed there. The two men sat, looked at the clear water, the weeds on the bottom, a couple of fish.

'Not worth bothering with,' Hampton said.

'You're a fisherman?' Tremayne asked, an attempt to overcome the man's reticence, to form a relationship.

Nobody was ruled out in Tremayne's book, not even if the alibi was cast-iron and the person had been a hundred miles away at the time of the offence, although Todd Hampton hadn't provided an alibi yet.

'I spent most of my time away from here. Sometimes in summer, I'd come here and throw a line.'

'Catch any?'

'Here's not the place for fish. On the other side of the village is better, but you need a licence to fish there.'

'Did you have one?'

'As a kid, no. Later on, I used to climb the fence at night, try my luck, catch nothing and then come home.'

'What do you reckon to this place?' Tremayne asked, looking back at the farmhouse and the barns.

'My father believes in it; my mother goes along with it.'

'You don't?'

'A good kick up the arse would do most of them as good as anything.'

'Is that the young man, full of vim and vigour, speaking, or is it what you believe?'

'I was a rebellious kid, and when I reached fourteen, father shipped me off to boarding school. The best thing he could have done for me.'

'You enjoyed it?'

'Fourteen going on eighteen. I always looked older for my age, and after a couple of miserable months, the new boy getting treated as everyone's lackey, I stood up for myself, bashed a few heads, and then it was fine.'

Tremayne approved of the man's take on life. Not that he had experienced bullies at school, and he had not had the benefit of a private school, only what his parents could afford, which was nothing. A state school, short on

45

quality teachers, long on cross-country runs and sports days.

'Eighteen, in the pub?'

'Sixteen. No one asked, not the places we went to. You're a man of the world, Inspector. I can see that, so you won't mind me being honest.'

'Honesty is what I strive for, although I think your father is sparing with it.'

'He's a good man, too smart for his own good. I doubt if I'm the first person to tell you that.'

'You're not. You called the people here losers.'

'Okay, maybe some have issues. Charlotte did, so has Ben, but for the others, I can't make them out. Not that I concern myself too much with them, but life's what you make of it.'

'Life has its ups and downs. You're young, on the up, but what of the others?'

'Father's harmless, and he does good.'

'Your mother?'

'You've seen the pictures?'

'I have.'

'One of my classmates got hold of one of the magazines, started showing it around the school. I beat the hell out of him.'

'What did the others say?'

'I was a hero. Not only had I flattened the school's boxing champion, although it was hardly Queensberry rules, I also had a beautiful mother. Personally, I would have preferred not to have hit him, and for my mother's past to have remained just that.'

'What else about your mother?'

'She was on a downward spiral when she met him. Did you ever watch the movie *Mr Chips,* the stuffy schoolteacher, the young woman?'

'My wife puts it on at Christmas.'

'That's how it was, very romantic. They're perfectly suited to one another, and you'll never get my mother to say anything against my father, no matter what.'

'Even if he committed murder?'

'You're good, Inspector. I'm not a fool, so you don't need to try your tricks on me.'

'It's a valid question,' Tremayne said. 'It needs to be asked.'

'Maybe it does, but I'll not believe bad of my father even if I don't always understand him. They both gave me a good upbringing, and I can only believe the best of them.'

The two men got up from where they had been sitting and walked alongside the stream. It was a cold day, and Tremayne turned up the collar on his jacket; Todd Hampton put his hands in his pockets, his jacket buttons remained undone. Tremayne had to admit the young man was a breath of fresh air after his parents.

'Do you hold with your father's views?'

'He looks for a better world, the same as we all do, but he's an idealist.'

'And you're not?'

'I'm studying law. That soon deals with the idealism. It's good to have people such as my father, and remember, it's only the last few years when he's collected people around him. Only since he became a minor celebrity with his weekly television programme.'

'Deluded fools?'

'Have you checked them all out?'

'We're working through them. Some have pasts they'd rather forget, and there are a few we can't make head nor tail of.'

'I can't help you much,' Todd said as he fastened the buttons on his coat. The air was getting colder, the farm receding from view; in the distance, the bleating of sheep. Tremayne couldn't help but reflect on that day in Avon Hill when the murderous mob had been coming for him and Yarwood and two uniforms, the frantic rush to the patrol car, the hurried trek across open land, the confrontation at the top of the hill, Yarwood almost dying.

That had turned out safely in the end, but here Todd Hampton was still a suspect. Tremayne knew that murderers came in all shapes and sizes, and being charming and agreeable company did not negate the possibility that the young man could have killed the two people. He was clearly capable of the subtlety to have killed Charlotte Merton, and he did have the strength to have hoisted Bess Carmichael up to her death.

'Did you sleep with Charlotte Merton? After all, you're a similar age to her, and she was an attractive woman.'

'I met her twice in the time she was here. I don't come down here often, what with my studies and a steady girlfriend, and the answer is no.'

'She put it about, to use the vernacular.'

'I know that,' Hampton replied. 'I know she had been with Ben.'

'How?'

'I was in the room next to them one night. I could hear the two of them at it like rabbits. From what I could hear, Ben resisted at first.'

'Why would he resist? He must have normal urges, the same as everyone else.'

'Hypothetically, and speaking as a future lawyer, a combatant of the police when they put forward dubious evidence, a forged confession, in court,' Hampton said, a broad smile on his face.

Tremayne took the joke in the spirit it was given.

'Ben has a temper,' Hampton continued, 'and that temper had got him into trouble on more than one occasion. Charlotte represented the outside world, the world of sin and bad thoughts, the place he no longer wanted to live in. You see, Ben's a gentle soul in a brawler's body. A man susceptible to drink and women. He would have made a good monk.'

'He's not religious,' Tremayne said. 'He told me that.'

'Nor is my father, but with Ben, it wasn't religion that he needed, it was hard physical work. The need to work each day to exhaustion; that's the pattern of his life. You've seen what he's done around the farm?'

'Very impressive.'

'He does it because he must. Charlotte was a distraction that he didn't want; she confused him, as she did others.'

'Others?' Tremayne asked. It was the time he would have cherished a cigarette. Ice was starting to form on the reeds on the stream's banks, the mist was swirling, and the interview was going well. He was receiving vital information. He fumbled in his pocket, looking for the non-existent packet.

Hampton, astute enough to realise, put his hand inside his jacket and brought out a packet of cigarettes. 'My father is always chastising me about them, but I'm over the age of twenty-one, and the occasional cigarette does no harm.'

Away from his wife, away from Clare, Tremayne took one of the cigarettes; a flame appeared from Hampton's lighter. Tremayne took his first drag of a cigarette in seven weeks; he coughed, he savoured the taste, he felt guilty.

'Sorry, can't do. Doctor's orders as well as the wife, and as for my sergeant, if she gets a sniff, I'll be in the doghouse for a week.'

'Heavy smoker?'

'I was, but now, it's purgatory. No cigarettes, half rations on alcohol.'

'Life's not worth living if you can't enjoy yourself.'

'The prerogative of the young. You've got time on your side, I don't.'

The two men left the stream and headed back to the farmhouse. Tremayne had one more question. 'Did your father sleep with Charlotte?'

'I want to say no, but the truth is, he probably did. Unlike me, my father has an open view on such matters, in that pleasure is to be garnered at every opportunity.'

'Your mother?'

'She had sown her wild oats well and truly before meeting father. She's devoted to him, as he is to her.'

'But he strays?'

'It's not something you talk to your father about, you know that.'

If he had spoken to his father about such matters, Tremayne knew, he would have received a good hiding with a leather belt.

'Charlotte Merton was pregnant,' Tremayne said.

'It wasn't my father.'

'Can you be positive?'

'I'm the only child. My mother told me that she had trouble conceiving due to my father's low sperm count. My parents are open about such issues, although it could be embarrassing to hear. Anyway, fertility drugs, artificial insemination and whatever else, and I turned up nine months later.'

    'You're sure of this?'

    'It wasn't my father. Maybe Ben? Maybe others?'

    'Who else?'

    'I'm not here that often. I'd not know.'

    Tremayne wasn't sure of that, but the conversation was at an end; at least for now.

Chapter 5

Bess Carmichael's death brought out the best in some people, the worst in others. Some were scathing about how she used to scrounge around the area, ferreting in the rubbish bins, taking whatever she could; others saw her as a harmless eccentric who minded her own business.

It was a Sunday, and the local church was full. The occasion, a remembrance for Bess, not that she had ever been in the church, although every couple of weeks she had found her way to the vicarage, and the Reverend Tom Walton, an eager, short and round man, had never failed to be charitable and to invite her in for a meal. It was his wife, Petula, as short and round as her husband, who had insisted on bringing her in, even though the smell could sometimes be offensive.

Bess, as would be recounted at the remembrance service, and later in the pub, aware of her hygiene, always doused herself from head to foot with the cheapest spray deodorant that she could find.

Clare attended the service, Tremayne did not.

At the church, the Reverend Walton offered prayers on behalf of the deceased and then spoke glowingly about the joy she brought to the village. At the back of the church, Harriet Huxtable sat, a hat on her head, wearing a buttoned-up overcoat and sensible shoes. It was her church, and each and every week she was there, cleaning and making the place ready for the Sunday. She placed the prayer books on the pews, polished the silverware, ensured the altar cloth was clean and pressed.

Harriet Huxtable, seventy years old and cheerless, was the soul of the church, having attended the Sunday service every week, only missing twice in the last sixty-five years. The first time, when a child, she'd missed due to having the measles; the second, three months previously, when she had tripped in her garden, catching the back of her shoe on a protrusion, and fallen over. Two nights in Salisbury Hospital, her ankle in a cast, and she was back in the village.

Even though her movements were still restricted and she was not as mobile as she once was, she'd not miss another church service. Clare sat next to the woman; she could see her seething each and every time the reverend made a reference to Bess.

Interspersed with the prayers, two people got up and spoke of Bess Carmichael, late of this parish.

One of those, a man Clare judged to be in his late seventies, early eighties, dapper in his tweed suit, his bow-tie, with a Poirot style moustache, spoke in clipped tones. 'Bess brought joy to us all with her cheery disposition, her eccentricity. We all forgave her whenever she erred. How could anyone stay angry with such a lovable person?'

Clare's ears pricked at the mention of 'erred'. Harriet Huxtable glowered.

Clare had only met the woman the first and second days at the farmhouse, and lovable was not a term she would have used. Sure, the woman had contacted the police and been open to questioning, giving a concise statement as to how she was walking across the field near to the ditch when she had seen the plastic sheet. There were inconsistencies in the statement which would have been brought up at a subsequent interview, although that wasn't going to happen now.

The first, after she and Tremayne had paced out the area, was why the woman was walking across the field close to the ditch. Her caravan was a half-mile away, and the village was to the north. Her route took her nowhere except to the farm, and she had no business there, and whereas no one would have said anything, she wouldn't have found anything of interest. The food would have been in the house, and any rubbish that they had was composted immediately and under lock and key, not because of theft, but to keep out the vermin, and the chickens, kept for their eggs, not for consumption, were in a wire enclosure. It wasn't locked, but there was a bar across to prevent a fox getting in.

Also, why did she get into the ditch? It was muddy, although the plastic sheet could have had value to someone who lived in a caravan, its wheels long gone, the axles raised from the ground with bricks. Jim Hughes and his team had checked the caravan out, found nothing of great value other than a stack of letters.

Later, after the church, and with most of the congregation at the pub – murder was good for business, the publican said as Clare paid for drinks – the dapper man came up to her.

'Colonel Angus Campbell, retired,' he said. He held out his hand: firm grip, military precision, Clare noted.

'Sergeant Clare Yarwood. You spoke highly of Bess.'

'I like people with spirit.'

'I only met her at the farm,' Clare said. 'Tell me about her, the type of person she was.'

The two of them were sitting in an alcove to one side of the bar. The volume of noise from the formerly subdued churchgoers was rising as the drinks kept flowing. Harriet Huxtable was noticeable by her absence; Clare would talk to her later. Those who despise and hate are often the best source of information.

'Eighty-five, not willing to slow down.'

'You spoke to her?'

'If she was in the village, but I can't tell you much about her history.'

'You asked?'

'Just inquisitive. After all, she lived in terrible conditions.'

'You're a man used to evaluating people. What do you reckon?'

'Her death or her background?'

'Both, but her background first.'

'As I said, I don't know. I like to think she came from money, a broken heart.'

'We'll check. I'll let you know if I can,' Clare said. She found the colonel an easy man to talk to.

'If it's not a romantic tale, a Victorian novel saga, then don't destroy the illusion. I'd prefer to keep my memory of her intact.'

'A softy at heart, not the authoritarian military man.'

'A pragmatist. I took troops into battle. Men with a background, a story to tell, were often the best. Those with a happy upbringing, no hardships and privations in their youth, often didn't have that edge, a hesitancy to pull the trigger. Bess did, that's why I liked her.'

'Her death?'

'That baffles me. She wasn't a gossip, and she didn't look in people's windows.'

'If she had seen anything at the farm?'

'Hard to say.'

'She contacted us about the first body.'

'Then her death is unrelated, or she saw something subsequently, overheard someone speaking. She could have been hanging around the farm, night or day. I've seen her in the village, very early morning, the sun not up. Winter, pitch-black, snow on the ground, and there she would be, looking in the rubbish bins, checking what people were throwing out.'

'Could it be someone in the village who killed her?'

'Charlotte or Bess?'

'Either. You knew Charlotte?'

'Everyone knew Charlotte. She always smiled when she saw you, asked how you were.'

'Any more?'

'I don't want to speak ill of the dead,' Campbell said.

'It's a murder enquiry. Questions need answers.'

'She was a troubled woman, and there were times when she wasn't happy, but always the smile. I could see through the veneer, but I wasn't there to help her, and besides, she had Hampton.'

'Your opinion of him?'

'Eccentric, a man too smart for his own good.'

'Capable of murder?'

'I'd say that Eustace Hampton is capable of most things. Whether that would include murder, I can't answer that.'

'A good man to have under your command?'

'A nightmare. Sometimes blind discipline is required. He would have been questioning my commands. Have you watched his weekly programme on television?'

'Esoteric,' Clare said, having watched two episodes the night before with Clive.

'He heads into the metaphysical, probability analysis, the universe, quantum theory and religious dogma. I can barely follow him, but I'll grant that it's interesting to watch, even if I don't understand a lot of what he's saying.'

'That's how I see it,' Clare said. She didn't say that Clive thought the man was full of hot air. 'Harriet Huxtable?'

'A sour woman, sees the worst in everyone, except for the Reverend Tom Walton.'

'A thing for him?'

'Only that he's closer to her God than she is.'

As Clare prepared to leave, Campbell spoke. 'I'm an admirer of your husband. He's doing a great job. You must be proud.'

'I am,' Clare said. It seemed that everybody knew who she was married to, and half of them always had a comment to offer. She had initially been embarrassed, but now she took it in her stride.

***

The two who had been absent on the days when Charlotte Merton and Bess Carmichael had died returned to the farm on the Monday. The first of them, a grey-haired man in his late seventies, had been attending the funeral of a relative. It had been checked and found to be true.

He reminded Clare of her grandfather, although he had been a sweet old man before he had succumbed to cancer four years previously, but Jacob Grayson was not sweet. In short, he was a cantankerous man who did not appear to belong at the farm with the others.

'I don't see why I should be answering your questions,' Grayson said. He was seated in his favourite chair in front of the fire. The others in the room had given the man a wide berth, although Eustace Hampton stood nearby.

'Jacob joined us two months ago,' Hampton said, almost apologetically.

Tremayne raised his eyes to Clare, who understood what he meant. Everyone, so far, had been dreamlike, as though nothing could disturb their perfect lives, not even when the children were removed from the farm.

Clare had checked on them several times, and in spite of the influence of their mothers at night, the children were starting to desensitise. Matilda, one of Gavin and Belinda Fitzwilliam's two daughters, had pulled Clare to one side at the hotel where they were staying and confided that she didn't want to go back to the farm. No reason was given, and Clare had not pushed it. After all, she knew Matilda and the other four children were still minors, and if there was something in their past that frightened them or left them bewildered, it was up to skilled professionals to deal with it, not a police sergeant, no matter how sympathetic.

At the farmhouse, the incongruous presence of Jacob Grayson loomed large.

'Mr Grayson,' Tremayne said, 'we're here on official business. If you would come into the other room, we can conduct our discussion in confidence.'

'Nothing this lot haven't heard before.'

Something was amiss.

The other returnee was a meek little woman who spoke quietly, almost in a whisper. Even though Bess Carmichael could have been killed by a man or a woman, the strength required to lift her would have been beyond Betty Iles.

With more cajoling, the threat of a police car and the interview room at Bemerton Road Police Station, Grayson acquiesced and followed Tremayne. Clare remained behind, dragging Hampton to one side.

'Why?' Clare asked.

'I know he can be a handful,' Hampton said. 'He's had a tough life.'

'A lot of people have, but you don't let them all in, or do you?'

'This place costs money, and whereas we all help, and I've got my television show, the sales of my books, we always need more to survive.'

'He's paying to be here?'

'He is, but he's a believer.'

A believer in what, Clare didn't know, unless it was bad manners. There was no way that Grayson belonged at the farm.

In the other room, Tremayne sat opposite Grayson. Clare joined them soon after.

'What's your story?' Tremayne said. Checks had already been made.

'I've decided to embrace an alternative lifestyle.'

'By being obstreperous?' Clare said.

'If you mean by being difficult, why don't you say it. I can't stand people who can't say it plainly.'

'Hampton is the master of convoluted English,' Tremayne said. 'The man's a master in the use of obscure words. He'd have me grabbing a dictionary.'

Clare couldn't envisage Tremayne with a book in his hand. The racing guide was his reading material, not that he understood the form of the horses, never learnt from his mistakes.

'Isn't the truth that you've invested a lot of money into this place?' Clare said.

'Smarter than you look,' Grayson's reply.

The man was a misogynist, Clare decided. She didn't like him, not one little bit.

'Some of us are,' Clare said, not wishing to get involved in verbal fisticuffs. 'It doesn't, however, explain why you'd want to put money into this place.'

'Not that it's any of your and your inspector's business, but I grew up in Brockenstoke, on this farm. My father owned it back then.'

'What happened?'

'A few bad years when the crops failed, and he was forced to sell below cost. He was a good farmer, but a bull-headed man who never listened to advice.'

'I imagine that applies to the son as well,' Tremayne said.

'Inspector, you understand, I can see that. I'd offer my apologies to your sergeant if she'd accept them.'

'Don't worry, Mr Grayson. I've dealt with more than my share of male chauvinism in my time. You're nothing special,' Clare said.

'I like a person with a backbone, not like them out there. Lily-livered, the lot of them.'

'Then why stay?'

'I'm bull-headed, the same as my father, but he never had the benefit of a good education. A couple of years, enough to learn to read and write, to add two and two and come up with four.'

'You had a decent education.'

'I learnt enough, left school at sixteen, worked for a couple of companies until I was in my early twenties, and then I went out on my own.'

'What sort of businesses?' Tremayne asked.

'Whatever. I bought and sold cars, renovated half a dozen houses, ventured into speculation, did well on the stock market. Buy low, wait your time. That's the problem, people are always in too much of a hurry, always wanting to get rich overnight.'

'You've got money?'

'Plenty, but that's all. An Ebenezer Scrooge, that was me. I rejected everyone and everything, lived a frugal and miserable life. I saw Hampton on the television and there in the background was my father's farm. I listened to him, tried to make head and tail of what he was talking about, not that I understood much or bothered with a dictionary either.'

'You saw a soft touch?' Tremayne said.

'There's something in what he talks about, but I spent my life being miserable and unpleasant to people. I contacted him, told him the family history, found out that the man was deep in debt. No idea why, as he's sitting on a goldmine. Just think of what he could charge to those who would pay to be here, instead of those outside.'

'That's not how he sees it,' Clare said.

'More's the pity. But there he is, broke, the bank about to pull the plug.'

'You struck a deal with him?'

'It seemed ideal. I'd bail him out, and he'd get the opportunity to rehabilitate me. Also, I'd be back home, something I had always wanted.'

'And in time, you'd slowly move the others out, claim the farm for yourself.'

'Hampton and me, we'd need to compromise. This place has to be on a strong commercial footing, and if he disagrees, then yes, I'd take it back. I own fifty per cent already, and the remaining money wouldn't be hard to come by.'

'You're a hard man,' Clare said.

'I'm a realist. The life that the man cherishes still needs money. Goodwill and love won't pay the bills. We know that, so does he, and his son knows it better than most.'

'You know Todd?' Tremayne said.

'I've met him on a couple of occasions. He's with me.'

'He said he was close to his parents.'

'He is, and Hampton's not a bad man, and his wife is a joy.'

'But you never married?'

'Charles Dickens could have written the book about me. No time for emotion or kindness, not then.'

'And now, you'd swap it all for a good life.'

'I don't regret my past, but I'd like to be back here, to be buried in the local churchyard. Is that too much to ask for?'

'I suppose not,' Clare said. 'It all depends on the future of this place. Who has committed these murders, whether there are to be more.'

'I can't help you there. I'll only be here a few days, then business calls.'

'Keep in touch.'

'You have my mobile phone number. If it's important, I'll come back.'

'Charlotte Merton?' Tremayne asked.

'A troubled woman.'

'Did you sleep with her?'

'I wasn't asked, which is, from what I understand, her modus operandi.'

'Who told you?'

'Ben. He's a good man, hard worker. No ambition, mind you, but I've got time for him.'

***

Betty Iles, the second of the returning community members, was not going anywhere soon. She had been at the farm for seven years and had only left it once. She would be interviewed later.

Tremayne and Clare found Tony Frampton. The man with a childlike mind was on the roof of the church, the Reverend Tom Walton down below.

'Dangerous up there,' Tremayne said as he looked up.

'He's cleaning the gutters, leaves get in them, the water freezes, cracks the gutter, lifts the roof tiles, and then we've got another sign outside asking for donations. Tony, he's got cat-like responses. He'll not fall, and he's fearless.'

Even so, Clare knew it was illegal to be on the roof without the appropriate licences and certificates.

'It's done,' Tony shouted. Clare studied the man after he came down; his face unblemished by stress, no wrinkles, no frowning, the face of a child, the body of a man.

They went in the church, out of the biting wind, although the weather didn't seem to worry Tony, dressed as he was in a blue tee-shirt, a pair of jeans, an old pair of tennis shoes.

The vicar handed Tony a cup of hot chocolate, his wife standing nearby.

'He's a dear, is our Tony,' Petula Walton said. 'So much work and he never complains.'

Tremayne smiled at the woman, as did Clare. However, it was Tony they needed to talk to. A simple man, regarded by everyone as harmless, he would be ignored by most. Indiscretions, idle words, all in front of him, and he might not even understand the significance. The man could be a treasure trove of information. However, weaning it from him would not be easy. As Ben had said, the man was not intelligent, barely able to understand what was being asked.

'You know Ben?' Clare said. She was sitting close to Tony, sharing a pew with him.

'He's my friend, is Ben.'

'You help him up at the farm?'

'If he needs me.'

'You were there in the last few days.'

'Ben wanted to move some material. I'm good for that, strong as an ox, that's what my mum says.'

'Did you see anything unusual?' Clare persevered. Direct questions, she knew, would probably evoke an incorrect response, Tony assuming that he had done something wrong.

'I only moved the material. It was Ben and me, that's all. He makes me laugh, does Ben.'

'How?'

'He calls me stupid, not that I am. He's my friend.'

Clare could tell that Ben had an insensitive side to him. The vicar and his wife stood nearby, glowing in their affection for the simple man. Tremayne felt a sense of frustration. He got up and beckoned the vicar and his wife to follow him.

'It'd be better to leave the two of them alone,' Tremayne said when they were in the church vestry. 'Yarwood knows what she's doing.'

With the other three no longer present, Clare made herself comfortable for the tortuous attempt to glean previously unknown facts from the man.

'Tony, you remember Charlotte?'

A look of horror on the man's face. 'She wanted to do things with me.'

'What sort of things?'

'I know what it was, but Tony, he's not interested. He likes to work for the vicar and his wife who makes chocolate cakes for me, and for Ben, he's my friend.'

'He says cruel words to you.'

'He makes me laugh. I like working with him.'

'Eustace Hampton?'

'He's kind to me, and his wife makes cakes for me too, not as good as Mrs Walton, though.'

'Do you know that Charlotte is dead?'

'Reverend Walton told me. Why?'

'Sometimes people do bad things.'

'Not Tony.'

'Not you, I know that, so does Inspector Tremayne.'

'Ben, he used to do things with Charlotte.'

'He told you?'

'I was there late at night. I was tidying up around the place. I could hear them in Ben's room. Tony doesn't want to remember. Ben's my friend.'

'But Charlotte wasn't.'

'I felt funny when she was near me.'

Clare could see the reaction of a normal man, obviously a virgin, in the presence of an available woman, unable to understand why he felt something.

'Did anyone else not like her?'

'Mrs Hampton didn't. I heard her arguing with Eustace about her.'

'What was she saying?'

'Tony doesn't listen, not to what people are saying.'

'I know that. You were there, you couldn't help but hear. It's important, what was she saying?'

'Eustace, that woman's got to go. Ben's screwing her, and God knows who else around here.'

'You have a good memory,' Clare said.

'I remember everything. I don't always understand. My mum said it's a gift, my memory, but I don't know.'

'It's a gift,' Clare said. The man, in his innocence, had an endearing quality. A grown man, the feminine instinct was to mother him as if he was a little child, which in effect he was.

'What else did you hear?'

'Nothing more. I didn't want to listen, not to other people's business.'

'Bess Carmichael?'

'Ben said she died.'

'What did you think of her?'

'She used to look in the rubbish bins. My mum said she was lonely.'

'What do you think?'

'She's not like Tony. She used to listen to what other people were saying.'

'Do you think she heard something up at the farm?'

'I don't know.'

Clare knew she had exhausted the conversation with Tony for now. If there were more he could tell, it would have to be for another day. However, Angus Campbell had said that Bess wasn't a snooper, didn't listen at keyholes, whereas Tony had said that she did. There was a variance in the two statements, a need to clarify.

Chapter 6

Tremayne took stock of the investigation, the first time that either he or Clare had had a chance to do so for several days. The interviews at the farmhouse had largely concluded, and the majority of the local villagers had been canvassed: their whereabouts on the key dates, their opinion of Eustace Hampton and his group, who they thought was capable of murder.

Nobody had firmed up as a prime suspect, although Ben, the community's handyman and ex-grievous bodily harmer, still held sway for the murder of Bess Carmichael, with Tony, the simple-minded child in a man's body, a long way behind in second place.

'It's what Tony said, not that he seemed to understand it. He said that with Charlotte near he felt funny, and then he had freaked out when she attempted a seduction,' Clare said, the two of them at the police station.

'There's a man in there wanting to get out,' Tremayne had said. Another long day, a few hours in the office, the obligatory report to deal with. Tremayne disliked the paperwork, and Clare, who would have admitted to enjoying it in the past, was starting to tire of it as well.

Not only were there two murders to solve, but there was also Clive and his mayoral duties, her need to attend the various functions. Not that she minded, but sometimes she'd rather curl up in a chair at home, stroke the cat and read a book.

At Clive's house in the cathedral close, the garden walls were high and solid, having been built in a time past when labour was cheap and manual work was heavy and for the desperately poor. She knew her neighbour on one side, a retired politician, only because of meeting him at a function with Clive. The neighbour on the other side she had not met, although Clive had told her that the woman who lived there was in her nineties, reclusive by nature, infirmed by age, and apart from her having a live-in nurse, Clare knew no more. A change from the easy friendship in Stratford sub Castle when she'd open the small gate between her cottage and her neighbours, the knowledge that if she was working late they would come into her kitchen, feed the cat, make sure that everything was in order. Clare missed the easy camaraderie of good people, the friendship that she had found there.

Clare focussed back on Tremayne. 'Maybe the man inside is not that suppressed. Could Tony, given a certain stimulus, become violent? Could he murder? Could that hidden adult be capable of criminal actions, morally wrong, and then his childlike simplicity unable to deal with the guilt, not even comprehending right from wrong,' Clare said.

'His upbringing, the doting mother, could have distorted his reality.'

'She'd be there telling him to put his cutlery together on the plate when he'd finished his meal, to say please and thank you, to look right, then left, then right before crossing the road, but what did he know of crime and murder and willing females?'

'Very little. It's an angle, not one I'm keen on.'

'Nor am I, but we're here to solve two murders, not to debate who we like or don't like.'

Which to Tremayne seemed to lead to Jacob Grayson. 'Now there's someone I don't like,' he said. He had adopted his favourite position on the chair, leaning back, his hands behind his neck. He stifled a yawn. Jean was waiting at home, a hot meal ready for him, although he wasn't sure that he wanted it, not that late. He felt the stiffening of his joints, the pain in one knee, sometimes both, the slowing pace.

An active man, he didn't want to deal with the reality, not yet, not ever, but a lifetime of smoking and drinking and arresting criminals, sometimes giving them a beating, was catching up with him. He wasn't yet sixty, but he felt older. He had to do something to improve his condition, and Jean's get-fit regime had helped. He knew that without her he'd be dead by now. But what he could do, he wasn't sure.

'Grayson's a pig of the first order,' Clare said. 'The man's got Hampton in a vice-like grip, and he's turning the lever slowly. He's not there to learn from Hampton; he's there to bleed the man dry, and as for reclaiming the family farm, that's nonsense.'

'You don't see him as sentimental?'

'He said it, Ebenezer Scrooge. He's not a Christmas story, and if Charles Dickens had modelled the miserly old man on Grayson, he'd have not finished the book.'

'Why the pretence? If the man's devoid of emotion, why not just break Hampton, kick him and the others out?'

'He derives pleasure from causing pain.'

'You're making a good case for him being a psychopath.'

'Psychopath, sociopath, Inquisitor General, Tomas de Torquemada, it makes no difference. The man's capable of murder, but almost certainly wouldn't do it. He'd manipulate others for his perverse pleasure, even Eustace Hampton.'

'Or his wife.'

'As you say. We need to follow through on Grayson more thoroughly, not to discount him as just a grumpy old man.'

***

The snow wasn't a given every winter in southern England, although this winter felt colder than most. Tremayne looked out of the window of his house, saw the white dusting, the lawn no longer green, and out on the road parallel lines where one car had driven up the street.

He looked around at his bed, saw Jean lying there still asleep. Outside it was cold and unpleasant, and there were murders to solve; inside it was warm and inviting. He knew which he preferred, but there was a responsibility, and Clare would be picking him up in forty minutes.

Jean stirred and looked up from the bed. 'I'll put the kettle on,' she said. 'You get ready. I don't want Clare waiting for you.'

'Yarwood won't mind.'

'I would.'

Forty-six minutes later, Clare beeped the horn of her car. 'Traffic delay,' she said as Tremayne got into the passenger seat. 'A bit of ice on the road and the idiots don't slow down. One of them is in a hedge not far from here.'

Clare, an experienced driver, a graduate of the police driving academy, handled the conditions with no trouble as she drove to Brockenstoke and the farm.

As Clare drove, Tony Frampton walked through the village. He said hello to Angus Campbell, the leader of men and treasurer of the church committee; he nodded to two other people as he wandered along, called in at the vicarage, a cup of hot chocolate ready for him.

If Tony thought about such matters, he would say that it was good to be alive and to be in such an attractive place with good people, but he didn't. He only thought of Ben and the job the two of them had for the day.

At the end of the village, determined by a narrow single-lane bridge over the river that had been built in the middle ages, he cut across the fields, an old walking track that had existed for centuries. He stopped by the stream that Tremayne and Todd Hampton had walked alongside; he threw a piece of bread to a couple of ducks.

Tony felt confused, but he wasn't sure why. He had liked Charlotte, even though she frightened him; he had liked the old woman, Bess, because she had been kind to him. But both were no more. He wanted to feel something, but he couldn't. He whistled as he walked, another whistle heard in the distance – it was Ben, their signal that they used to communicate, to grab the attention of the other when they were working together.

'Busy day,' Ben said, slapping Tony on the shoulder. 'Are you up to it?'

'I am, Ben,' Tony said, forgetting what he had been thinking about, unsure of what he had seen the day that Charlotte had died. In the mind of a simple man who remembered everything, forgot nothing, a hidden compartment where unpleasantness lurked.

71

***

In the village, Harriet Huxtable went about her business. She had cleaned her house, fed the dog; it was as disagreeable as she was, and it bit everyone who came to the door. She had an appointment at the church, one that was of her making, and each day without fail she would be there, cleaning here, cleaning there, fussing over this and that, complaining to the vicar if he was around, which wasn't often as the man preferred to keep away when she was present.

In confidence, to his wife, he would admit to uncharitable thoughts about Harriet Huxtable.

Her routine that day, however, had been disturbed by a knock at her door. The dog, a Jack Russell Terrier, leapt out of its basket in a flash and ran to the door, barking, its teeth bared.

Harriet Huxtable opened her door, but not before she had looked through the spy hole.

'Down, dog,' she said. The dog retreated back to its basket.

'We've a few questions,' Clare said, her teeth chattering. Tremayne was turning a shade of frozen-to-the-bone blue.

'Come in, you're making the place look untidy,' Harriet said. Before the murders, she would have told anyone that asked – no one did – that the one thing she disliked were unwelcome guests who interfered with her routine.

'We spoke the other day,' Clare reminded her.

'Will this take long? I've got a busy day.'

Tremayne was warming up. Their car was parked down the road, the road having been blocked by a lorry that had jack-knifed on an icy patch, the snow on the road now turning to slush. The walk, brisk in Clare's case, hesitant in his, had chilled him. Clare, dressed for the weather in a fur-lined jacket and fully-lined boots, found the weather bracing; Tremayne in a dark blue suit, wearing an overcoat, yet still keeping to black leather shoes, did not.

'It depends,' Tremayne said. 'We were on our way out to the farm, but there are still a few questions we have for you, for almost everyone.'

'I told your sergeant all that I know, precious little as it turns out.'

'We're aware that you disapproved of Bess Carmichael,' Clare said.

'I did, but that doesn't mean I killed her, or does it?'

'If we killed those we disliked, there'd be a lot fewer people in the world,' Tremayne said. 'We don't suspect you of her murder, but we're not sure who is guilty. Hate's a motive, disapproval's another, but there are other reasons. Tell us why you disliked the woman? We'll find out in time.'

Harriet Huxtable visibly shrank in her chair. The dog, sensing its mistress's emotional state, got out of the basket and rested its head in her lap – an empathetic response.

'We have some letters that were removed from her caravan.'

'You don't need to check. I can tell you what they will confirm.'

Tremayne and Clare had come into the house without a firm agenda, and no previous plan, and now, a revelation. In the cities, even Salisbury and especially London, nobody knew anything about anyone else, but in a small and seemingly charming village, the type of place that people hanker to retire to, scratch the surface and there, laid bare, would be all the wickedness of the world.

'Is this a statement?' Clare asked, not sure how to proceed. Harriet Huxtable had not been seen as a person of significance, just a miserable woman who had lived in the village all her life.

'It's not something I've ever wanted to talk about,' the woman said. 'Is this in confidence? Or will you need to tell others in the village?'

'It's a murder investigation,' Tremayne said. 'We can't give you that guarantee. However, we will treat what you tell us with the sensitivity it deserves.'

'It doesn't deserve that. It's horrible.'

Clare set her iPhone on the table. 'You don't mind if we record this?'

'I've no option, do I?'

'Not really, but we'd prefer you to agree.'

'Very well. If you, Sergeant, could make us all a cup of tea, I would be most obliged. I don't think I can do it, not now.'

Clare left. Tremayne patted the dog's head – it reminded him of the animal that Jean took when she had left him all those years before, the dog that he had trained to fetch his slippers without chewing them first. Neither he nor the woman spoke in Clare's absence.

'I'll be mother,' Clare said on her return, remembering that was what her grandmother would say as she had poured the tea.

The dog sensed that it had fulfilled its role and went back to its basket.

Harriet Huxtable sat up, cleared her throat and took a sip of the tea, too strong for her, but she said nothing, not to Clare.

'I wasn't born in this village,' the woman said. 'I know everyone thinks I was, but that's not the truth. I arrived here when I was very young, too young to remember, and apart from a handful of occasions, this is where I've remained. But that's not what I'm about to tell you.'

Harriet took another sip of tea, looked over at the dog, around the room.

'I was adopted,' she continued. 'My parents, my adoptive parents, gave me this house when they died. I loved them.'

'We weren't aware of this,' Tremayne said.

'Why should you be? I was fourteen when my adoptive parents told me the truth of my birth; how I had been the result of an incestuous relationship between my mother and her father, my grandfather.'

Clare gulped, almost spat out her tea; Tremayne sat calmly. He had heard variations on the story over the years: incest, patricide, matricide, brother killing sister, sister killing brother. Even so, what the woman was saying disturbed him.

'My parents...I mean the adoptive ones, you realise that?' Harriet said.

'We do,' Clare said.

'I could do with another cup of tea.'

Clare took hold of the teapot, her hands shaking from the shock of what she had just heard. Somehow, she managed to complete the task, although some of the tea spilt into the saucer as she handed it to the woman.

'They died when I was twenty-two, a car accident. It was tragic, and for years afterwards, I couldn't talk about it, barely left the house. Money was never an issue. I started to do some research on where I had come from, a need to connect with someone.'

'You knew some details?' Clare asked.

'My parents had told me enough, and there were adoption papers which I found later.'

'How did you take it?'

'I was fourteen. How do you think? I felt cheap, dirty, the child from hell. After that, I changed, kept to myself. It's hard to believe, but I had been popular, outgoing, attractive. I've only hardened since then.'

'We appreciate this is difficult for you, but we need to know about Bess Carmichael,' Tremayne said.

'As I said, I started to make enquiries, not so easy back then. I travelled up to London, checked with the various adoption agencies, the government departments tasked with such matters. It took me two years before a kind soul took pity and helped me.'

'You found out?'

'Eventually. I contacted my mother, found that she was alive.'

'Your grandfather?'

'In time, after I had made contact with her, she told me that he had denied any responsibility and had thrown her out of the house.'

'He's dead now?'

'A long time, before I found my mother.'

'Is that the end of the story?'

'It's only the beginning,' Harriet said. 'We met a few times, realised that time and the circumstance of my birth could never allow us to do anything other than to recognise the fact. My mother had been fifteen at the time of my birth, and she had only seen me once after the birth; she was not a maternal woman, and my heart had hardened.'

'Your mother now?'

'My mother was Bess Carmichael.'

'I thought that was where it was heading,' Tremayne said.

'But you were unfeeling at the church, showing your displeasure,' Clare said.

'She arrived in the village over twenty years after we had severed contact. She never spoke to me, not once, nor I to her. We'd exchange glances, nothing more.'

'It's not easy to listen to,' Clare said.

'It's the truth,' Harriet said. 'She needed somewhere to live, and being near to me was obviously important to her. I regret her passing, but I can't feel anything for her. My heart broke a long time ago; it won't heal now.'

Outside the house, the weather had improved, a ray of sunshine penetrating into that otherwise depressing room with that sad story.

Tremayne and Clare left the woman and her dog and walked back to Clare's car. Five minutes after they had gone, Harriet Huxtable pulled her front door shut – there was still a church to clean.

Chapter 7

Harriet Huxtable's bitterness had come as a surprise to Clare, although her own relationship with her mother was tenuous, and in the past, she had always felt the need to lecture Clare, telling her to find a better job, to find a man of substance, to settle down, to give her grandchildren. That had changed since Clare married Clive Grantley, and although he was older than the mother would have preferred, she had eventually accepted the compromise.

Yet in the village, a mother and daughter, both of whom had been shamed by the same man, had not felt able to connect, to forgive, to spend time together.

'You can see why the woman's got a perpetual down on the world,' Tremayne said. Clare's car had now been retrieved after the lorry that had been blocking the road had been moved to one side. Even Tremayne had been emotionally touched by the woman's confession, although Clare knew that he would never admit to it.

In the village, as they drove through, the publican was out in front of the pub. Clare stopped the car, and she and Tremayne walked over to where he was.

'Cold for the time of year,' he said.

'About to get colder,' Tremayne said. 'You've got some answering to do.'

They hadn't planned to confront the man, not yet, as enquiries were continuing behind the scenes. In Salisbury, a task force had been set up, or to be more correct, three sergeants and a constable, as well as a police informer that Tremayne used on occasions. Their function was to find out if the publican, Walter Plumpton

– although no one called him Walter, to his patrons he was Wally – was dealing drugs, and if he was, where had he obtained them and who else were his customers.

Publicans were invariably cheerful: your best friend, the person with a joke or a story, a reason for you to stay in the convivial atmosphere of a cosy bar. But not Plumpton. He had the look – the extended belly, the bulbous red nose, the flushed complexion, the sweaty brow, even the smell of stale beer – but his joviality always seemed contrived.

Although, as Tremayne saw it, the man was going to be out of the pub soon enough due to declining business, and he didn't have much to be happy about.

Inside the pub, not open as it was still early, the three of them sat at one of the tables in the bar. It was an old building, the sort of place that should have exuded old-world charm but didn't.

Tremayne had his back to the wall, Clare was sitting across from him, and Plumpton was at ninety degrees to each of them, his chair reversed, his forearms resting on the back of the chair.

'I've got plenty to do,' Plumpton said.

Neither Tremayne nor Clare was moved by his statement. Harriet Huxtable had had plenty to do and then she had sat down and told them a tale that sent shivers up the spine, and besides, what did the publican have to do. The pub was clean enough, although uninviting, there was wood in the open fire, the barrels had been dealt with, and a local lady beavered away in the kitchen at the rear preparing sandwiches for those who wanted a quick snack, meals for those who'd be in later.

'You were friendly with Charlotte Merton,' Clare said. She didn't need to elicit a response; she was merely confirming a fact that Plumpton had already stated.

'I liked her,' Plumpton said.

Tremayne took a more direct approach. He looked the publican straight in the eye. 'Mr Plumpton,' he said, 'Charlotte Merton was a drug addict, injecting heroin. Did you know that?'

'I did.'

'So, what did you do about it?'

'Nothing. I wasn't her father.'

'She told you?'

'Not in as many words. Where's this leading? I get the feeling that you're lining me up for something or other.'

'How did you know she was taking drugs?'

'Because I'd been there. I've been clean for a long time.'

'Where did she get the drugs?'

'How the hell should I know?' An angry reaction from Plumpton. The red of his face took on a more intense shade.

'What's your history?' Tremayne asked. 'We're not accusing you, not yet.'

'But you're checking.'

'Nobody's innocent, not with us.'

'You'll find nothing against me,' Plumpton said.

'Charlotte was pregnant, did you know?' Clare asked. Tremayne had softened the man up; it was for her to go in for the kill. She hadn't liked Harriet Huxtable before, but now she pitied her. She knew that pity was not an emotion she'd ever feel for Plumpton.

'It wasn't me.'

'Did you know?'

'Of course I didn't. Do you think that she and I were screwing?'

'More than one person has intimated that you were, and Charlotte had told one person. Now, denial or no denial, that's not what's important here, as we'll get to the truth eventually, we always do.'

'Why I deny it, or whether I was screwing her?'

'Both, either,' Tremayne said.

A head appeared around the door to the rear of the bar. 'I've finished,' the cook, a woman in her mid-thirties, said. 'I'll be back later when you open.'

Plumpton left his seat and walked over to her and handed her some money. He looked over to where the two were sitting. 'Twenty seconds and I'll be back.'

'He can't go far,' Tremayne said.

'What do you reckon?'

'Guilty.'

'Of what?'

'That I don't know. Doesn't make him a murderer though.'

'We're not getting far in Salisbury. Plumpton may be innocent of all crimes,' Clare said.

'Then why was Charlotte sleeping with him?'

'Another secret to be admitted.'

'I've had enough for one day,' Tremayne said. 'A harrowing tale from Harriet Huxtable.'

'I thought you were unmoved.'

'Conditioned, but there's always another surprise when you're least expecting it.'

Plumpton returned, carrying a tray. 'Maria's prepared pies for later. They're still hot, I'm sure you'd both appreciate one.'

They did, and for a moment Clare saw a different man, a man untroubled, a man innocent.

The three ate the pies in relative silence; a glass of orange juice for each had also been on the tray.

'Plumpton,' Tremayne said as he wiped the crumbs from his mouth, 'let's assume you're not guilty of anything other than bad judgement.'

'Let's,' Plumpton agreed. 'Fancy a pint?'

Clare looked over at Tremayne; nothing needed to be said.

'Not now,' Tremayne said. A pint would have finished off the pie nicely, but it wasn't to be.

'Mr Plumpton, let's go back to Charlotte,' Clare said. 'We're certain that you did sleep with her, as did others. We're aware of her need.'

'I knew she was troubled, and we'd talk, sometimes about the pub, sometimes about Hampton. We got along, exceptionally well as it turned out; she, the beautiful, yet troubled woman, and then me, an overweight beer drinker who's going broke. I like to think there was more to it than that, but I was never under any illusion. I was glad whenever she was here.'

'And now she's dead?'

'Murder, not a good way to go, if it was that.'

'What else could it be?'

'I don't know, but she was on a downward spiral, a spiral that had only one end.'

'She was lost?'

'I had been there, I could see that she would never stop, not for long, no matter how much Eustace Hampton tried to get through to her.'

'I'd not say no to another pie,' Tremayne said.

Clare sat back on her chair, folded her arms in disgust at her senior, his willingness to eat more than he should, and then come lunchtime, more food, and back at home with Jean at night, another meal.

Tremayne leant across the table. 'Yarwood, take that look off your face. I needed to talk to you before he came back.'

'About what?'

'Assuming Plumpton's on the straight and narrow, and he had slept with Charlotte, what do we have?'

'Not a lot.'

'That's where you're wrong. What would Charlotte have told him? If we're down at the farm, it's closed mouths, but up here, the woman, not a true believer, could have been indiscreet, seen Plumpton as an outlet.'

'Hardly a bedmate.'

'Father figure, confessor, like-minded troubled soul. We're not here to judge, only to find out the truth.'

'You want to angle the conversation towards Hampton and the farm?' Clare said.

'That's it. Push him if you have to.'

***

The intention for the day had been to revisit Hampton's farm, to follow up on previous conversations, to attempt to get through the blanket that covered those who lived there, to see what glimmered through cracks in the responses.

Yet so far they'd seen an unpleasant woman, an overweight publican. The first had revealed a hitherto unknown fact, but whether it had got Bess Carmichael murdered seemed unlikely.

However, Wally Plumpton represented a serious motive. If she had been pregnant, if it had been his child, how would he have reacted, how would someone else? What if someone else had fallen in love with her, only to be discarded thanks to the woman's fickle nature, her promiscuity, her need for a narcotic?

All of the options figured large in Tremayne's calculating mind. He knew that Clare, although younger and less experienced than him, would have seen the possibilities as well.

'Mr Plumpton,' Clare said on his return – he had brought three pies, two bottles of beer and a glass of wine with him. She was not about to complain, and she had to agree that the man was hospitable – 'were you the father of Charlotte Merton's unborn child?'

'Even if I admitted that we had slept together, which I'm not, it wouldn't have been my child.'

'Why's that?'

'I was married young, a childhood sweetheart. Back then, I was thin, a star athlete at school, even ran for the county, under fifteens. At eighteen we got married, not because we had to, but it was a council estate, and my parents, old-fashioned values, could see that we weren't going to keep our hands to ourselves for much longer. And we weren't, but they didn't know that. Anyway, we got married, a child within eleven months, another within a year, and so on. By the time she was twenty-five, there were five children, another on the way. That's when she said to me, enough is enough. I had the operation, shooting blanks now.'

'Your wife?'

'We were married for a long time, twenty-two years, and four of the children had left home, another was about to fly the coop, and the sixth, pretty as a child, subject to illness as she got older, died at the age of nine.'

'Sorry to hear that,' Tremayne said.

'As I said, twenty-two years and the ardour that had drawn us together had waned, and I'd had more than one encounter with drugs, a predilection for drinking. We drifted apart, no more than that. We keep in touch, meet up now and then, talk about the children, but she found someone else, I didn't. Not a bad word to say about her.'

'If we check, we'll find this to be true?' Clare said.

'Scout's honour. It's true, not something I'd lie about.'

'But you've lied about Charlotte.'

'She reminded me of my wife in some ways. Easy to talk to, pleasant to be near.'

'Did you love her? It's a motive, as good as any. The discarded lover, the wanton woman.'

'I offered her a place at the pub, not that I'll be here much longer. I wanted to look after her, not to impose myself on her.'

'Come on, admit it,' Tremayne said.

'Charlotte was here in the pub; it was raining outside, and she was melancholy, wanting to talk. One thing led to another, and yes, we made love. It wasn't screwing, or whatever else you want to call it, it was genuine affection. She made me feel young and virile; I made her feel normal.'

'What happened?'

'One day later, she's off the planet, heroin. I tried to get through to her again, but she was another person. We stayed friends, but we never made love again, and then, she's up at the farm with Ben, even attempting to seduce the young Einstein.'

'It's better than "Stupid Tony",' Tremayne said.

'Not much better,' Clare snapped.

' Nobody means harm by it, certainly not me. Tony's a good worker, and most people in the village have kind of adopted him.'

'Eustace Hampton?' Clare said, changing the subject away from the simple-minded man.

'It was Charlotte who said that he helped to calm the demons in her. She didn't say how or when, but I don't think he touched her.'

'Would you have known?'

'I think so. Charlotte, when she was in one of her better moods, would talk. That's how I found out about Ben and Tony. If Hampton had tried it on, no reason to with that wife of his, she would have told me.'

'What else did she tell you?'

'It wasn't only Ben at the farm, I know that. Another beer?' Plumpton said, looking over at Tremayne.

'Not now,' Tremayne replied. 'Who else?'

'Gavin Fitzwilliam, the embezzling accountant.'

'We're not aware of the embezzling,' Clare said.

'Neither was Charlotte, not until the man broke down in tears and told her about his life, the guilt he felt over sleeping with her. I can't be sure if it was true or not, but it probably was. It seems his wife had him on short rations.'

'What else went on at the farm? Do you know?' Tremayne asked.

'According to Charlotte, group sessions, holding hands, attempting to connect with your inner self. From what I could see, nonsense. And Charlotte was a perceptive woman, intelligent if given a chance, but the demons had her.'

'A religious interpretation?' Clare asked.

'Drugs, nothing religious about them. They're evil, that's all I know. I had a good woman to see me through the worst of it, Charlotte had no one.'

'And you wanted it to be you?'

'Why not? I wasn't asking anything from her. She knew that, and, at times, she seemed to listen, but at others, she was a brick wall, impervious to reason, susceptible to others.'

'Hampton, a master manipulator of people, could have been pulling the strings.'

'He could have, but I think you need to look further. Gavin Fitzwilliam has secrets, one of them from his wife. What about the others?'

Tremayne lifted the collar of his coat, buttoned it up tight.. He shook Plumpton's hand, told him that he was still under suspicion and that his history would be checked, as would Fitzwilliam's involvement with Charlotte. Clare also shook Plumpton's hand, said she was sorry about Charlotte.

With the pub empty, Wally Plumpton went into his small office at the rear of the building. He looked at the pile of letters on his desk. He slipped a paperknife through the top of one of the envelopes and opened it. It was, as he expected, a final demand from the bank: ninety days and they would foreclose, sell the property and the land on which it stood.

Plumpton sat down, looked out of the small window. He felt sad.

Not only was his future uncertain, but he had also felt love for that misguided, troubled woman. He leant down and opened the bottom drawer of the desk. Inside, something that he had never wanted to use again. He applied a tourniquet to his upper arm, went through the procedure that was second nature to him and injected the drug. Relief coursed through his body. He would forget for now.

Chapter 8

The focus at the farm, on the next visit after Harriet Huxtable's early-morning bombshell and Wally Plumpton revealing some of the truth, if not all, was Gavin Fitzwilliam.

It was just after midday, and the once pristine covering of snow in the farmyard was gone, replaced by slush. There was no way to avoid walking through it, Tremayne and Clare wiping their shoes on a mat outside the front door of the house.

Inside the house, unhurried activity. Over near the barn, the noise of two men at work, cutting firewood by the sound of it, occasional laughter.

Levity was not encouraged and rarely encountered in the house. A smell of cooking wafted through the building. There was the indistinct chatter of two women as they worked in the kitchen. Over to one side of the main room, a woman was embroidering, another at a spinning wheel, while a third fussed with the wool being fed into it, a dimmed light providing some illumination, the weak sun coming in through a window.

The children were still not at the farm, but a hearing had been scheduled, with the return of the children back to their homes to be decided.

Clive, Clare's husband, had confided that the children would probably be allowed to return home as no evidence had been presented to prove that they were in harm's way at the farm; on the contrary, they were polite and intelligent, even if quieter than most other children of their age.

Gavin Fitzwilliam was found over at the barn, the noise Ben and Tony were making more noticeable there. The man looked up as Tremayne and Clare entered his makeshift office.

'Online these days,' Fitzwilliam said. He was dressed in a suit and tie.

'We've a few questions,' Tremayne said.

'I thought you eschewed technology,' Clare said. She wasn't feeling very accommodating. After all, Fitzwilliam's daughter had confided that she didn't want to go back to the farm, and the man was an adulterer.

'In the house, but the place needs money, and online accountancy doesn't take a lot of my time, just a few clients these days. I've also got a couple of companies that forward work to me: analysis of a company's finances, profit and loss, asset management, whether it's viable or not. You'd not believe how many people fiddle the books.'

Tremayne knew one person, and he was looking straight at him.

'I don't understand you people,' Tremayne said. 'I don't have a clear idea of what it is that you and the others are hoping to achieve here. Outside there are cars, the children go to school, you have a laptop, Hampton's got a mobile phone, drinks a pint of beer. What is this place?'

'A place for people yearning for a better life, a return to old-fashioned values.'

'Murder doesn't figure high on the list of old-fashioned values, does it?'

'No.'

'Nor does *fornicating* with a heroin-addicted young female,' Clare said. Being sanctimonious on the one hand, hypocritical on the other, did not sit well with her.

'What!' Fitzwilliam exploded.

Tremayne was pleased – a reaction.

'We have proof that you had sexual intercourse with Charlotte Merton,' Clare said. She didn't, it was only an aspersion, but she wasn't going to let the facts interfere with placing the man on notice.

'It's a lie, a damn lie.'

Blaspheming, this is getting better, Tremayne thought.

'Yarwood's softened you up,' Tremayne said. 'Now I'm going in for a killer blow.' Instinct told him that Fitzwilliam was more than he seemed, and Wally Plumpton had said that the man had a dubious past, courtesy of information from his one-off lover, Charlotte Merton – or maybe it was more than the once, but that wasn't the point, not now.

'You're the sort of people we try to avoid,' Fitzwilliam said. He had stopped pretending to work and looked up.

'And what sort of people is that?'

'You live by your own creed, unwilling to accept that there are alternatives, other choices that can be made.'

'Living here under the one roof, holding hands, screwing the weak and defenceless.'

'Charlotte wasn't defenceless, and she wasn't weak, either.'

'You're admitting to having had relations with the woman?'

'I said she wasn't weak or defenceless. Unfortunately, that's the problem with you, too ready to believe the worst in people, to condemn out of hand.'

Tremayne, willing to take the man's reaction, knowing that out of anger and frustration came truth, continued. 'Don't give us the sob story, or outright denial that you are a poor misunderstood man and that life has dealt you a bad hand.'

'What if it had?'

'We've got two things against you,' Clare said. 'One is your relationship with Charlotte Merton. Withholding a vital fact doesn't bode well for you.'

'I can't tell you something if it isn't true.'

Fitzwilliam was shaking, angry. Tremayne needed him more riled.

'Embezzling, what's that all about?' Tremayne said as he leant over the top of the laptop. 'Does Hampton know that you're a crook?'

'Eustace looks for the best in people, something you apparently can't do.'

'Fitzwilliam, let's be honest with each other. I've been a police officer for over thirty years. I've got a nose for a villain, and you're one. Also, we're conducting enquiries into your history, previous clientele, Inland Revenue. Either you tell us the truth, or we'll find out anyway. Now, what's it to be?'

'Inspector Tremayne is right,' Clare said. 'It'll be worse for you if we find out something you could have told us here and now.'

Fitzwilliam closed the lid of his laptop, sat back on his chair, reached over to the coffee machine on the top of a filing cabinet. Clare interceded and poured three mugs of coffee as the man wasn't as steady as he should be. He was broken. Tremayne felt satisfaction; Clare felt some sympathy, although it wasn't a lot.

'It was five years ago,' Fitzwilliam said. 'I had a partner, someone I went to school with. We had been firm friends for years, and I trusted him. He was entrepreneurial, and I was ambitious for money. He was into finding rundown businesses, fixing them up, milking them for as much as he could, and then selling on or writing them off as a tax loss. He was good at what he did, not illegal, just taking advantage of other peoples' misfortune.'

'He'd not be the first,' Tremayne said.

'Nor the last, but he did have a conscience, sort of.'

'Then greed sets in.'

'That was it. He hadn't really hurt anyone, not to any degree. Some people had gone bankrupt, but they had taken the gamble, had been willing to break others, so the two of us slept easy.'

'Can this be verified?' Clare asked. She could see where this was heading, the man admitting to an error of judgement, not a crime, attempting to give as little as possible without incriminating himself.

'It's the truth.'

'That's not what Yarwood asked you,' Tremayne said. 'It appears that you, Mr Fitzwilliam, would benefit from a spell down at the police station.'

Clare could see Fitzwilliam deflate, the realisation that spinning a good tale wasn't going to work.

'Very well,' he said. 'It was the two of us, both aggressive and determined to make our mark. He was my school friend, that much was true. We were young, full of ourselves. I had just met Belinda, and we were going to move in together. It was Dominic's idea on how to make quick money. It was good at first, two young men out on the town, making our mark, driving good cars, a woman on our arm, or in Dominic's case, both arms.'

'Where is he now?' Clare asked.

'Somewhere in the sun. I'm coming to that. Dominic was pushing the envelope. We started small, a corner shop, made a few thousand. We ploughed the money back in, bought a bigger shop, higher turnover, and then a chain of coffee shops – good money in them if you know what you're doing, which we did. He could spot a bargain, I could do the sums. Neither of us had much in the way of civic responsibility, no concern if we were fudging the numbers, not paying our taxes.'

'Young men on the make rarely do,' Tremayne said. He was sitting calmly, his hands folded, an indicator that the police station option was still possible.

So far, Fitzwilliam's second attempt at an explanation sounded plausible. Salisbury had its fair share of 'wide boys', young men who would use whatever means, nefarious usually, to make money; men who brushed the edge between dubious and illegal. It was a term his father had used, although Tremayne liked the phrase too, and Fitzwilliam was shaping up by his own admission to be one of them.

'We had a few ventures going, but then we became greedy, especially Dominic. We had lined up an engineering company that was supplying racking to supermarkets. They were doing well, although times had moved on and the Chinese were eating into the market, the same as they do with everything. I'd taken a job there, finance director. I was young, but I was well-credentialled, a record of making money for myself.'

'They knew about your other ventures?' Clare asked.

'The management was staid, a family concern. The managing director was in his late eighties; the manufacturing manager, the man's grandson, was in his early forties. The grandson wanted change; he needed people who knew what to do, he needed me. And besides, he was Belinda's brother.'

'That meant that Belinda had money.'

'In trust, not to be given until the old man had died, and then only a small amount. Her father was still alive back then; he was to inherit.'

'Was he keen for change?'

'He wasn't interested. A falling out with his father, and he'd set up an IT company, doing well, even today, although the man's retired, gone to Portugal. His only interest in his father's company was that it made money and it was his when the old man died.'

'What happened?'

'I made recommendations, offloading unwanted property, automating the process, reducing the staff numbers. All good and largely implemented, although the MD wouldn't reduce as many of the staff as I had wanted. At the end of the first year, the business was making a small profit, and it carried little debt. Dominic was out there buying and selling, but I was still the finance director.'

'Why?'

'Belinda was pregnant, so a steady income was handy, but mainly because it was what Dominic and I had planned. Besides, it didn't need two of us out on the street. I was a numbers man, that was all. The plan was honed between Dominic and me, Belinda's brother was in the dark, although in the end we offered him twenty-five per cent.'

'Which he accepted?' Clare said.

'He wanted out, a life of ease.'

'Illegal?'

'No.'

'It will be,' Tremayne said, starting to tire of the convoluted tale.

'If I had creamed off the top, we could have taken sixty to seventy thousand pounds, but we were up and coming men of worth. I did the figures, falsified the tax returns, upped the profit, lowered the loss.'

'You borrowed money.'

'That we did. It took a couple of banks, an impressive proposal and we had the money.'

'How much?'

'Two million pounds, give or take a few thousand either way. A tip, if you ever want to borrow money. Put a proposal together, long on facts and charts, short on the negatives, and never ask for a rounded-off amount. Two million sounds as though it's a figure out of mid-air. Two million, one hundred thousand, four hundred and thirty-seven pounds sounds professional, as though you've done your homework.'

'Which you had?'

'We spent almost as much time coming up with the figure as preparing the proposal. It was feasible what we were presenting, although the market was turning against us.'

'Then what?'

'The money's in the bank, to be drawn on as needed, subject to bank approval. We stipulated that; made us sound genuine.'

'The money's locked up, what then?'

'At the company, a flurry of expansion activity, an increase in orders. We lowered the price, knowing that with the expansion it would be a lot cheaper to produce.'

'Shouldn't you have waited until production costs were down?' Clare asked.

'I knew what we were doing. I had the costing down to a fine art. I could see that the hit we were taking was starting to impact on the bottom line, but neither the manufacturing manager nor the MD could understand how I was structuring it.'

'It blew up in the end?'

'Of our choosing. The banks were releasing the money, over one million eight hundred thousand pounds. I'd kept them in the loop, kept updating them with what we were achieving, kept up with the charts and graphs. They were putty in our hands. But then came the day. I set up transfers of the company's money into various accounts; on the face of it, they were to pay for services rendered by the various contractors, but they weren't.'

'Bogus?'

'Legit. Never get too greedy.'

'And then, the pièce de résistance, you moved the embezzled money to other accounts.'

'It wasn't embezzled. The only ones who were hurt were the banks. We celebrated hard and long that night.'

The company?'

'Gone now. So has the MD, although the manufacturing manager, he got his twenty-five per cent, is still around. Besides, I never liked him and the banks, not wanting a scandal, wrote off the debt.

'Why are you doing online accountancy if you had so much money?'

'Thirty-six hours later, Dominic's skipped the country, my share of the money now in his account. All I had left was enough to buy into this place…'

'Buy?' Clare said.

'Figuratively. We don't own anything here, enough money for our share of the upkeep of the place. That leaves us with enough to look after our children.'

'Would you be here if you had an option?'

'It's been good for the girls.'

'That's not an answer.'

'Eustace Hampton is a good man.'

'Criminal action against you?'

'For what? Belinda's brother diversified into other engineering projects, using my skill as his guideline for financial management. One year later, another profit. Some good came from what we had done.'

'*Charlotte Merton?*' Tremayne said.

'It was in the afternoon, no one's at the farm. It was just her and me.'

'We've heard variations on this story from others,' Clare said.

'Either you want it, or you don't.'

'It's a common theme,' Tremayne said.

'It wasn't often,' Fitzwilliam said, 'and if I don't tell you now, then you'll have your minds in the gutter.'

'It's there now.'

'Charlotte had other lovers.'

'A break from the monotony of this place...'

'Don't you like it here?' Clare interrupted.

'Belinda and the children, especially Gwyneth, do.'

'But you don't?'

'It gives a man time to think.'

'But not enjoy.'

'I miss the old life, the cut and thrust...'

'The illegality of it,' Tremayne added.

Fitzwilliam sat still, said nothing to Tremayne's jab at the truth.

'Charlotte Merton?' Clare asked. She was tired of another man taking advantage of a weak and defenceless woman, no matter how it was justified.

'You'd not understand,' Fitzwilliam said.

'Only too well. It's the same old story; my wife doesn't understand me, the pressure of work, the need to bring in money.'

'Don't you get it?'

'Get what?'

'The last deal we pulled wasn't the only one. We upset a few people on the way, people who remember, remain angry…'

'People who could be violent,' Tremayne said.

'It's Dominic they'd rather have, but I'm here in the country, he isn't. If they found me…'

'Is that likely?'

'Two murders, a police investigation, your checking here and there, attempting to validate my alibi. What hope have I?'

'It still doesn't explain Charlotte Merton.'

'Okay, have it your way. She was here, so was I. She started coming close, teasing, making suggestive comments. I tried to back off, but she wasn't having any of it.'

'And you gave in.'

'We had to find somewhere to hide. If it hadn't been for Gwyneth and Matilda, the two of us would have left the country, but they're our responsibility. They needed to continue with their education, to grow up in England. And then there was Eustace, a family friend, inviting us to join with him.'

'He knows of your past?'

'He has no idea of what would happen if certain individuals found me.'

'Your wife? Does she share Hampton's vision?'

'Not at first, but she was tired of her old life. High stress levels, cut it fine with the money. Sometimes there would be a fortune squirrelled away in a bank somewhere, other times just a few thousand. I don't go along with Eustace on a lot of things, but I sleep better here.'

'Was Hampton having sex with Charlotte Merton?' Clare asked.

'I don't know, not about Eustace, and that's the truth, not if she was determined.'

'And if the man is weak.'

'All men are weak, including me.'

'We've not found anything to verify what you've just told us. The Fraud Squad might,' Tremayne said.

'That's because Dominic and myself led double lives. A lot of business is conducted over the internet, via the phone, so we had little physical contact with anyone. He used a different name most of the time, the same as I did.'

'It still doesn't explain why you're hiding away,' Clare said.

'It was in our early days when we were starting out. Both of us were younger, more careless. If you're out to make money, the detail mustn't be known to those you're short-changing. It was the chain of coffee shops that I mentioned. We knew that one of the shops was prime real estate, ripe for redevelopment. However, zoning laws were against it, but I'd done some checking, found a loophole. We took advantage, sold the building, made a hefty profit.'

'No law broken, *caveat venditor*,' Tremayne said.

'Seller beware,' Fitzwilliam said.

Clare looked at Tremayne, surprised that he knew the term. *Caveat emptor* was the more common one.

'Only the vendor didn't see it like that. He learnt of the deception later. He was Italian, from the south, Mafia country, and whereas he'd been charming when he sold us the business, he wasn't so charming later on, when Dominic skipped the country, and I hotfooted it down here.'

'The Italian?'

'If he found out where I am, he'd be after his money, and I could be another murder for you to investigate.'

'Verifiable?'

'If I gave you the name that I used, yes.'

'But you don't intend to do that, do you, Mr Fitzwilliam?' Clare said.

'Not a chance.'

'It'll come out eventually.'

'Then I'll say this. If I become the next death, it will be on your consciences.'

Chapter 9

A key in her pocket, Maria Connelly entered the pub, surprised that it was locked. She went into the kitchen and switched on the oven in preparation. The remainder of the pies that Plumpton and the two police officers had not eaten in the morning were in a cabinet, still warm. She turned up the temperature, knowing that by five in the afternoon, most would have been sold.

As was usual, she would leave later for forty-five minutes, pick up her two children from school, a boy of six, a girl of eight, take them home, ensure they were fed and wait for her husband to come back from his work before returning to the pub.

In the main bar, there were no lights, only an eerie silence. Outside, at the rear of the building, Wally Plumpton's car, its engine cold. Maria called out his name – no reply.

Gingerly, with a sense of foreboding, Maria inched her way through the building. Typically, Wally's presence was only too apparent, and the man never exercised, never walked, never went anywhere without his car.

She opened the door to his office, saw him slumped over, the effect of too many drinks.

'Wally, it's time to open up,' Maria said. It wasn't the first time she'd seen him passed out.

Maria looked around the office, gave no more thought to the situation and left the room. The pub could stay closed until she came back later; she would open up if Wally wasn't capable.

***

Inside the farmhouse, Miranda Hampton sat close to the log fire, her hands stretched out in front of her, attempting to keep them warm.

Tremayne and Clare had seen the photos of when she was younger, and even though the woman had aged, she still remained attractive. Clare only hoped that when she reached Miranda's age, she would look half as good as she did.

'The media attention is unsettling,' Miranda said.

'It was to be expected,' Tremayne said.

Another of the women in the room gave Clare and him mugs of tea. 'No sugar, sorry. It's not good for you,' she said.

To Clare, it was fine; to Tremayne, tea without sugar wasn't tea, it was tasteless hot water. Nevertheless, he'd drink it. The cold outside and in Fitzwilliam's small office had cut through him like a hot knife through butter. Jean's wish to take a cruise somewhere warm seemed all too appealing.

Tremayne remembered his two visits to Singapore on a previous murder enquiry, the death of Clive Grantley's brother. The heat had been intense and unpleasant, but not as uncomfortable as the biting cold he felt now, and his joints ached.

'The negative publicity has caused the cancellation of Eustace's weekly programme.'

'How will you manage?'

'They're recorded. The money is not the immediate issue, the murders are. One or two of our flock are thinking of leaving.'

'Who?' Clare asked. She had taken a seat alongside Miranda, the chance to warm herself by the fire. Tremayne sat on a chair to their side.

'Betty Iles is one of them, but then, she always seemed not to belong.'

'We spoke to her once,' Clare said. 'A sister who had been ill.'

'She wasn't here when the two died, and she's thinking of going back to her sister, not that they get on.'

'How about you, Mrs Hampton?' Tremayne asked. 'You've led an interesting life.'

'My past seems glamorous, but it wasn't. A succession of lovers, most of them bad, a constant battle to stay slim, easy when you're in your late teens, not so easy later on. Here's where I'll stay, by Eustace's side, the one constant in my life, the one person who'll never disappoint.'

Tremayne wasn't so sure, as Eustace Hampton still came with a question mark. If Charlotte Merton had seduced Ben and Fitzwilliam, although neither had held out for long, what about the holier-than-thou Hampton.

'Jacob Grayson?'

'He was a different man when he first came here, exceedingly charming.'

'As soon as the ink was dried?'

'We could pay him back now, but he doesn't want it.'

'Have you offered?'

'Eustace would rather let it drift, hope that it'll work itself out.'

'You wouldn't.'

'Eustace is right. Too much is made of confrontation, of unnecessarily worrying.'

'Do you have a voice?' Tremayne asked.

'I have a view, if that's what you mean. I trust my husband, and whether we're here or in a council house, then I'd want no more. I had the life of plenty in my youth. Now all I want is a quiet life with my man.'

Clare had to agree with the sentiment. Life continued, good and bad, whether a person liked it or not. It was up to the individual to decide what was important, what was not.

***

Maria pulled the first pint from the beer tap on her side of the bar.

'Wally's not here?' Tremayne said as he took the pint glass from the woman.

'He's out the back, drunk.'

'Do you sometimes help in the bar?'

'Not often. My husband's with the children, and I expect Wally to appear at any time. It's best to let him sleep it off.'

'I should check,' Tremayne said. He took another drink of his pint, a bite of the hot pie in front of him, and lifted the entrance to the bar. He walked through the door at the rear, soon finding where Wally Plumpton was, head down on his desk.

Tremayne had stared death in the face too many times. He stood at a distance and watched the man, looking for the tell-tale signs, but there were none: no movement of the body as it breathed in and out, no sound emanating from the man.

'Brockenstoke, the pub, and pronto,' Tremayne said over the phone to Jim Hughes. 'We'll need an ambulance as well, just in case.'

'In case of what?'

'Just following procedure. The man's dead, that's all I know.'

'Have you touched anything?'

'No need to. He's been dead for a few hours. We spoke to him earlier in the day, so we can narrow it down.'

Tremayne left the room and walked back to the bar.

Maria was taking a pie out of the cabinet. A man sat in one corner of the bar.

Clare was sitting on a barstool, sipping her wine. 'Wally Plumpton?' she said.

'Maria, you'll have to close up,' Tremayne said, not replying to Clare. 'This is a crime scene.'

'He's dead, isn't he?' Maria said, holding her hands to her face.

'For several hours. We'll need to get a statement from you.'

'Murder?' Clare asked.

'Not sure. I've touched nothing. We'll wait for Hughes to give his opinion. No signs of violence.'

Clare went over to the only other occupant of the bar and explained the situation. The man lived two doors down, his address given, along with a phone number. He drank his beer and left; a statement would be taken later. The publican had died long before he had entered the bar.

Maria sat with Tremayne and Clare. Ten minutes later, a patrol car drew up outside, and the two officers set up the crime scene tape, made sure that no one attempted to enter the pub.

Jim Hughes arrived within the hour, apologised for the delay, but his team's workload only got larger, and budgetary constraints had meant that he had lost two of his staff, one of them finding a better paying job in

London, the other intending to take a six-month break to travel and recharge the batteries.

'I found him lying there earlier, head on the table,' Maria said. Tremayne had poured her brandy to steady the nerves.

'Not the first time, you said earlier.'

'Wally was a drinker, although he handled it well, but sometimes…'

'Sometimes he drank too much and became difficult.'

'He would bang into things, literally blind drunk, but never violent, not with me.'

'You've known him for a long time?'

'Four, nearly five years. I help out, prepare the food, clean around the place. It's not much money, but it's cash, and I can be there for the children. Every little bit helps, and my husband, Joe, he doesn't bring in much, but he's a good man, good father.'

'Let's go back to earlier today,' Clare said. 'We were here, and Wally was fine then.'

'I left before you did.'

'What time did you return?'

'3.30 p.m. on the dot.'

'You're very precise.'

'I had to pick the children up at twenty past four off the bus. I make sure that I keep to the schedule, as I don't want to leave Wally with unfinished work, and I don't want to be late for the children.'

'We left here at 11.50 a.m., so that gives a window of three hours and forty minutes. Long enough for him to get drunk?'

'If he started on the heavy liquor, not that he did often, only when he got bad news.'

'Did he ever confide in you?'

'He was close to his children, not that he saw them often, and he was on good terms with his ex-wife.'

'No one in the village?'

'Not that I know. He was a creature of habit, an unadventurous man.'

'Did you like him?'

'Yes, very much. The reason I worked for him.'

'Bad news, you mentioned it before. Any idea what would upset him?'

'The pub wasn't making money. The pub two villages away has put up the shutters, and Wally knew he wasn't going to survive.'

'A lot of money lost.'

'I don't think it was only that. He didn't want for much, just this place, a convivial life. He had nowhere to go, money or no money. He told me once that he wanted to die behind the bar.'

'Macabre,' Clare said.

'Not to Wally,' Maria said. 'He was an uncomplicated man. The pub was his life; it was him.'

Jim Hughes came into the bar, beckoned Tremayne to one side.

'Suicide or an accident,' Tremayne asked.

'There's a syringe, and he had injected himself. I'd say he overdosed, but you'll get that from the pathologist in due course. Also, a letter from the bank, ninety days or else.'

'How long has he been dead?'

'What time did you leave him?'

'11.50 a.m.'

'Thirty minutes to one hour after that. You and Clare were the last two people to see him alive.'

Tremayne left Hughes and went back to Clare and Maria. 'He OD'd on heroin,' he said.

107

'How tragic,' Maria said. She left the pub; it would remain closed for that day.

'Overdosed or intentional?' Clare asked.

'We'll never know. It's not foul play. He could have been a murderer. However, we'll not get a confession from him, not now.'

Chapter 10

Tremayne wasn't convinced that Wally Plumpton could be Charlotte Merton's murderer. To him, it was too easy, and there wasn't the evidence to wrap up the investigation into one of the murders, not yet.

It was a new day, warmer than the previous one, and both of the police officers were hopeful that they'd get through it without another body. Optimistic they knew, as murders invariably followed a pattern, and if Tremayne had been a man who believed in fate – he wasn't – he would have said that he was jinxed.

'Two murders, one suicide,' Tremayne said as he and Clare entered the farmhouse. Their presence had been expected.

'Sorry to hear about Plumpton,' Eustace said. He was sitting close to the fire, a laptop resting on his knees.

'I didn't think you went in for those, not in the house,' Clare said.

'The situation's changed. It was meant to be a place of tranquillity, a place where troubled souls could congregate, to gain benefit from others.'

'Not a murdering den of reprobates,' Tremayne chipped in, another of his attempts to elicit a response, Clare recognised. She wasn't sure that it would work, not with Hampton.

'Inspector, your choice of the vernacular is direct; unfortunately, it may have an element of truth.'

Clare was wrong; Hampton had reacted, and it appeared that the once proud leader of the small community was feeling the pressure. She knew that Tremayne would press the advantage.

'You're coming around to my way of thinking,' Tremayne said. Clare could see from the man's posture that he was pleased with himself. But then that was her boss, a man who kept applying pressure where needed, then backing off a little, then reapplying it. Murders, as he had told her, take time to solve, and those who kill are often rational people in irrational circumstances.

'It's Jacob,' Hampton said. 'The man wants us out.'

'Why now?'

'He phoned to let me know.'

'He said he wasn't about to pull the plug on you, not yet.'

'His childhood memory is being tarnished by what has happened.'

'I don't think Grayson is a man who cares about anything like that, do you?'

'It's unimportant. He has the legal right to do what he wants.'

'Naively you allowed him to gain the upper hand.'

'You're right, Inspector. I placed my faith in a man who couldn't be trusted.'

'Hampton, the world's not as you'd like it to be and pretending otherwise is sheer lunacy.'

'It doesn't have to be that way.'

'And you were going to change it.'

'It's a new world. Haven't you read about climate change, the earth's resources being consumed, the rainforests destroyed?'

'You believe you have the solution? Grayson was never to be trusted.'

'In time there will be a rejection of technology, a return to simpler times, the self-sufficient family.'

Tremayne and Clare had met Jacob Grayson the one time, and they hadn't liked him; how could Hampton? But then Tremayne was right; Grayson was street smart, but in the rarified atmosphere of a university, where academic debate dominated, there was the naivety that Hampton admitted to.

'It's not only Grayson, is it?' Tremayne said. He had taken a seat alongside Hampton. 'People who shouldn't have been trusted, Fitzwilliam, for instance.'

'Gavin pays his way.'

'And that's the reality,' Clare said. 'There are bills to pay, rates on the property, maintenance of the vehicles. Isolating yourself from society isn't going to work, not in England, not anywhere, unless you find a remote island, live off the land.'

'Miranda and I have discussed our future,' Hampton said.

'Before you leave, if that's what you're intending,' Tremayne said, 'there's still the matter of a couple of murders. What can you tell us about them?'

'If Grayson follows through, we'll leave, find that island, that clearing in the forest, live off the land…'

'And get bitten by mosquitoes, eaten by a wolf, starve to death in the winter. I read fairy tales as a child. You and your wife are not leaving, not until we've wrapped up our investigations.'

'It may be beyond your control. Grayson intends to have us out of here in seven to ten days.'

'Your people?'

'I've not told them.'

'We want to be here when you do.'

***

Tremayne was neither concerned about Grayson taking the farm, nor about Eustace and Miranda leaving. What concerned him was another variable: whether ownership of the farm could be another reason for murder.

Todd Hampton was still at the farm, even though he could have left before, and the two of them found him at the back of the house, a cigarette in his hand, blowing rings into the air.

Clare found something disturbingly uncomfortable about him, although she couldn't pinpoint what it was. He was a good-looking young man of above-average height, carrying a few pounds more than he should, a pleasant smile, a straightforward manner. Strangely, he reminded Clare of a younger Tremayne, more so than of Hampton.

'Any success?' Todd said as he shook Tremayne's hand first and then Clare's. His grip was clammy, and she felt as though she had just held a dead fish, but it was clear Tremayne liked the man.

'I thought you would have left,' Tremayne said.

'I was going to, but here's interesting. You never know what's going to happen next.'

'Todd, what do you reckon?' Clare asked.

'I've got my money on another murder.'

'You've heard about the publican?'

'Murder?'

'Suicide. Why, do you reckon it could have been?'

'No one here has any idea why the two women were killed.'

'Did you have sex with Charlotte Merton?'

'Well, I certainly didn't with Bess.'

Clare realised that Todd's politeness hid an acerbic tongue.

'That wasn't the question,' Clare pointed out.

'The situation never presented itself,' Hampton said. 'I wasn't here, not often.'

'If you had been here, and she had come on strong?'

'I'm a young man, what do you reckon?'

'That's a yes, then.'

'If it had, I would have taken advantage, who wouldn't? Anyway, the woman was messed up, and I kept my distance. She was trouble and if I had, and my girlfriend had found out, that would have been the end of a great romance.'

'I've been talking to your father,' Tremayne said. He was dressed for the weather: a heavier coat, more suitable footwear, a hat and gloves. The cold didn't concern him as much as it had the day before.

'Grayson?'

'You know?'

'Father told me, not that he'll worry too much.'

'Why's that?'

'The man believes in karma, whatever is whatever. To him, every cloud has a silver lining.'

'You'd disagree?'

'It's not for me, but it suits the two of them. As long as they're together, they'll be fine.'

'Would they do something foolish?' Clare asked.

'Overdose on pills, a joint suicide?'

'Something like that,' Tremayne said.

'It's always the two of them, that's for sure.'

'It's a possibility, that's what you believe?'

'Losing the farm wouldn't be sufficient. They would find somewhere, make home-made bread, grow vegetables, live off their love for each other.'

'Your remark about Bess Carmichael was in bad taste,' Clare said.

'She was a nosey person. I caught her once listening in on Fitzwilliam and his wife. If anyone knew what was going on, here or in the village, it would have been her.'

'She would have known who Charlotte had been with?'

'She would have watched, would Bess. I liked her in some ways. Most of them at the farm are dead from the neck up, but Bess, in her disgusting caravan and eating out of rubbish bins, was always entertaining. Why Charlotte was murdered, I can't guess, but Bess had the dirt on everyone.'

'A motive?'

'The problem is who did she have enough on to warrant murder, and why here?'

'Her death at the farm puts the focus on here. It points to someone belonging to the farm, when it could have been someone from the village, from anywhere,' Tremayne said.

'That, Inspector Tremayne and Sergeant Yarwood, is for you to find out,' Todd said. 'As for me, I'm back off to university and my girlfriend. Mother and father will survive, no matter what.'

Hampton stubbed his cigarette out under his foot and walked away.

Tremayne and Clare remained for a couple of minutes, taking in Hampton's conversation.

Finally, Tremayne turned to Clare. 'I don't trust him.'

'I thought it was only me.'
'It takes time to see through him.'

***

Sunday came around soon enough; another remembrance service, this time for Wally Plumpton.

Standing in the pulpit, the Reverend Walton. 'Wally was an important person in all our lives,' he started.

Tremayne, tired from the investigation, hopeful of a break for a few hours, a lie-in at home, breakfast in bed, was sitting in the second row of pews, Clare to one side of him.

He was there because Clare had been insistent, and because a church service is a good time to observe: those they knew, those they didn't.

To their right, on the other side of the aisle, Harriet Huxtable. She held a bible in her hand and was dressed in black, although she did not show any sign of remorse at Plumpton's passing. Directly in front of Tremayne and Clare sat a neatly-attired woman with a hat; she was dressed in black, the same as Harriet. However, she had a handkerchief in her hand, and two younger people on either side, their arms around her.

The woman had briefly introduced herself earlier as Plumpton's ex-wife, confirming that she had spoken to him one week before his death, and had met with him three months previously. And yes, they remained friendly and devoted to their children, she said when Clare had asked.

Later, Maria would be opening up the pub, a get-together to raise a drink to a man who was not as popular as the vicar was saying, but a decent man all the same.

That is, Tremayne thought, if he hadn't been trading drugs for money or favours; if he hadn't been a murderer.

Pathology had confirmed that Plumpton had had a vasectomy.

In the church, a good turnout. Eustace and Miranda Hampton sat towards the rear. Gavin Fitzwilliam – his wife was not present – sat next to Eustace.

Colonel Angus Campbell sat on his own, the opposite side of the church to Tremayne and Clare.

'Sadness has come to our corner of paradise,' Walton said.

Tremayne drifted away as one speaker after another got up to say a few words about the dead man, Maria included.

One of Plumpton's children climbed into the pulpit, said a few words about how they all missed their father, that he never forgot their birthdays, was always there for them. The son was the spitting image of the father, the red face, the bulbous nose – a drinker.

However, he never mentioned Charlotte Merton, not that he would have been expected to. It didn't stop Walton though.

'Let us not forget the others,' Walton said. 'Charlotte Merton, although not many of us knew her, was always ready for a conversation, always willing to pass the time of day with whoever.' Tremayne latched on to Walton's last word – whoever.

And that was it. Was it just because she was liberal with her favours, or was there something else, a reason that he and Clare had not thought of.

'Bess, dear sweet Bess Carmichael,' Walton said. Tremayne wanted to stand up and say 'go easy on the sweet', but he didn't. Clare looked at Harriet Huxtable, saw no reaction as her mother's name was mentioned.

***

'I had to come,' the woman's first words. The small bar at Plumpton's pub was full. Maria, a resilient woman, Clare had to admit, had organised someone to help serve the drinks, and she had stocked up on extra food.

'You didn't like Wally Plumpton,' Clare said.

A small glass of sweet sherry in her hand, Harriet Huxtable, a woman who by her own admission had never once been in the pub before, said in a whisper, her mouth close to Clare's ear, 'My mother.'

'You seemed unemotional when we were at your house.'

'She was my flesh and blood, and yet we couldn't talk to each other. How could I have done that?'

'Families are complicated,' Clare said. Back at the woman's house, she could have said that she was vexatious, a heart of ice, someone who deserved the scorn of all who knew the story, but she hadn't; stunned at the time as the woman had revealed the truth.

'I miss her. She was my only relative, can you believe that?'

'I can. You've never married, the circumstances of your birth, the life she had led.'

'I spoke to her once, about five years ago.'

'What happened?'

'It was up near that caravan of hers. We couldn't avoid each other, and for the first couple of minutes, nothing.'

'After that?'

'We hugged each other, cried, but it was no good. Too many memories. We parted, never spoke again.'

'You did no more for her?'

117

'Every Christmas, I'd make sure there was food for her around the back of my house, but I did not see her or utter one word. That makes me a wicked woman, worse than her, worse than Charlotte Merton.'

'Let's come back to Charlotte,' Clare said. She looked across the bar, saw Tremayne talking to Plumpton's family. Their eyes met, Tremayne understanding to leave his sergeant alone with the woman.

'She was a fallen woman. In the bible...'

'This is the real world, Miss Huxtable. She was murdered for a reason we don't know.'

'I couldn't speak to her, not even when she said hello.'

'Because of who she was?'

'I acted wrongly. She hadn't harmed me, and even if she sinned, what concern was it of mine? I should have been charitable. If I had, she might still be alive.'

The noise level of people talking, drinking too much, continued to rise. Clare took hold of the woman's arm and walked out of the pub with her.

'Now, what were you about to say?'

'I knew about her and Wally Plumpton.'

'How?'

'I saw her come out of the pub one morning very early, around two o'clock.'

'Are you in the habit of walking around the village at that hour?'

'Insomnia. I've always suffered from it.'

'He didn't kill her.'

'I know. She walked away from the pub, heading back to the farm across the fields.'

'And what?'

'She met someone. I wasn't following, not on purpose, but it was a clear morning, and I could see the two of them.'

'How long ago?'

'Ten days before she died.'

'Who was it?'

'Hampton's son.'

'Todd?'

'I don't know his name, only who he is by sight.'

'What else did you observe?'

'I saw them embrace, and then…'

'You saw them make love?'

'Against a tree.'

'You averted your eyes?'

'I should have, but I couldn't.'

'Why not?'

'One day, there'll be a service for me at the church. Do you know what they'll say? A spinster of the parish. They'll not say chaste, untouched, an old maid, but that's the truth. My mother had known love, even if it was carnal, incestuous. I never have, never will.'

Harriet Huxtable put down her glass and walked away.

Clare did not follow, only watched the confused, embittered, lonely woman walk back to her house.

Chapter 11

Clare, not pleased with the decision to allow the children back to the farm, spoke to Belinda Fitzwilliam in a café not far from where she lived with Clive.

Belinda, in her early forties, was dressed in a heavy coat, a long skirt and boots. To Clare, her appearance was markedly changed from when she had first met her at the farm. A few weeks, and the woman's inability to say much, other than to meld into the group at the farmhouse, was gone. In its place, an independent woman who wanted to talk.

'Wally Plumpton committed suicide,' Clare said. She had ordered latte for each of them.

'I can't say I knew him, not well. Gavin would talk to him occasionally, but neither of us drinks alcohol.'

'Because of the farm?'

'I don't enjoy it, and Gavin used to drink too much. He's a bad drunk, never hit me, but he'd start to get loud, shout at the children. It was an agreement we had when we rejected our previous life. We've both kept our promise to each other.'

'I'm not pleased that the children are going back,' Clare said. She was probing, trying to find corroboration of Gavin's story, not wanting to cause friction between husband and wife. Neither were strong contenders for murder, not yet.

The motives were there for Charlotte: jealousy, love, hate, anger at rejection. With Bess, apart from the contradictory statements that she was nosey or she wasn't, it wasn't so clear. The woman's lifestyle offended a few, but it was hardly a motive, and Harriet, the woman's daughter, even though full of remorse and bitterness in equal measures, wasn't a suspect, no more than the others in the village. Where Bess had been strung up still pointed to someone at the farm.

Tremayne would say that this is when it gets interesting: when all the pieces of the puzzle come together. Clare had to concede to his wisdom in such matters, but there still remained the possibility of further murders, and she didn't want the children back at a murder scene.

However, as Clive had said the night before when they had discussed the matter, 'It's a cost on the council paying for the hotel, and where's the proof that they'll come to any harm?'

He was right, she knew that, but she had seen the change in the children, the difference in Belinda Fitzwilliam, as well as in Tommy Yardley, nine years old and a livewire, running up and down the hallway in the hotel – they would be glad when he left. His mother, Eva, perilously thin, although the breakfasts at the hotel had fattened her up, was delighted to be returning.

But then, Clare had observed that the woman was easily led, easily controlled by her heavily tattooed husband, John. The man's explanation for the decorations: too much drink, too many years in the navy.

His explanation, as with the others at the farmhouse, of a better life, the right place for the children, hadn't held true, and Yardley had been found to have a conviction for robbery with menace, a five-year term in prison.

Clare liked Tommy, cheeky as only a nine-year-old boy could be, but his mother she found to be without a personality, not an independent thought in her head. In short, Eva Yardley could bore for England, whereas her husband, calm at the farm, could steal for the country, and probably still did. Two days a week, he would leave the farm, not telling anyone where he was going, not even kissing his wife goodbye, not that she would have ever asked what he was up to. Clare could see that if it was a crime, or another wife somewhere, a mistress, she wasn't the sort of person to care, not outwardly. Inwardly, she could have, but that was not known.

John Yardley had been questioned about his time away, and his story about visiting his mother, helping her as she was old and disabled, had been proven to be untrue. The man had not been at the farm when Charlotte and Bess had died, and even though his alibi was false, he wasn't an emotional man, and didn't seem to be concerned about them one way or the other.

He had only one redeeming feature, his love for the young Tommy, who was a good-natured tearaway, but would soon enough transpose into a carbon copy of his father. Even at nine he rarely listened to his mother – and she was too timid to discipline him.

The other two children returning to the farm, Sally and Bronwyn Reece, Sally the older at thirteen, Bronwyn, twelve years and one month, were both intense. They were not twins, although they acted as if they were. If one had a blue jumper, the other did. If it was jeans, the same colour, as with their shoes.

'They've always been that way,' their mother, Margaret, had said. Their father had died three years previously. Neither of the girls would speak of him, even when Clare had asked, although Margaret, a proud woman, her head held up high, her appearance always immaculate, would, although only to say that he was missed by all three.

Clare could not relate to Margaret Reece; however, she liked Belinda Fitzwilliam.

Belinda drank her latte, enjoyed the breakfast that she had ordered. 'Gwyneth doesn't want to go back,' she said.

'Matilda told me that, as well,' Clare said. 'What do you intend to do?'

'It's up to Gavin.'

'You'll do what he says?'

'He cheated my brother, him and that Dominic.'

'We know about that, and your husband told us that his partner absconded with the money.'

'Gavin's not the murderer, I'm sure of that, so I'll be open with you,' Belinda said.

'We can't discount him, not yet.'

'It doesn't matter. Gavin would have told you that Dominic moved all the money out of the offshore accounts, put them somewhere where Gavin couldn't find them.'

'He did.'

'Half-truths, but then Gavin talks in riddles. He's a clever man, knows how to massage the figures, but he plays it too close to the edge sometimes.'

'People get hurt, get cheated,' Clare said.

'Get angry, and then come looking for revenge and their money back.'

'Your brother?'

'He told you that much. That's Gavin, careful with the truth. Okay, he short-changed my brother, but he still came out alright. He's not the problem.'

'Gavin mentioned that someone was looking for him.'

'He would have left the country, but I wasn't going to, and the children were going to stay with me.'

'He said he wouldn't leave because of them.'

'Did he tell you that our money is still intact?'

'He said he was freelancing, attempting to pay the bills. According to him, the people who were looking for him weren't the sort to listen to lame excuses, more likely, a knee-capping.'

'Eternally optimistic, that's Gavin,' Belinda said. 'He'd have offered to work for them.'

'Which they might have accepted.'

'It's immaterial now. The girls and I are going to live with my brother, better for all of us.'

'And Gavin?'

'He'll not come with us. He can go and join Dominic, wherever he is. He'll have to find another woman, now Charlotte's not available.'

'You knew?'

'She wasn't the most discreet. She blurted it out to me.'

'Do the girls know?'

'I hope not. I don't want them to feel disappointment with their father. He cared for them, the same as he cared for me, but the man's either on the up or he's dead. Whichever it is, I don't want us to be there. My brother has a big house, plenty of room for all of us. One day, Gavin can come and visit, stay if he wants, but that's his decision. The girls need stability, and they don't need Eustace and his nonsense.'

'Anything I should know about what goes on there?'

'Nothing, just meditating and philosophising, that's all. It's good for some, not for others.'

***

Todd Hampton had little to say for himself when Tremayne caught up with him. He had stayed an extra night at the farm, the reason not given, and for the present, unimportant.

Tremayne, not concerned that people tell the occasional lie – even he did when he had lost more on the horses than he'd care to admit to Jean – did not appreciate untruths in response to direct questions, especially when it was a murder investigation.

The two men walked away from the farmhouse, over to the stream where they had spoken once before.

'It's time you started telling the truth,' Tremayne said.

Hampton looked away, avoiding eye contact, acting nonchalant. 'I don't know what you mean, Inspector.'

'Your relationship with Charlotte Merton.'

'I told you before. I've got a girlfriend, and sure, Charlotte was easy on the eye and one or two others were messing around with her, but I wasn't one of them.'

Tremayne walked away, Hampton walking alongside him. At the end of the track, close to the narrow bridge that defined the start of Brockenstoke or the end of it, depending on which direction you were travelling, he stopped.

'This tree,' Tremayne said as he leant against it.

'It's an oak tree. Judging by its girth, it's over a hundred years old, maybe as much as one hundred and fifty.'

'It's not the tree that's important; its what you were doing here up against it ten days before Charlotte died.'

'I wasn't here. I hadn't been here for three weeks until I arrived the other day.'

125

'Then you've a doppelganger. You were seen. Now, why were you here, and why didn't you visit your parents? And don't give me "my girlfriend doesn't understand me" drivel.'

'You're mistaken, Inspector,' Hampton pleaded, not as convincingly as before.

'Don't try my patience. If you came down here, a bit on the side, then say it. Otherwise, you're a hostile witness, and there's one thing I don't appreciate, it's people who lie. Makes me think about what else they're lying about. If they could be a murderer, for instance. Are you a murderer, the father of the unborn child?'

Hampton leant against a nearby fence post. 'It was Charlotte, she asked me to come down.'

'Why?'

'She told me she was pregnant, and the child was mine.'

'Your reaction?'

'Alarmed. A promising career, a girlfriend that I want to marry, down the drain if it became known.'

'Is that why you killed her?'

'Quite the opposite. I'm career-driven, and in time will be a great lawyer. What I feel – felt – had to be put to one side.'

'You cared for the woman?'

'There was something about her, a joy for life, remarkable considering the life she had led. It was refreshing, and my girlfriend, a beautiful and clever woman, all that a man could want, is conventional in her thinking, predictable. I intend to marry her, but it will be a dull life, and that's fine by me, but with Charlotte, you could dream, talk nonsense, laugh, irrationally fall in love.'

'What did you intend to do?'

'I couldn't be with her, it just wasn't possible, but somehow I wanted to be.'

'She slept with other men here. How could she be sure it was yours?'

'She couldn't, and I knew about the other men. Why I could forgive her, I don't know, and she told me it was behind her, and she was willing to devote herself to me, to forsake the others, to not take drugs anymore.'

'Did you believe her?'

'I parked my car up a lane not far from here, met her at the tree. I wanted to tell her that it couldn't be, but it was a cold night, and she was there. I couldn't resist her, never could.'

'Did you see her again?'

'Never. I went back to university and my girlfriend. There was no solution, and I couldn't believe the child was mine. I knew about Ben and the publican, suspected Fitzwilliam, even thought of my father, so it didn't seem possible that she could be sure, but she was adamant. "It's yours, Todd", she kept saying.'

'Did she love you?'

'In her own way, I think she did. But life had mistreated her, the degradation of selling herself for drugs had made her weak. She was doomed, regardless of what she might have wanted.'

'Yet you fell for the woman?'

'I felt protective of her.'

'Men have been convicted on weaker evidence,' Tremayne said.

'I knew that if she lived, then one day she would tell someone, probably my father, and my girlfriend would find out. My career would be dashed, as well.'

'You would be found guilty for what you've just said.'

'Circumstantial, and you know it. Inspector Tremayne, you've been around, what do you think?'

'I think you've either used me as a subject for your courtroom skills or you're telling me the truth; I'm not sure which of them I prefer.'

'I didn't kill her,' Todd Hampton said, 'Not Charlotte, not ever.'

The two men walked back to the farmhouse, shook hands and parted. Hampton went into the farmhouse; Tremayne got into his car.

Chapter 12

It was a Wednesday, three days since the service at the church for Wally Plumpton, three days since Harriet Huxtable had revealed more about herself.

At the farm, the departure of Betty Iles: the hugging, the promise to keep in touch, the going-away present, but it was a façade, Clare could see that.

She had not gone to the farmhouse to see that person leave but to see two others return. The first was Eva Yardley; her son, Tommy, was at school. He'd be arriving on the school bus in the afternoon, along with the two Reece girls.

Clare could only imagine the reaction of the people at the farm on seeing the previously subdued Tommy running up and down, being cheeky with everyone, causing mayhem, although the depressive air of the farm would soon calm him.

The welcoming back of Eva and, five minutes later, Margaret Reece, was more subdued than when Betty Iles had left, who had got into the back of a taxi and been driven off, not once looking back at the place that had been her home, not looking at those who had been her friends.

Coldness in the woman, or was it the people at the farm? Whatever it was, Clare didn't like it: too sterile, too contrived, lacking in reality.

Regardless, she intended to stay and observe, noting that Gavin Fitzwilliam stood apart from the others, awaiting the arrival of his wife. She wasn't coming, and it was clear that she had not informed him.

Tremayne had updated Clare as to what Eustace and Miranda Hampton's son had admitted to. He was in two minds about his guilt, although the man's forced admission had weighed in his favour.

That afternoon the hyperactive Tommy Yardley was soon running up and down in the farmhouse, out in the yard and not wiping his shoes on his return.

In the end, after Tommy had screamed through the farmhouse for the third time, opening the fridge door, failing to close it, grabbing an apple out of a fruit bowl without asking, Eustace Hampton reacted. He took the boy's mother to one side and spoke to her. Clare attempted to listen, but could not hear, and besides, her focus was on the assembled group. Over in one corner, the Reece sisters, almost as if they were joined at the hip.

Eva Yardley, regardless of her wish to be at the farm, had changed. Not dramatically, but subtly. Clare could see the woman in discussion with Eustace, looking over at her son who had been temporarily distracted by a book he had found.

Tommy was a handful, and Clare conceded he did need some gentle discipline, but that was all.

John Yardley came into the farmhouse, touched his wife's arm, gave her a kiss on the cheek and went over to where Tommy was sitting. The young boy's reaction on seeing his father was unexpected: he ran out of the building, leaving the book opened on the floor. A smile from the father, and then he left in pursuit of his son.

There was tension in the Yardley family, and it was possibly destructive. Behind the calm exterior, Clare wondered if John Yardley did at times deal out discipline to the young boy. If he did, it was contrary to the spirit of the community and strictly against the rules laid down by Eustace Hampton.

Margaret Reece, removing herself from the two women she had been talking to, went over to her daughters, and sat down with them, the young girls welcoming her into their midst.

Clare reflected back to a time past when Harry had died, and her mother's reaction. Her mother had not been conciliatory, and barely helpful in any way in dealing with her grief, the reason Clare had found herself back at work within a couple of months. Tremayne had taken the correct approach, not expressing outright sympathy, only putting her straight to work, giving her no time to feel sorry for herself.

Was that the same with the Reece three, each relying on the other, helping them through a difficult time, or had the husband been pushed to one side, finding another woman, preferring to be out drinking with his mates, before finally overturning his car late at night while incapacitated? Clare had read the report on the man's death, although it was conjecture as to why the mother and daughters were as close as they were.

A cup of tea was placed into Clare's hand. She didn't know who had given it to her, but she was glad of it. Outside it was cold; inside it was stiflingly warm, and the air was heavy with the smell of the open fire, the musty odour of people whose clothes were washed in a large tub, not in a washing machine, the water recycled to conserve it.

'It's good to see them back,' Miranda Hampton said as she came up to Clare.

'It must be,' Clare responded, observing that the complexion of the former model and socialite was fresh and pale, not tanned like some of the others.

'It's a shame it's not to last.'

'Do they know?' Clare looked over at the others in the room.

'Not yet. It's changed, you must have seen that.'

'Are you sad?'

'For Eustace, not for me.'

'You're not convinced?'

'I am, but Eustace is an idealist. I've had more experience of the world; I know what is out there, but my husband has enjoyed a cloistered existence, tied to academia, his beliefs shaped by the philosophers of old.'

'*Plato's Republic*?' Clare said.

'You've read it? Admirable if you have.'

'The philosopher-king. We were all naïve back in our youth, believing that our generation could take humankind to another level, justice for all, equality, no poverty or war.'

'Eustace still believes it's all possible.'

'Did you read the book?' Clare asked.

'I tried, Eustace intent on educating me, read the first chapter. After that, I'm afraid to admit, it lost me.'

'It's a smart person who can understand it on the first reading. Your husband probably did.'

'He studied it for his PhD.'

'Inspector Tremayne's spoken to your son.'

'I know, Eustace doesn't.'

'What do you know?'

'I know that Todd liked Charlotte. I saw myself in her at that age, but I never found drugs, not until later, and never heroin; although I found men, plenty of them. Some only wanted one thing…'

'Which they got, according to the magazine articles of the time,' Clare said, sure that the woman wouldn't be offended.

'Exaggerated most of the time, but there was a modicum of truth.'

'Why? You were a beautiful woman, you still are.'

'It seemed decadent, and it was exciting. In truth, it was shallow, and eventually I tired of it. I ceased to play the game, to party all night, and then the phone stopped ringing, the chauffeur-driven car no longer at the door, no private jet waiting to fly me off to some exotic location. Eustace was my saviour.'

'Is he still?'

'Very much so. He needs to be told about Todd and Charlotte at some stage, but not today. Would you agree?'

'His reaction if he's told?'

'Disappointment. Todd is more like me than his father, easily infatuated.'

'Was Todd infatuated with Charlotte?'

'He saw it as love, but he has a girlfriend at university. Have you met her?'

'Not yet.'

'She's hard, the person for Todd.'

'Love?'

'Her for him. Todd is easily distracted, but she'll keep him close, the same as I do Eustace.'

'Is Eustace's head turned by a pretty face, a wiggle of the hips?'

'His head in a book and he'll take on board the philosophical argument in favour of infidelity, attempting to construct his own. Idealism is all very well in the confines of a university, but out here it serves little purpose.'

'You'll not be sad to leave here?'

'We'll find somewhere remote. Eustace can write; I can look after my man.'

'And Todd?'

'He can visit when he wants, but his girlfriend will never come.'

'She disapproves?'

'Of us, she does. A hard woman, as I said, but I like her, even if she doesn't like me and loathes Eustace.'

'How long before you tell everyone that they're leaving?'

'Five days. It's long enough for them to make alternate arrangements.'

***

After the excitement of the return of the children and their mothers, normality returned to the farm. Gavin Fitzwilliam dressed in his suit and tie and went to his makeshift office each day, sat behind his laptop, continued to work. In the house, Margaret Reece and Eva Yardley returned to their duties, the children catching the bus to Salisbury in the morning, returning in the afternoon, the boisterous Tommy still active, but more manageable now, still irritating some, being ignored by others.

In the village, Harriet Huxtable went to the church every day, and Maria opened the pub of an evening – in honour of Wally, she would say if asked.

The Reverend Walton continued to visit his ill and aged parishioners and to spend time preparing sermons for those that attended on a Sunday, though not many did, most preferring to go down to the coast if the weather was good. Petula Walton, his ever-loyal wife, continued to make cakes, ensuring that some went to Tony Frampton, the simple-minded man that everyone accepted and liked, although it didn't stop the disparaging comments, especially from Ben who continued to refer to him as 'Stupid Tony'.

Tremayne was laid low for a day with a severe cold. Clare was still at the village and the farm every day, and making sure to be at the police station too, sometimes till late at night, checking on facts, writing reports, so much so that Clive had commented on one occasion that he missed her, and he wasn't a demonstrative man, not the type to say 'I love you', even though he did.

To Clare, he was the rock in her life, and she had to admit to feeling sublimely happy with the man, an unusual emotion for a police officer used to the underbelly of society, delving into people's dirty linen, being told things that would make some people cringe, others shocked.

Such was the situation with Harriet Huxtable, 'spinster of the parish', as she had said that time in the pub. Clare had spoken to her since, and the woman had closed up, both verbally and emotionally. No more revelations, no gossip, nothing, only the church and the vicar.

As content as Clare was, Harriet Huxtable was the opposite. Clare could find sympathy for the woman, but not empathy. The woman was not an empathic person, not a person to feel any strong emotion for, not love or hate, and after a lifetime in the village she had not one friend, not one person who came over for a bite to eat, a gossip.

Colonel Angus Campbell, his presence in the village unmistakeable, walked around in a brisk military fashion, always immaculately dressed, speaking to everyone, enquiring after their health, their children and their well-being. Clare wasn't sure if it was an affectation, or whether it was the years of military discipline, the rank that he had held, that had given him the bearing he displayed, the concern for others a requisite of command.

On the fourth day since the return of the children, an unexpected face appeared in the village.

Clare had seen her get off the bus from Salisbury at midday, a small case in one hand, a handbag in the other.

'Miss Iles, you weren't expected,' Clare said.

'It's her, impossible. I can't live with her,' she said as Clare drove her to the farm.

Betty Iles, with a perpetual frown, a downcast appearance, Clare had reasoned, was a woman who accepted life on its terms, not hers, and if it dealt her a bad blow, she'd just accept it and continue. The only thing that did bring out a reaction was her sister.

'You've come back for good?'

'As long as I've got,' the woman's response.

She was in her seventies, frail and constantly sniffling with a cold, always taking medicine in the morning, not that Eustace held with drugs, medicinal or otherwise. Clare had had a great-aunt who had looked the same, spoken in the same negative manner, rarely smiling, and yet she had lived to over a hundred, a message from the Queen to celebrate the occasion. Betty Iles looked as though she'd outlive most of those at the farm, even Eustace.

***

Clare and Tremayne were keeping close to the farm, although the murder enquiry wasn't progressing as well as it should have been. And now, the superintendent, Tremayne's and Clare's boss at Bemerton Road Police

136

Station, was asking questions, concerned at budgetary constraints, the tying up of valuable personnel on an investigation that was rapidly becoming a cold case, to be filed in the too-hard basket, unsolvable.

He and Tremayne were sparring partners, with a mutual respect for each other; one of them not wanting to retire, attempting to stay healthy, a jaunty swagger in the station, a slouch outside of it; the other, driven by key performance indicators and results, burdened with a shrinking budget, the need to reduce staffing levels, the need to solve crimes by computer, the power of the internet, forensic analysis.

Each was willing to concede that the other was correct to some extent. Technology served its purpose, critical to the superintendent, an adjunct to Tremayne who maintained a belief in out-at-the-scene policing, knocking on doors, observing people's reactions. He held with being at the scene of the crime, reading the body language, looking for the missing clue.

'It's like this,' Tremayne said as he sat down with Gavin Fitzwilliam. 'We've got two murders, your wife's done a runner with your daughters, and you're sitting here like a lemon.'

'I still need to provide for them,' Fitzwilliam said, his head buried in his laptop.

'From what you've told us, limited as it was, you could be another statistic soon.'

'Not if I'm here.'

'Your wife and children leave, and you've made no effort to contact them. Why's that?'

'I have, by phone.'

'You short-changed her brother, and we know they're with him. What's the relationship between him and you? Hostile, friendly, what is it?'

'It's not good.'

'You cheated him, that's the truth.'

'He's no fool, and yes, we cheated him, and good for us. I've no guilt regarding him. He was willing to come in with us, to hoodwink the banks.'

'Is he likely to do something against you if he knows where you are?'

'He'll try and get some money from me, not that I have any.'

Tremayne got up from where he was sitting. Fitzwilliam's office was cold, and his right leg was cramping.

'We've been told that your partner didn't take off with the money, and you've got plenty hidden away overseas. We can't prove that, but if it's true, then your wife's brother could come here.'

'If he knows where I am.'

'Fitzwilliam, don't insult me. Your wife might not tell, but do you expect your children not to. They're still young, probably see you in a benevolent light, more than I do. You're a rogue of the first order, a criminal without a doubt. It may well be a white-collar crime, but the Fraud squad, and you've been accused of embezzling, could be down on you like a ton of bricks. What would you say to that?'

'Are they likely to? Have you told them?'

'I'm Homicide. It's two murders that concern me. In due course, you'll be subject to a full audit, although if you've shifted the money to where it can't be found, if you've wiped all records in this country, they might not get very far.'

'You have a flair for fiction, Inspector,' Fitzwilliam said. The laptop was now closed, a clear sign to Tremayne that the man was rattled.

'Of course, there is still the Mafia connection. They won't need proof, just you strung up somewhere, electrodes attached to your genitals, a handle to crank.'

'They are Italian, not Mafia.'

'You'll talk, people like you always do. You're on a precipice. Either you tell us, and we'll try to protect you, or you take your chances.'

'My conscience is clean.'

'Have it your way, but we intend to talk to your brother-in-law, see what he has to say. Which leads us to the two dead women. Charlotte could have known something, threatened to blurt out the truth, as to how you were a big man, plenty of money, and that you and she could have headed to the sun.'

'It wasn't like that.' Fitzwilliam thumped the table.

'Or Bess Carmichael, a woman who looked in windows, could have seen something, came into your office, deduced what was going on.'

'She wasn't that bright. Don't credit that old woman with something she wasn't.'

'She had had a rough life, lived badly, but she could have been smart, known a crook when she saw one. Maybe she threatened you, asked for money.'

Tremayne knew the man was not going to confess to fraud or murder, not even sure that he was guilty of either. Cheating another businessman out of money wasn't necessarily criminal, although not paying tax on the profit was illegal; that could be dealt with in time.

Tremayne realised, however, that his statement that Bess Carmichael could have seen something, whether it was Fitzwilliam or someone else, was plausible.

Chapter 13

In the four days since Betty Iles had returned to the farm, five people had left. Two were a married couple in their late sixties who had never fitted into society, preferring the periphery. Alternative life-stylers, their definition; no-hopers, Tremayne's translation. People who dropped out, dropped in, drifted through life high on one recreational drug or another were of little value to Tremayne, and he gave them scant regard.

The two gave a forwarding address, a commune in Wales. Clare checked, but it was extreme: no phones, no electricity, no running water, just ramshackle shacks. According to the local police who had confirmed the place existed, it was a sad attempt to live as man had lived in the past. Even so, the police sergeant had said they weren't averse to taking money if offered, eating the fruits of the forest in summer, shopping at the supermarket in the winter with the dole money.

The other three, two women and their male companion, departed soon after the geriatric hippies.

The Fraud squad had been informed of Gavin Fitzwilliam and were conducting checks. The only condition imposed by Tremayne was that their enquiries were discreet and that the man was not to be approached by them in case it interfered with the murder investigation.

Betty Iles was a conundrum: meek, hardly saying a word, sitting on her own most of the time.

Fitzwilliam continued to spend his days in his office, always dressed in a suit. 'I dress for the office,' he had said. 'Casual, and I can't focus.'

Tremayne always wore a suit during working hours, although not with Fitzwilliam's sartorial elegance; Tremayne wore his as if it was a bag of potatoes, the pockets bulging, the tie askew, the shirt collars pointing in whatever direction they wanted. Jean made sure he left the house smart, but the lumbering man soon adjusted the suit to his liking, or it could have been that what he was wearing gave up in disgust and adapted to the man.

But that was Tremayne, a man who affected a style, but was razor-sharp in dealing with a crime.

Jacob Grayson, the most contentious of the farm's inhabitants, also wore a suit. He was a coarse man, a man that Clare didn't like, but then nobody appeared to.

Checks had been made, the same as for everyone who had known Charlotte and Bess. His childhood at the farm had been confirmed, although it had been glamorised by Grayson. His father had owned the farm for two years, lived in it for thirteen.

For the first eleven years, Grayson senior had leased it on an annual basis at a competitive rent. A copy of the lease had been obtained. However, a condition of the contract was that after the first ten years, if the property were to be offered for sale, it had to be first offered to the sitting tenant; to wit, Grayson senior. At year eleven, the owner had passed away, and the farm had been sold to the tenant at a favourable price; so much so that two years later Grayson had sold it on for a good profit.

If Grayson senior had been involved in the previous farm owner's death, surmised, never proven, then Jacob Grayson's assertion that his father had been a farmer, nothing more, was untrue.

It could be that Jacob Grayson had learnt murderous skills at his father's knee.

***

Bess Carmichael, her death inadvertently taking a secondary position to that of Charlotte Merton, nevertheless remained a focus. Charlotte's history before arriving at the farm had been easier to ascertain; her transition from rebellious child to a rebellious teenager, the drugs forging the inevitable downfall from promiscuity to prostitution, then pulling herself up from degradation, finding a job, only to relapse and end up back on the street again.

'Charlotte told me once that she had never been so happy as here,' Eustace Hampton said, as he and Tremayne walked alongside the stream at the back of the farm. 'She had a problem with men, she told me that.'

'Nymphomaniac, is that what you're saying?' Tremayne said. Even though the weather was cold, and there had been a frost the previous night, he enjoyed the ambience of the small stream and the track beside it.

'Inspector, that's not what I meant.'

'She initiated sex with more than one man, or don't you know that? You're the all-seeing, all-knowing fount of knowledge around here. You must be aware of this?'

'People seek affection for many reasons. It's not always physical.'

'Are you saying it's emotional? Her and Wally Plumpton?'

'And Ben. I know about those two.'

'How?'

'I observe, the same as you do, the body language, what a person says, the expression.'

'We've got your son with her, and God knows who else,' Tremayne said.

'Gavin Fitzwilliam,' Hampton said. 'Yes, I know about him and Charlotte.'

'And if he were a criminal, answerable for crimes committed?'

'We judge the person, not the deed. We are all guilty of one crime or another, regrets from our past.'

'As you are, Hampton.'

'What happened at the university is old history.'

'A woman committed suicide.'

'She was troubled even when I knew her.'

'Is that your justification for sleeping with her, discarding her when you'd had enough, finding another younger?'

'Inspector, our relationship may have been inappropriate, ill-advised, but both of us were adults. University is not a school, different rules apply, rebellion is fomented, protests are held, relationships are formed.'

'The woman died because of you.'

'She died because of depression.'

'You have a penchant for younger women,' Tremayne said.

'If you're referring to my wife, we've been married for over twenty-six years. I don't think you could hold up our relationship as proof of what you're trying to make me admit to.'

'Which is?'

'That I had sex with Charlotte.'

'Well, did you?'

'This is not the first time you've asked the question, and the answer remains the same. I am innocent of what you're accusing me of.'

'Would you agree to a DNA test?'

'If it will prove, once and for all, that I wasn't involved with the woman.'

'It'll prove if you were the father of Charlotte's unborn child.'

'Take your test, eliminate me from that at least.'

'We know that Wally Plumpton wasn't, but then he had had a vasectomy.'

'They can be reversed.'

'We have the fetal DNA. It wasn't him, and if you're certain you're not the guilty party, then who was it?'

'Ben, Gavin?'

'It raises interesting questions, doesn't it?' Tremayne said.

'You're the police inspector, you tell me. I'm just a malingering defrocked university professor, an oddball, in your opinion, that is.'

'You belittle yourself, Hampton. I don't form opinions of people based on my personal views, not during an investigation. I interview, I question, I evaluate the person, look for proof, look for a motive.'

'And the motive for Charlotte's death? The father of the child?'

Tremayne knew that Hampton wouldn't see it being as simplistic as that. The man would have weighed up the facts, understood that a DNA sample would not only eliminate him as the father of the unborn child, it would also eliminate his son, as the Y chromosome passed along the male line.

'Fitzwilliam wouldn't have wanted the child to be born, although his wife knew about him and Charlotte.

144

Plumpton would have been delighted, as he was fond of Charlotte. You, on the other hand, wouldn't want your perfect marriage to be affected, nor would you want your wife to be hurt. And what about your community here? What would they say?'

'It's not mine.'

'And then we have the possibility that one of her lovers, not sure if we know who they all are, could have found it abhorrent that the woman was carrying another man's child.'

'Ben?'

'The man can be violent. We also have Tony Frampton, harmless as everyone believes, but he's a strong man, and Charlotte made a play for him, scared him half-senseless.'

A smile from the usually sombre Hampton. 'I bet she did. I did like Charlotte, the woman had a spark. In time…'

'You hoped to save her from herself.'

'She would have made a good wife for Todd.'

'Her past would always be there.'

'She would have made him happy. His career would not have suffered, not as much as you'd think. She'd be a tainted woman, but Todd will be brilliant when he completes his studies, and Charlotte would never have let him down.'

'Hampton, you should get your head out of the sand,' Tremayne said. 'If you believe what you've just said, you're not as smart as people give you credit for.'

'Her heart was pure, and Todd liked her.'

Tremayne reflected on the conversation that he had had with the son on a previous occasion by the stream. Todd had liked the woman up against the tree, but Tremayne knew that his father liked her more.

It was the father who saw that if he couldn't have Charlotte, then his son would. And as to the hogwash that the son's career would still flourish, that was nonsense. The man would be the butt-end of jokes amongst his fellow lawyers, the under-the-table comments from the prosecution when he was defending. And Charlotte's need for a man was not emotional, it was physical.

***

Colonel Angus Campbell presented himself at the police station in Salisbury. 'I didn't want to say anything, not at the pub, not at the service for Plumpton,' he said.

The three of them were in the interview room; Tremayne and Clare on one side of the table, Campbell on the other.

'Withholding evidence is an offence,' Clare said.

Campbell sat upright, square shoulders, his chest pulled in, his moustache freshly-waxed. In the breast pocket of his jacket, a handkerchief neatly folded, the triangle showing at the top.

'It's about Bess Carmichael.'

'We still don't have a motive for her death,' Tremayne said.

'She lived in that disgusting caravan, but I found her intriguing. She was more my age and sometimes, not recently, not for many years, we'd talk.'

'About what?'

'This and that, general conversation. Over the years, snippets of her past would come out. How she had had a child when she was young.'

'Anything else?'

'When she first arrived in the village – it seems a lifetime ago, although it was probably only twenty to twenty-five years – she was in her early sixties, I was a few years younger, recently widowed.'

'A romance?' Clare asked.

'It was hardly that, not something you as a young woman would understand. It was companionship, and for a couple of years, we'd spend time together.'

'The caravan?'

'Contrary to what people might tell you, although most wouldn't remember, she didn't arrive with the caravan. Sometimes she'd stay with me, other times she'd board at the pub.'

'What happened?'

'Age happened. We drifted apart, rarely spoke, and since the turn of the century, we've not exchanged a word.'

'Why?'

'The woman started to disintegrate.'

'The caravan?'

'It appeared one day, no idea from where. Bess moved in, and it and she became one. As it fell to pieces, so did she.'

'The sorrow in her life that you spoke of?' Clare said.

'A child. A girl, although she died at birth. Apart from that, I can't tell you much about her life. She was educated, and she told me that she had worked for the government in London, lived overseas, never married.'

'A child and not married; didn't you think that strange? She came from a different generation, people would not have regarded that the same as they do today.'

'She never wanted to talk much about herself. She helped me through a difficult patch, my wife had died, recently retired.'

'What if we told you the daughter was alive, what would you say?' Tremayne asked.

'Did Bess know?'

'She did.'

'It's Harriet, isn't it?'

'We're not at liberty to discuss it,' Tremayne said, regretting that he had given the man the lead; pleased that it opened up further questions and possible answers.

'A military man, trained to observe,' Campbell said. 'Trained to keep secrets. Neither Harriet nor anyone else will know from me.'

'If what you've figured out is true, what more can you tell us?'

'I used to see the two of them sometimes in the village, careful to avert their eyes, and then Harriet, at Christmas, ensuring there was food for Bess.'

'What did you think?'

'I thought it was odd at the time, but now…a shared history so shameful that neither could deal with it, drawn together as mother and daughter, repelled by the very idea. It must be a dreadful secret.'

'You came here to tell us about Bess,' Clare said. 'What else can you tell us?'

'Observations only, you must understand.'

'We understand.'

'It was a week before Bess died. I was out for my daily walk, not that I go far, not these days.'

'You saw something?' Tremayne said.

'I'm not far from the caravan. There's a spot on a hill that I sometimes climb, or to be more correct, hobble up. I can see Bess and where she lives from there.'

'Why would you keep a watch on her?'

'She's old, and no one checked on her, although it appears that Harriet did.'

'What does that mean?'

'I'm looking down at the caravan; I often do, once a week if I can. Harriet is outside talking to Bess.'

'You couldn't hear?'

'Not a word. It's windy, and I'm too far away.'

'Were they friendly?'

'I couldn't tell, not from where I was. In all the time I've checked on Bess at the caravan, I've never seen Harriet.'

'You came here to accuse Harriet of murdering Bess?'

'Not directly. To be honest, the memory sometimes plays tricks on me; it was only when I saw Sergeant Yarwood talking to Harriet in the pub that I remembered back to that day. It's odd, though. You'd have to admit to that, the two of them related, mother and daughter. I'm right, aren't I?'

Tremayne could see that the investigation would not be advanced by lying. 'You are.'

'Not a word from me, you can trust me on that.'

'Anything else?' Clare asked.

'There was another person.'

'Where?'

'In the caravan. I don't know why Harriet was there, but the person in the caravan would have heard everything.'

'Who was it?'

'Charlotte. No idea why, and I don't believe Harriet knew. But whatever the truth, two of the three are dead.'

'Do you believe Harriet to be a murderer?'

'You'd better ask her. I've no idea.'

'If mother and daughter had said something to each other, who knows,' Clare said. 'Secrets could have been revealed; something one or the other woman didn't want to be known.'

'That's up to you and your sergeant to find out,' Campbell said, addressing his comment to Tremayne. 'As for me, I've told you what I know. If you'll excuse me, I'll take my leave and head back home.'

Chapter 14

The focus had shifted. Angus Campbell had thrown the enquiry back to Harriet Huxtable, a woman who had been in the company of the two dead women days before they had both died.

As usual for a weekday, the woman was found in the church.

'We need to talk,' Clare said.

Harriet continued to work, oblivious to the presence of the two police officers.

'We have new evidence,' Tremayne added.

The woman moved away, as though she were on her own. Clare was confused, as she usually didn't say much, but the woman was invariably polite. Clare grabbed her by the shoulder and turned her around.

'Oh, I'm sorry. I didn't hear you. It's my hearing aid, I turn it off in here.'

The explanation had been accepted, and with the hearing aid switched on, the woman was once again polite. Clare led her over to one of the pews where the two women sat down.

Tremayne sat in the pew in front of the two women, off to one side. At the front of the church, Reverend Walton entered, took one look at the three and left.

'It's my life, don't you see?' Harriet said.

'You don't have many friends,' Clare said.

'None, not really. There was a lot when I was young, and ten, maybe it was fifteen years ago, there was another woman in the village, Mrs Everton, but she passed away. The occasional cup of tea, a chat over the garden fence, no more than that.'

'No one else?'

'The bastard child, the child of incest, who would want to be friendly with me?'

'It wasn't your fault,' Clare said. 'No one would have held you responsible, and how would they know?'

'I knew, that's enough. In here, I'm not judged, but outside, I would be open to ridicule.'

'Miss Huxtable,' Tremayne said, 'tell us about the time your mother arrived in the village. Go back to then.'

'It was a Sunday, my busiest day. She knocked on my door, hoping that I would be pleased to see her.'

'Were you?'

'The church, people in the village, the gossip, how could I?'

'You rejected her?'

'I told her to find a room at the pub, not that I visited her there.'

'Sinful?'

'I don't hold with hard liquor. It was before Plumpton; a man and his wife, the O'Rileys.'

'Irish?'

'From Liverpool. His wife was a rosy-cheeked, smallish woman, a pleasant smile. Her husband was a rough man, coarse language and a roving eye. No idea what she saw in him, but they were always together, always sharing a joke.'

'Where are they now?'

'He died in the pub one day, a heart attack.'

'An alcoholic?'

'I don't think so. He was fond of the occasional drink, men are. His wife would drink too much sometimes, but she was such an endearing woman, I would forgive her.'

'A friend?'

'Not close, you'd understand.'

Neither Tremayne nor Clare could, although they weren't about to comment.

'A publican's wife and me. What could we have in common?'

'Friendship is not judgemental,' Clare said. 'You either like the person, or you don't. Did you like her?'

'I did. We used to meet in Salisbury, or she'd come over to my house, always the back gate, through the fields. She said I was silly, but that was what I wanted.'

'Is she still here?'

'After her husband died, she rented a small cottage not far from here. Five years after he went, she died as well.'

'And you were alone by then?'

'That's not why you're here, is it?' Harriet said. She leant forward and ran her hand over the back of the pew in front of her. 'I'll need to clean it before Sunday.'

Clare could tell that the woman was nervous, talking about matters that had remained hidden for years.

'How long did your mother stay at the pub, and why did you tell us that she appeared one day with the caravan?'

'I'm not sure if I did. Painful memories, don't you understand?'

'Miss Huxtable, Harriet, we can't,' Clare said. 'We're investigating two murders and honesty is demanded. Now let us have the truth, or we'll have to tell you what we know.'

Harriet got up from the pew and walked to the front of the church. She entered the nearest pew to the altar, sat down and then adopted the position of prayer.

'A confession?' Tremayne said.

'It seems unlikely. She's a devout woman.'

'She receives sustenance from her religion. Her way of dealing with all that's wrong with her, not that she's anything to be ashamed of.'

For close to five minutes, Harriet had her head bent low. Eventually, she resumed a sitting position, and then returned to sit alongside Clare.

'I needed guidance,' Harriet said.

'Did you receive it?' Tremayne asked.

The woman didn't answer, only started to talk. 'My mother stayed in that pub on and off for two years.'

'Why didn't you tell us this before?' Clare said.

Harriet Huxtable ignored Clare and continued her story. 'I tried to be friendly with her, but it was impossible, and then…' She paused for what seemed an eternity but was closer to fifteen seconds. Neither Tremayne nor Clare said anything.

'I had seen my mother as the victim, the same as I was. But then, she engages in immoral behaviour.' Another pause, longer than the first. 'I don't think I should talk about it in here.'

'I'm sure he'll forgive you, just this once.'

Harriet looked up at the altar, mouthed 'I'm sorry.'

'My mother formed an illicit relationship,' she said.

'They were both single,' Clare said.

'If they had married, but they didn't. It was fornication, a sin.'

'The man?'

'Angus Campbell, but you know this already, don't you?'

'We do, but we wanted you to corroborate it.'

'I could never forgive her after that.'

Tremayne knew that the woman by her own admission was capable of murder, incapable of rational thought, a bigot, a hater of her own mother.

'The caravan?'

'I don't know. It appeared one day, and she moved in. I rarely saw her after that.'

'Angus Campbell?'

'Men are wicked, immoral, devoid of anything other than animalistic lust. I held no hatred against him, only despised him for his gender.'

From what she said, Clare could see that she was not only embittered but also held distorted views, regarding every man as wicked and every woman who acted contrary to her narrow views as a Jezebel, a creature of no worth, not worthy of life.

Harriet took the initiative and moved to the vestry. The church was cold and in the vestry there was a small heater.

'Harriet, you should have told us before about your mother and Angus Campbell,' Clare said after the three had settled themselves.

A knock on the door: Petula Walton. 'I thought you could all do with a cup of tea,' she said as she placed a tray on the table.

Clare looked up at her and said 'Thank you,' although she thought her to be a nosey bat. Tremayne said nothing, only scowled. He got up as she left, walked over to the door and turned the key in the lock.

'Harriet, you've cleared up one misunderstanding; however, there is something else that we need clarity on,'

Tremayne said. 'I'd advise you to be totally honest with us.'

'Memories suppressed for so long, how can I?'

Harriet Huxtable's heart, Clare knew, was icy cold, devoid of compassion.

Tremayne did not psychoanalyse people, not the way his sergeant did. He had never had the training, or the instinct to see through to the person's psyche. He did, however, see all the clues pointing to the pious Harriet Huxtable as a murderer.

Even though the vicar's wife's intrusion had not been warranted, the tea was still a pleasant interlude before the main event. Clare drank hers with no sugar, Tremayne added two spoons. Harriet added three spoons, necessary to overcome her bitterness, Clare thought but did not say.

'I don't want you to underestimate the seriousness of the questioning from here on,' Tremayne said. 'You have become our primary suspect for both murders.'

'I don't know why,' Harriet replied. 'I've done nothing wrong. An old woman, that's all.'

'Harriet, your age is not a factor, your attitude is,' Clare said. 'Let us go back to before your mother died.'

'I'll try.'

'Good, then you can tell us the last time you saw your mother.'

'It was in the village. She was looking in bins, prowling around.'

'The question will be re-asked,' Tremayne said. 'It is important for you to consider your answer. The last time you saw your mother, and the truth this time.'

Harriet said nothing, only looked around the room, the vicar's cassock hanging on a hook, a bible on the table, a notebook on a shelf.

'Your answer,' Clare said after a suitable delay.

A hesitant whisper. 'I went to her caravan a few days before she died.'

'Thank you. Did you go there often?'

'Never. It was the first time I'd approached it, although I'd seen it from a distance.'

'Why this time?' Tremayne asked.

'I wanted to make my peace with her. We're both getting old, and I didn't want her to die without saying goodbye.'

'Nothing you've said up to now has given us any indication that you were concerned about her.'

'She was my only relative; it seemed important on that day.'

'Why that day?'

'I wanted to talk to her one last time.'

'It sounds as though you or she were about to die,' Clare said.

'I had received a letter,' Harriet said.

'Do you have a copy?'

'It was horrible, accused me of all sorts of things.'

'The truth,' Tremayne said. 'It's more important than ever.'

The woman picked up her handbag and took out an envelope. She handed it to Tremayne. He withdrew the sheet of paper inside and started to read.

'Don't, please. It's too horrible.'

Tremayne read it and handed it to Clare.

'It's not blackmail, no demand,' Clare said. 'It has to be read. I'm sorry, Harriet.'

Harriet Huxtable, the bastard child of a wanton woman and her father, the spawn of Satan. I know all about you and what you are. And soon, everyone will know you for what you are, and I will be glad.

It's people like you, hypocritical, holier-than-thou, who make me sick.

I give you notice that the truth will be revealed and your whore of a mother will be driven out. In the past, it would have been dunking in the water, burning at the stake, two witches, but even I can't organise that.

But I can rally the community in the village to have you and her driven out with only the clothes that the two of you are wearing, the two of you rotting in a hole in the ground. Then, and only then, the peace of the village can be restored.

'It's been typed, difficult to trace,' Clare said.

'We'll let Forensics try,' Tremayne said.

'Any more?' Clare asked of the ashen-faced Harriet.

'Who could write such a letter?' Harriet's voice was tremulous.

'It explains why you met with your mother; it doesn't explain how the writer intended to achieve his objective.'

'It's a narrow-minded community. He would have succeeded.'

'Or she,' Tremayne said.

'It's a *man*,' Harriet said. 'It's always been that way through history, the man exerting his right, the downtrodden woman in the fields, breeding his children, slaving day and night for him.'

Tremayne struggled for the word for the opposite of misogyny. Misandry, he remembered, and Harriet Huxtable had it bad.

'Harriet, we can understand your anger at the letter,' Clare said, placing her hand on the woman's arm,

158

'but it still doesn't explain why you visited your mother, not fully.'

'I wanted to say goodbye, nothing more. I felt more upset about the letter than with her.'

'Let us go back to the caravan,' Clare said. 'That final time you visited?'

'She was surprised to see me.'

'Who broke the ice?'

'I did. I asked how she was.'

'Did you tell her about the letter?' Tremayne asked.

'Not at first. It had been so long since we'd spoken, and we were virtual strangers.'

It was a sad story, Clare knew, the mother tainted for life through no fault of her own; the daughter who couldn't forgive or forget, needing somewhere to place the blame for her birth, unable to rationalise. Two women, so close, yet so far from each other.

'What else?' Clare said.

'We stayed there, outside of the caravan.'

'You didn't go in?'

'I wasn't asked, and I wouldn't have anyway. I live an organised life, everything in its place; my mother did not.'

'When you told your mother about the letter?'

'She asked to see it, but I wouldn't show her.'

'It would have helped if you had.'

'I read it to her; she laughed, told me to take no notice. Said what does the opinion of a crackpot mean.'

'She was right,' Clare said. 'If you had been open with people, none of this would have happened.'

'What do you mean? The letter or the murders?'

'Probably both,' Tremayne said.

'You left her at the caravan?' Clare said.

'I did. The last time I saw her. If I had known, I would have hugged her, but I didn't.'

'What would you have done if the truth had been revealed.'

'I would have killed myself. I would have had no option.'

Clare did not respond to the woman's statement, but understood that her mental condition was parlous.

'Were you aware that there was another person in the caravan?' Tremayne said.

'Whoever it was, he would have heard.'

'It wasn't a man,' Clare said. 'It was Charlotte Merton, and she's dead, like your mother. Circumstantial, or is there more?'

'Am I next, an old woman with nothing to live for apart from eternal damnation?'

'Damnation?'

'Those who commit suicide are condemned to everlasting torment. Am I to be one of those?'

'That's your decision,' Tremayne said. 'As for us, we still need to find the murderer. If it's not you, then it could be whoever wrote that letter.'

Clare looked at the letter one more time and then at the notice at the entrance to the church, noticed similar spelling errors.

'Harriet, who typed up the notice for the church about putting the prayer books back on the shelf as they leave?' Clare asked.

'I did. Is it important?'

Forensics would not be troubled. The writer of the hate mail was known, although why Harriet Huxtable had written it to herself was a question for another time.

Chapter 15

Tremayne sat in his office. Even though she was gone, he reflected, Charlotte Merton's past history was still clouded in mystery, and nobody at the farm recollected her talking much about herself or where she had come from.

'She turned up at the farm one morning, a small backpack, a coat under one arm, a plastic bag in her hand,' Eustace Hampton had said. 'And that was it. Said little, other than she was looking for a place to rest.'

Tremayne, glad of the small fan heater under his desk, warming his feet and his legs, easing only slightly the aches that his lower body felt, went over the case.

Charlotte Merton was the key to it, of that he was sure, but Bess Carmichael figured large in the investigation as well. Was Bess an unrelated murder or was her death tied to Charlotte? Were they looking for two murderers or one?

They'd spent too long on this case, Tremayne knew, and soon the presence of the station's superintendent would become a regular fixture in the office. The two men had crossed swords when the superintendent first took up tenure, with his desire to sweep out the old, bring in the new, lower the average age of those at the police station, make sure they were all computer savvy, politically correct, and degree educated, especially inspectors and above.

Tremayne knew that in the modern police force he wouldn't have risen above a junior rank, but in his time what mattered was competency, bringing in the results, ensuring that you had your contacts out on the street, the ability to bring in a favour, kick a villain up the rear end.

But now it was computers, which the detective inspector did not share an affinity with; political correctness that meant that he had to treat a suspect, no matter how disreputable, with respect; and worst of all, the endless fascination for policing learnt in a classroom, great in theory, pointless out in the hard world.

Tremayne relied on experience at the coal face, instinct to know the truth, or in most cases, the lie, and knowing when something was amiss, the sixth sense he called it, that told him that something wasn't right.

Harriet Huxtable's story had been plausible, and so had Angus Campbell's. But now, in the cold light of the following day, the weather outside Tremayne's window threatening, the dark clouds ready to let forth with another downpour, he wasn't sure.

Outside of his office, Clare focussed on her laptop, aware that her senior was running through the facts, looking for the inconsistency, the intangible that tied the loose ends together. A silence had settled over Homicide, the ancillary staff busy at their work, no one saying much, the printer in the alcove at the end of the office printing out more paper, most of which would end up in the recycling bin, a telephone ringing in the distance.

Tremayne got up from his seat and came and sat down next to Yarwood. 'Angus Campbell and Bess Carmichael,' he said. 'I've been thinking about what he said.'

'A problem?'

'When he was asked why he and Bess had split up, he said, "age happened". She would have been in her early sixties, and he would have been fifty-seven or fifty-eight. It's a flippant comment, neither of them was that old, nor ready for a nursing home.'

'You think there's another reason?'

'I can understand Campbell's loneliness, the sorrow of Bess Carmichael; it's just the "age happened" comment that I can't accept.'

'Relevant?' Clare said, closing her laptop, putting on her coat, grabbing her car keys off the desk. When Tremayne had something on his mind, staying in the office was not the way he solved it. She knew they would be leaving soon.

As the two of them walked out of Homicide, they saw the ominous figure of the superintendent coming up the corridor. 'Tremayne, a word with you.'

'Sorry, got to dash,' Tremayne said as he hurriedly walked past the man.

'He'll not be pleased with you giving him the brush off,' Clare said.

'We both know what he wants.'

'Your job?'

'It'll be his damn key performance indicators and what are we doing to solve the murders. That'll be first on his list, and then he'll get around to my health, and aren't the long hours getting to me, have I considered retiring, handing over to someone younger, to you.'

'I'm not sure I'm ready.'

'You're ready,' Tremayne said.

Clare accepted the compliment, knowing that a thank you was not required. Her boss was a man who showed emotion rarely, affection never. The two of them, the master and his apprentice, as it had been when they had first paired, had over the years changed to master and junior, although within the last eight months, after a couple of difficult murder investigations, it had become master and equal.

Clare was gratified, confident in her ability, not wanting to be without Tremayne. They worked seamlessly, each gaining strength from the other, each using the other as a sounding board.

Clare pulled the car up outside Angus Campbell's house. He was in the front garden, marching up and down, striding out. To Tremayne it looked comical; to Clare it was reassuring that the man was determined to prolong his life, and for his age, he was an imposing figure.

'Campbell, a moment of your time,' Tremayne shouted over the white-painted fence.

'If you don't mind a walk,' Campbell's reply.

Tremayne did but said, 'A walk it is.'

Clare watched the two of them walk away: the retired army officer, his back straight, his head held high, his walking stick making a methodical tapping sound as he used it to steady himself; the police inspector, his hands in his pockets, his shoulders drooping, his back hunched. The age difference was over twenty years, but Angus Campbell, the older of the two, seemed fitter.

***

Clare walked over to the pub. Inside, although it was early, Maria was busy.

'Someone's got to keep it open,' she said as she worked in the kitchen.

'The foreclosure?'

'I had someone out here from the bank the other day. He's given the place another three months.'

'Generous?'

'Nothing of the sort.' Maria was a woman who, Clare knew, had good commonsense, someone who could have made something of the pub if she had the money, which she didn't.

Her husband was on a basic wage in Salisbury as a bus driver, and they had two children to look after. Clare had met the husband on a couple of occasions, and whereas he was affable and devoted to his wife, he wasn't a go-getter, content to drift along, with his loving wife and two well-behaved and smartly turned out children.

'What is it?'

'Public relations, the young man they sent out admitted to it. The village has got a reputation – two murders, a publican who commits suicide due to the bank's pressure. How do you think it'll read in the local newspaper, on the television, if the media got to hear that the man had taken his own life, his dead body sprawled over the bank's ultimatum?'

'Is that what he said?'

'I gave him a few pointers, something to take back to his manager.'

'You're a sharp woman, Maria. Plumpton must have loved having you here.'

'He was a good man, I liked him. But he was like my husband, well-meaning, a pushover. That's my lot, falling for good men.'

'As long as they make you happy.'

'I'll tell you, Sergeant…'

'Clare.'

'Clare, it is. If I didn't have Joe, and thankful that I do, then I would have taken Wally, made something of this place.'

'Of him?'

'I wouldn't have changed him one bit, other than to have kept him away from drugs. A few too many drinks occasionally don't do much harm, but I've got a sister who became addicted.'

'Where is she now?'

'At home with my parents, and they're too old to be nursemaiding an adult woman. They try, and I'd have her here with me if I could, but the children are too young. Maybe, in time.'

'Did you feel affection for Wally?'

'I'm committed to my husband. I was only telling you what a good man Wally was.'

'Your plans?'

'I let the bank know, subtly, let them think it's their idea, that if they gave me six months, no repayments, I could turn the place around, make a small profit, pay off some of the debt.'

'Wally's family?'

'Wally had no money, even if this place had been sold, and I've asked his ex-wife and his children if they'd be interested.'

'You're planning on keeping the pub open,' Clare said.

'Boutique beers, a gourmet restaurant, the possibilities are endless. It can work, but not as a staid English pub.'

'The bank, do you reckon they'll go for your idea?'

'I can be quite persuasive if I need to be, and adverse publicity to the bank would be damaging.'

'Especially if you were on the television, in the newspapers, on social media, calling them cold-hearted, the memory of a good man killed by the bank's intransigence in his hour of need, a woman he was fond of murdered. I'll bring my husband out if you bring it off.'

'Will he open it for us?'

'He's an intensely private man, but for you, I'll see that he does.'

'I hope you don't mind me bringing it up, but you know about pubs.'

Clare stood for a while, didn't feel as though she wanted to say anything, felt disloyal to Clive.

'Sorry, I shouldn't have mentioned it,' Maria said.

'For a long time, I was sad, but now I've got Clive. The past is where it belongs. Let's not talk about it, not now. Clive knows, so does his daughter, but you never truly forget, do you?'

'I'll never forget Wally, big old lovable Wally,' Maria said.

Clare considered the possibility that Wally and Maria had been involved, but discounted it.

'A pie?' Maria said.

'Why not?' Clare said, the two women at ease in each other's company. Clare could see a friendship developing: the wife of a bus driver, the wife of the mayor. And Clive would open the resurrected pub in due course, she'd make sure of that.

***

Angus Campbell hobbled up the hill from where he had seen Bess Carmichael's caravan and the three women.

Tremayne, walking alongside him as Campbell took his morning constitutional, did not hobble; he puffed, and he ached, bending over halfway up to catch his breath, eventually cresting the hill.

Jean had been making sure that he walked regularly, but with her, it was twice around the block and on the level. With Campbell, it was a route march, up hill and down, along the country trails, through the main street in the village, across the narrow bridge at the end. Tremayne was, he knew, out of condition, and he had put it down to his age, but Campbell was older than him, and if the man could manage, then so could he.

'It's good for the soul,' Campbell said when Tremayne had finally stopped wheezing.

'I need to ask you about something you said the other day,' Tremayne said, not willing to indulge in a conversation about his health or lack of it, the fear of a heart attack if there was another hill to climb.

'What's that?' Campbell said, taking in deep breaths, exhaling.

'The reason you and Bess Carmichael broke up.'

'You're putting too fine a point on it. We didn't break up as we had never been together, not totally.'

'You and she were younger. The relationship was physical.'

'If that's a policeman's way of saying we were sleeping together, then say it.'

'Were you and her having sexual relations?'

'We were, not that it was often, and there were no platitudes of love, no mention of forming a permanent arrangement, moving in together, plighting our troth. As I told you before, we were glad of the company, nothing more.'

'You said "age happened" when you were asked why the relationship had ended.'

'You've strained to keep up with me just to ask what I meant?'

'Neither of you were that old.'

'It was just a comment, nothing more. She was set in her ways; I was set in mine.'

Tremayne accepted Campbell's explanation. 'You don't miss much in this village,' he said.

'Is that a roundabout way of asking if I killed either of the two women?'

'It wasn't, but it's an interesting speculation,' Tremayne said. 'You're certainly fit enough to have hoisted Bess up, and capable of injecting Charlotte in the neck.'

'You'll not get far with that,' Campbell said. 'I was concerned for Bess, and Charlotte, mixed up as she was, was too young for me, and besides, my interest in women was long ago, not that it was ever that strong, that is.'

'What does that mean?'

'I was glad of my wife, glad of Bess for a while, but I'm a loner, always have been. Age happened was a way of me saying that I wasn't interested in spending more time with her. I wanted to be on my own, but she was clinging, looking for something or someone. Not that I knew the truth of her past, only what she told me. If I had, then I might have acted differently.'

'Stayed with Bess?'

'I would have been more sensitive in terminating the relationship. You can't blame Harriet either for her stern face, her rudeness.'

'We got the story from Harriet as to why she was at the caravan.'

'Do you believe it?'

'Not totally, not even you telling me you're innocent. For a man of your age, you're still fit and active.'

'There was gossip about Bess and me at the time, but it's long been forgotten, not sure if anyone remembers. You've not lived in a small village, Tremayne?'

'I was glad to get away, join the police force.'

'You must remember what happened there, who was sleeping with who? Who was having an affair?'

'I minded my own business; it made more sense than creating waves.'

'Harriet lived her life with shame, hating her mother, hating herself,' Campbell said. 'But why? For no good reason. We had our detractors, Bess and me, even the vicar, not Walton, he's a recent arrival, but two reverends before; terrible body odour, the breath of a rhinoceros.'

'You're acquainted with the animal?' Tremayne was amused at the man's putdown of someone who had caused him grief.

'Not personally, but he was extreme in his views. He got up in the pulpit. It was a Sunday, two weeks before Easter, and he started quoting from the bible, finding passages, the need of a man to take a wife, the evil that had descended on the village. He was having a go at Bess and me.'

'What happened after that?'

'I never went into the church again, not while he was there. Walton's a wet blanket, but he's not a bible basher, more willing to accept the status quo, to counsel the fallen, to offer hope.'

'The vicar who caused you problems?'

'A year later, the river was flooding. He was down there late at night, fell in. They found him face down, a mile downstream.'

'Foul play?'

'It was a long time ago. The man preached during the day, went on a bender in the vicarage at night. Not that any of us knew that, not until the police checked the vicarage, found his stash of alcohol. Walton's a much better man, more my style.'

'You go to church now?'

'Regular as clockwork, every Sunday.'

'Religious?'

'I believe, no reason not to, and besides, it does a person good to have a routine. And you were close to passing out as we walked up here.'

'It concerns me,' Tremayne said.

'You need to push yourself.'

'I might take you up on that suggestion,' Tremayne said.

'You won't. You would have made a good soldier, brave no doubt, no problems with killing the enemy, but you don't have the rigour and determination to have risen in the ranks.'

'Not officer material?'

'Sergeant Major, able to keep the troops on their toes.'

Tremayne knew that Campbell was right. 'Bess Carmichael, you never answered the question.'

'I believe I did. I'm a loner, and Bess was troubled. It got between us. I wished her well, and I hope she did of me, but we rarely spoke afterwards, and then not at all for many years up to her death.'

'But you always kept a watch out for her.'

'Someone had to, and for a while, it had been fun. You can't forget that, can you?'

Tremayne had no answer as the two men walked down the hill and back to the village.

Chapter 16

Media interest in the farm and the village continued to wane, and the formerly frequent intrusions of one journalist or another had withered, so much so that Eustace Hampton was once again being asked for his views on alternative lifestyles.

Not that this change ended the exodus, and three more had left the farm. One of the three, Eddie Cummings, was an apathetic man with grey dreadlocked hair. Clare had seen him around the farm on several occasions, and he had been interviewed, his alibi checked, but most of the time he kept to himself in a rundown shed at the back of the house. He was an artist, and whereas he was generally uncommunicative and rarely cheerful, his art was vibrant.

Clare had been interested in one of his pieces, and when she had asked for a price, she had been stunned by his reply.

'It's two thousand pounds,' he had said.

Hampton had told Clare later that Eddie was highly regarded, and that several of his works hung in art galleries, and that two thousand pounds was cheap for one of them. However, as much as she had liked the painting, Clare decided that Clive would not, as he preferred the old masters, not the modern trend of impressionism, and not dramatic colours across a canvas.

Eddie was the first of the three to leave, a Mercedes Benz transporting him away, with not a word to the others at the farm other than to slap a wad of money in Hampton's hand as he left.

'Best of luck,' Hampton said.

'It's you who needs the luck,' Eddie said, and then he was gone.

'Why here?' Tremayne said as he stood alongside Hampton looking at the money.

'He said this place gave him inspiration.'

'Did you believe him?'

'He paid his way, caused no trouble, and he slept in the shed, even though we've better accommodation.'

'You'll take whoever you can, Hampton,' Tremayne said. 'Not fussy as long as they pay.'

Hampton took a step back, leant against the farmhouse, looked across the yard at the barn where Gavin Fitzwilliam sat with his laptop. 'Charlotte couldn't pay, neither could Ben. My hopes for this place were not commercial, just enough money to get by, but, Inspector, I might have been wrong,' he said.

Tremayne could see that Hampton's self-assured demeanour had taken a battering since Charlotte Merton's death.

After a few more minutes, two women, the knitters of the community, came out of the front door of the house. The elder of the two, a dowdily-dressed woman – she always wore black – kissed Eustace on the cheek.

'Thanks,' she said before returning to the other woman and putting her arms around her.

'We'll miss them,' Hampton said to Tremayne.

'Not much money in knitting, is there?'

'They sold it sometimes, and they had their pensions.'

'What will become of them now?'

'I don't know. This was their home for six years, and they never spoke of anyone else, not relatives or friends, and no one came here to see them. I'll worry for them, but they have found here tainted.'

'It is. Don't you feel it?'

'I can rise above it. They can't,' Hampton said, looking over at the two women.

'We have their address,' Tremayne said.

'Can you know, truly, about anyone?'

'Your faith in the goodness of man shaken?'

Tremayne sensed it more keenly than before. Hampton's previously implacable belief in the farm and in his fellow man was not as resolute. It was a side that hadn't been seen before, but the police inspector was glad to see it. Experience told him that the end of the investigation was near and that people, relaxing a little, dropping their guard, would start to make mistakes.

'Sergeant Yarwood?' Hampton asked after the two women had walked out of the farm gate.

'She's in the village.'

'She's an attractive woman.'

'No doubt she is; she's also a competent police officer. What is it, Hampton? What do you want to tell me?'

'Let's get away from here, a pint of beer.'

'It's early in the day, but if that's what you want.'

'It is.'

Tremayne left the car at the farmhouse and walked with Hampton along the track that he had traversed on several occasions now.

'Grayson intends to evict us in the next two days,' Hampton said.

'Can he?'

'It's not Miranda and me, you must understand.'

'You'll survive, Hampton. Men like you always do, even if you're strange.'

'You don't like me very much, do you?'

'I don't understand where you're coming from. I had a tough upbringing, a career. No time to philosophise, only to get on with it, make the best of an imperfect world, but you see it differently.'

'Academia, a fertile, enquiring mind. I had doting parents, ensured that I had the best of everything, the best schools, trips around the world. And then the university, and now here. Money's never been an issue for me, not that I ever wanted more than needed to live a modest life.'

'You've got money?'

'Enough to survive.'

'That's not what you told us before.'

'I told you that I had to take money from Grayson. Survival is a lot cheaper. It's someone at the farm who's the murderer, it has to be,' Hampton said.

The two men stopped at the oak tree where Todd Hampton had his romantic tryst with Charlotte.

Hampton continued to talk. 'I've not told Miranda.'

'Told her what?'

'I agreed to give you a sample of my DNA. I've changed my mind.'

'The truth can't be avoided, not even for one's own family. We always find the guilty person. Maybe not today, but they always slip up.'

'Why is that?' Hampton asked.

'While we're here, Yarwood and me, everyone's watching what they say, what they do. In a few weeks, when we've got another murder to deal with, our presence will not be so obvious, and those with something to hide will make a mistake.'

'If you're not here, how will you know?'

'Someone will tell us, and we'll be back. The pretence can't last forever.'

'It was here, Todd and Charlotte, wasn't it?'

'That's what he told me.'

'I've always held with right over wrong, the truth at all times, even at the expense of family.'

'Are you trying to say in your convoluted way that you think Todd murdered Charlotte?'

'No, I don't think that. I know who killed her.'

'Who?'

'His girlfriend. She's a hard woman.'

'Your proof?'

'It's the only logical answer. You see, Charlotte's baby was Todd's, I know that now.'

'How?'

'He's more like his mother than me, but he was brought up to believe the same as both of us. He phoned me last night. It was late, and Miranda was fast asleep.'

'He told you the child was his?'

'Charlotte had told him, the day before she died.'

'He wanted Charlotte?'

'The weak, sentimental side of him would, but not the aggressive, ambitious side. He knew what needed to be done, for Charlotte to get rid of the baby, but he was confused. There was only one person who could resolve the impasse – his girlfriend. She's hard, is Emily, as hard as they come. When you meet her, you'll see. She wouldn't let a minor inconvenience such as Charlotte interfere with her life or the man she had chosen.'

'The woman behind the throne?'

'She's here with Todd this afternoon.'

'You asked her to come?'

'If she's guilty, she has to pay. I told her it was a family conference, a discussion about Todd's career.'

'What will Todd's reaction be?'

'He'll hate me for it, but what else can I do? I can't allow him to be with a murderer, can I?'

'You should have told us before.'

'I didn't know about Todd and the baby. I thought it was someone else's, possibly Plumpton, Fitzwilliam, Ben, even Tony; but not Todd's.'

'If Todd didn't kill Charlotte, then it makes no difference if he was the father or not.'

'Todd killed Bess,' Hampton said as he walked away.

***

The local shop, always a place for information, was quiet when Clare went in, an agreeable-looking woman in her sixties behind the counter.

'Sergeant, what can I get you?'

Clare had spoken to her before, realised that she was full of innuendo with no substance. Shirley Jenkins, the shopkeeper didn't know about Harriet and her relationship to her mother, nor did she know about Angus Campbell and Bess, even though she had lived in the village for fifty-two years, the owner of the corner shop for twenty-three of them.

Clare picked up a bar of chocolate, not that she wanted it, only to engender conversation, and placed it on the counter. 'I'll take this,' she said.

'Anything else? A few are moving out of Hampton's place.'

Gossip was good for business, and Shirley Jenkins was probing. Clare had no intention of giving her anything of value, but she'd play along for now.

Tremayne had phoned; Todd and the mysterious girlfriend were due within the hour. Until then, she'd engage the woman in the shop in idle chat.

'A few,' Clare said.

'They say that Hampton gets up to some funny business.'

Nothing original in the woman's line of questioning. A group of people who did not follow the norm were always suspected of something or other. She and Tremayne had spent enough time at the farmhouse to know that nothing untoward was happening.

'They say they summon evil spirits, not that I believe it.'

She did if it was good for business.

'And what about the children? You moved them out soon enough, but they're back now. Do you hold with what they do up there?'

'And what's that?' Clare asked.

'You know.'

Clare knew what she was inferring, mind in the gutter, basing her views on what she had seen on the television, movies not based on reality.

The Fitzwilliam daughters were doing well away from the farm. Clare had phoned, and so far Gavin had kept his distance, which wasn't surprising as Fraud was homing in on him and his partner, found to be living in Thailand, the extradition laws weak enough to make sure he'd not be coming back to England. The bank accounts overseas, the proof to prosecute Gavin Fitzwilliam still not watertight, and the Italians they had cheated found to be unsavoury characters. Fitzwilliam was right to be fearful of them.

'What do you believe happens to the children?' Clare asked.

'You know.'

'I'm afraid I don't. If you have any proof…'

'It's what people say.'

The shopkeeper was talking nonsense, and Clare thought her to be a silly empty-headed nonentity, but she persevered. The children at the farmhouse – the ebullient and troublesome Tommy Yardley still running around but more agreeable than before, attending school every day, and the two Reece daughters, Sally and Bronwyn – were fine. Clare had spoken to them in Salisbury. She had been in the city centre with Clive, on their way to a function, and the two children, along with their mother, had been shopping.

Margaret, the mother, had been excited to meet Clive, and the two girls had been polite and had shaken his hand, Bronwyn even asking for an autograph.

'It's next week, we've got to stand up and make a speech on people we've met,' Bronwyn said.

The two girls, whether they were meeting Clive or at the farmhouse, continued to remain close to each other, holding hands most of the time, including with their mother.

Clive had thought them a lovely family, although they had been at the farm when two women had been murdered.

'What do people say? The farm? Who killed the two women?' Clare asked, persevering with the shopkeeper.

'People talk, not that I hold with it, you know that. Maria and Wally Plumpton's wife. People are talking.'

It was true that Plumpton's ex-wife was in the village; Maria had introduced her to Clare. So far, she had not spoken to her in depth. And if Maria and the woman were together, it boded well for the pub staying open,

Clive doing the honours, cutting the ribbon, making a speech.

'What are they saying?'

'The two of them, up there, very cosy.'

'Are people putting two and two together, coming up with five?' Clare said, more irritated than she should have been.

'They say that they killed Wally. That it had been planned all along, so they could get his money.'

Village gossip, Clare knew, could be either trivial and forgettable or vindictive and in bad taste. The shopkeeper preferred the latter.

'Harriet Huxtable spent yesterday with Angus Campbell at his house,' she said.

Clare took a magazine out of the rack next to the counter. 'I'll have this,' she said, not intending to read it. Harriet and Campbell were interesting; it was relevant. The other nonsense had not been.

'What about Harriet and the Colonel?'

'There are some that say he was never a colonel, only a sergeant.'

Angus Campbell's military record had been checked and confirmed. The man had served with distinction and had led troops into battle, as he had said. It was irksome, hearing disparaging comments about him.

Clive had been a victim of the fickle nature of people when his brother's body had been found: openly accused on one occasion in the street of murdering him, and then, when Kim, his daughter, had spent the night at his house, the gossipmongers had been out in force.

Clive, intensely private, had chosen not to douse the flames by telling the truth about the relationship of father, mother and daughter. He remained cynical, yet obliging when those former slanderers approached him with the hand of friendship and respect when the truth had reluctantly been revealed.

'The man's record has been checked,' Clare said. 'He was a colonel.' She felt that the shopkeeper should know the truth, although whether it would be passed on, she didn't know.

Yet, as Clare left the store –Tremayne phoning to say that Todd and his girlfriend had arrived – she was concerned that Harriet Huxtable and Angus Campbell had spent time together. What had they spoken about? Had Angus told Harriet that he knew who her mother was? Had Harriet told him? Could the two even be friendly to one another?

Chapter 17

Emily Walker came as a surprise to Tremayne and Clare. Eustace Hampton had said on a couple of occasions that she was a hard woman, but in front of the two police officers was a demure woman with good manners, a slim figure. She barely came up to Clare's shoulders, and when she had shaken Tremayne's hand – 'So pleased to meet you, Inspector' – she had had to crane her head upwards to make eye contact.

The ogre had been revealed as a forest nymph, although Clare knew that initial impressions may be false.

Harriet Huxtable was embittered and showed it, but at times Clare had seen a timidity in her, an unwillingness to let anyone get too close; a woman who had wanted to be loved, to love, but had had neither. And Maria, the woman that Wally Plumpton had relied on to keep the pub tidy, the patrons fed, who was showing her entrepreneurial talent in convincing the bank and Plumpton's former wife to let her have a chance at making a viable business, had changed from when Clare had first met her.

Emily Walker came from a wealthy family; her father was now known to be Ian Walker of Walker Constructions, a company that had built shopping centres, office blocks and residential developments the length and breadth of England.

'I thought it was a family discussion,' Emily said, looking over at Eustace and then at Todd, who sat a little distance away to one side of her.

'I'm sorry,' Eustace said. 'Inspector Tremayne and Sergeant Yarwood weren't involved in my deception. The air needs to be cleared, the aspersions need to be addressed; the truth told, not only by Todd and you but by all of us.'

A pause while the young woman mulled over the situation. 'I don't believe it is wise for me to stay here any longer,' she said. 'I cannot approve of this, nor do I believe that I can help the investigation.' She looked over at Tremayne. 'That is what we're here for, isn't it?'

'Eustace believes that you and Todd being here is worthwhile. I'd suggest that you stay for now.'

'Todd, I cannot believe you're a party to this,' Emily said, looking at her boyfriend, who continued to sit back, not sure what to say next.

'I'm not. My father has taken this on himself, although why I don't know.'

'I told the inspector two facts,' Eustace said.

'And that's the reason we're here?'

Tremayne stood up, moved over to the fireplace, his back to it, even though the fire was giving little heat. Miranda Hampton had said nothing so far.

'Eustace has made certain accusations,' Tremayne said. 'I can't be sure if he believes what he told me. However, there's another possibility.'

'Which is?' Todd asked.

'That he wants me to confront you and Emily with these allegations and allow the two of you to deny them, to convince my sergeant and me of your innocence.'

'What have you done?' Miranda said, aghast that her husband had placed her son in harm's way.

'Todd has a bright future ahead of him, and Emily is the person we want him to spend it with,.' Eustace said.

'Thank you,' Emily said. Clare didn't like the way the woman smiled, remembering that Hampton had said she was a hard woman.

'What are we accused of? What have you told the police, Father?' Todd said.

Tremayne interrupted. It was his investigation and squabbling between father and son was not warranted at present.

'Emily, you have remained outside of the current investigation,' Tremayne said.

'I've not been here, and I didn't know either of the dead women. Todd knows my view of this place, as do his parents.'

'You see it as worthless?'

'Inspector, a person is judged by what he does and what he achieves. Communing with nature, group hugs, sitting under a tree and meditating are all very well on a weekend retreat, but not in reality. Todd's father is a clever man, an academic, a man who could have imparted knowledge to those who wanted to learn, yet he's here with a bunch of reprobates, drug addicts, fallen women, and who knows what else.'

'That's a damning criticism.'

'It's nothing more than I've said to Todd before, and he's in agreement with me.'

'You said it the last time you were here,' Eustace said.

'More succinctly. This time it looks as though I will be asked to defend myself.'

'What are you studying at university?' Clare asked.

'Law, the same as Todd.'

Clare knew that if ever she needed a defence lawyer, it would be the demure and slim Emily that she'd choose. In that delicate package resided a determined woman, a person who would seduce the jury and the judge with her eloquence, who would deliver the winning argument.

Tremayne cleared his throat, looked over at Clare, before focussing on Emily. 'Miss Walker, Todd's father, is convinced that you killed Charlotte Merton,' he said.

Todd Hampton was on his feet, Miranda Hampton had her face in her hands, and Clare took mental notes, watched the body language.

Of the six in that room, only one remained immobile: Emily.

'How dare you,' Todd said.

'It's wicked, what have you done?' Miranda said, lifting her head.

'What Eustace has done is to bring new impetus to this investigation,' Tremayne said. 'You, Miss Walker, do not seem to be moved by what has just been said.

'I learnt at the feet of a master.'

'Your father?'

'He's a remarkable man, the son of a miner, a poor education, no perceivable chance to improve himself, but he did; rung by rung up that ladder. Many tried to take him down, none succeeded.'

'What do you believe is behind Eustace's accusation?'

'His parents approve of me, although they don't like me that much.'

'That's not true,' Miranda interjected.

'Don't worry. Your love for me doesn't matter. I love Todd, and I intend to marry him, regardless of your blessings.'

The woman's hardness was becoming apparent. Tremayne could tell that even though she was young, she was tenacious. Accusations of murder weren't going to faze her.

Todd sat down. He moved his hand towards Emily; she pushed it away.

'Inspector Tremayne, I will answer your questions to the best of my ability. If at any time I feel that you are acting incorrectly, or you're attempting to badger me with your smart tricks, I will phone for a lawyer, a man that my father uses, a person who will deal with these slanderous accusations.'

'I have done what was necessary,' Eustace said. 'My conscience is clean.'

'I don't care whether your conscience is clean or otherwise,' Emily said. 'You are to be my father-in-law soon enough. We will be civil to one another, but remember this, I never forget and I certainly never forgive. That may be possible for you and your deluded disciples, but not for me.'

'Miss Walker, if I may come back to the accusation. Did you murder Charlotte Merton?' Tremayne said.

'No. Next question.'

'Had you met the woman?'

'I saw her once, that's all.'

'Your impression?'

'I believe I've already mentioned what I think of the people here.'

'Please answer the question,' Tremayne said. 'We'll accept that you regarded her as a deluded disciple. What else?'

'Spaced out, looked as though she had led a rough life. Probable drug addict, attractive to some.'

186

'How much of that evaluation came from Todd?' Clare asked.

'You asked my impression of what I saw, not what Todd told me. I summed up the woman the day we were here, the day I told Eustace what I thought of this place.'

'You're a hard woman,' Tremayne said.

'On the contrary, I'm a realist. I say it as it is, no need to gild the lily. Todd's parents know my views; I know theirs. We agree to disagree, but an accusation of murder I can't accept. That's below the belt. My father wouldn't have stooped that low.'

'You're close to your father?'

'We fight sometimes, but yes, I am. Great men deserve love and respect. Eustace could have been, but all that intelligence down the drain, wasting away in the country.'

'It's not a waste, not to me,' Eustace said.

'Not to me, either,' Miranda acknowledged, once again close to her husband. 'Did you kill Charlotte? I was fond of her.'

'Why? Because your son couldn't keep his trousers on when she was around?'

'You knew?' Tremayne said.

'My father used to put it about, not that I agreed with him. Todd isn't any better, and besides, I've made my decision. Todd had better believe, and I know he does, one indiscretion I'll accept, not more.'

'Not many women would,' Clare said.

'At least he hasn't murdered anyone, has *he*?' Emily said. She was looking directly at Clare, making eye contact.

Clare, who had been willing to give the woman credit for her resilience in an uncomfortable situation, realised at that instance that she detested her with a vengeance. It was clear that Emily Walker had compiled a portfolio of the persons associated with the murder. She knew about her and Tremayne, she knew about Harry Holchester and what he had been to her and the crimes he had committed. If she was that calculating, Todd wouldn't have a chance, and she would not have committed murder. She may have paid someone else to, or coerced somebody, but Emily Walker wasn't stupid enough to be found guilty of murder, of any crime, not even a parking ticket or a fine for speeding. She was a dangerous woman, and the Hamptons' future, parents and son, good or bad, would be of her choosing.

Clare looked over at Tremayne. He knew what she was thinking.

'Emily, we know that Todd had sex with Charlotte on the one occasion.'

'Once? He told me about that night up against a tree. He was almost proud of it.'

'Why tell you?'

'Todd's like his mother, dependent, needy. I like her, so did my father once.'

Everyone looked over at Miranda.

'That's nasty, Emily. Even for you,' Miranda said.

'My wife's past belongs back there,' Eustace said as he put his arm around his wife.

'Is this true?' Todd asked.

'I was wild, high on life, on drugs. It was a more permissive time, at least for those who could afford it. I can't remember Emily's father, but it could be true.'

'If I can be accused, so can others.' Emily said. 'Besides, my father said it was just the once at a party, Miranda high as a kite. He told me when I started going out with Todd.'

'Any reason?' Tremayne asked.

'It was years before I was born, years before Todd was. We're not siblings if that's what you're thinking.'

'Eustace, why did you accuse Emily of murder?'

Hampton shifted uncomfortably; he removed his arm from around his wife, and she moved away.

'I knew that eventually the police investigation would stall and you would be looking for other possible suspects.'

'We hadn't regarded Miss Walker as a suspect before.'

'It was better to meet her here than at her family home or the flat she shares with Todd.'

'Would it have made a difference?'

'On her home turf, her guard would have been up. And without Miranda and me here, she wouldn't have been so scathing. You needed to see the true woman.'

'Are we seeing that, Emily?' Tremayne asked.

'He's right. I wouldn't have said as much, and if it had been my father's house, there would have been a lawyer with me, someone more experienced than I am.'

'Would we have learnt more there or here?'

'You've not learnt anything here. I couldn't have killed Charlotte Merton, not capable.'

'You're capable,' Clare said. 'But you're smarter than that, aren't you?'

'Sergeant Yarwood, you're married to an important man. You must know how the elite live.'

'Your research?'

'I asked a company to check out everyone involved. That's how I know that Todd had been with Charlotte on more than one occasion. I also know that Inspector Tremayne has health issues and you're covering up for him.'

'I said you were a hard woman before,' Tremayne said. 'I was right, wasn't I? A realist wouldn't go to the lengths you have.'

'"Know thine enemy". Sun Tzu, *The Art of War*. You must have heard the saying. My father has it in gold-embossed letters in a frame on the wall behind his office chair.'

'He also said "know thy self", Emily,' Clare said. 'Do you, or are you just a pretentious twenty-one-year-old spoilt brat trying to be like your father, and failing miserably?'

'I like her,' Emily said, looking over at Tremayne. 'Perceptive, direct, able to quote Sun Tzu.'

'A good education is not the province of the rich,' Clare said.

'The daughter of a hotelier, the wife of the mayor. Grant me some credence. Your hobby is policing, and no doubt you're good at it. I don't have to work any more than you do, but I intend to be a lawyer, Todd at my side. As for the research, why not?

'I knew that at some stage you'd get around to me, and you'd find me obnoxious, overbearing, too smart for my own good, a person who could have lawyers here in a couple of hours. However, I didn't murder either of the two women, nor am I upset by their passing: one of them a drug-addicted woman of low repute and dubious morals, the other the incestuous mother of a woman in the village.'

'How did you know that?' Tremayne asked.

'The same way that you did. It appears my research might be better than yours, and Miranda and my father met at a party, and a few times after. Seeing that I'm under pressure here, maybe I should reveal a few more facts.'

'If your research is that good, are you able to tell us who murdered Charlotte Merton?'

'Miranda.'

'Eustace accused you of Charlotte's murder. He also believed that Todd killed the older woman,' Tremayne said, waiting for the reaction.

Clare moved over to Miranda and put her hand on her shoulder, looked down at her and whispered, 'Not now.'

Tremayne stood between father and son, the younger up on his feet ready to do battle.

'Sit down, Todd. You're making a fool of yourself,' the indomitable Emily said. 'Can't you see that the inspector is baiting you.'

'It was an accusation,' Tremayne said after the situation had calmed.

'Father, I don't understand,' Todd said. 'Why? Do you hate me that much?'

'I do it out of love,' Eustace said. 'This would have dragged on for much longer, and if you or Emily are guilty, then your mother and I will be there for you.'

'Do you really believe that I could have killed Bess Carmichael?' Todd said.

'You couldn't have killed Charlotte, I know that, as does Emily,' Eustace said.

'He was infatuated with the stupid woman, thought he could redeem her, the knight in shining armour on his white steed. Sentimental nonsense,' Emily said. 'You, Eustace, and you, Miranda, have raised the man I intend to have at any cost. A man who needs guidance.'

Tremayne pitied Todd Hampton, a man doomed to purgatory, a woman watching over him, checking that he didn't drink too much, ate the right foods, made love at her command.

'Is that true, Todd?' Clare asked.

'She was lost, needed help. Some of Father's beliefs have rubbed off on me, but I wasn't about to leave Emily for her, I couldn't.'

'Because she's your rock?'

'I need to overcome my father's belief in the goodness of man, the need for a simpler world. I'm too intelligent, too young for that.'

'You see,' Emily said. 'Can't you see that I'm right.' She folded her arms and sat back on her chair, a smug look.

You cow, Clare thought, averting her eyes from her, looking over to Miranda who was totally confused as to what was going on.

'Emily, why do you believe that Miranda killed Charlotte?' Tremayne said.

'Miranda had lived on the wild side in her heady modelling days. Plenty of men, plenty of drugs. She understood heroin better than most. She would have known the effect that injecting the woman in the neck would have, and how to ensure she died.'

'But why? What would she gain?'

'She'd gain me. She knows her son, knows what he needs.'

'He needs you,' Miranda said, her voice weak and trailing off at the end. Eustace moved over to be near her. She moved away from him.

'Todd was confused. He wanted us both, but he couldn't. In the end, Miranda made the decision for him.'

'But it can't be proved,' Clare said.

'It's a motive and a good one, don't you think?'

It was, Clare knew, but she didn't want to give the woman the satisfaction. 'There are stronger motives,' she said.

'Father, why would I have killed the old woman?' Todd asked.

'She had seen Emily on the day Charlotte died. She was going to tell the police.'

'I never knew that,' Todd said. 'Is this true?'

'It's true,' Emily said.

'It seems that you have some explaining to do,' Tremayne said.

'I didn't kill either of the two women. If Charlotte were around, she'd confuse Todd. I came down here, parked up near the old lady, took no notice of her. I thought she was just crazy. I didn't know her history then. It was later that I found out she was the mother of another woman in the village.'

'Who?' Eustace asked.

'It's not important, not now,' Tremayne said. 'Please continue, Miss Walker.'

'It was the day Charlotte died. I saw her out the back with the chickens, no one was around, no idea why, but there she was.'

'You spoke to her?'

'I did. I could see why Todd was interested. She was attractive, or she could have been, but the years had taken their toll on her. A sympathetic woman could have taken pity on her, but I'm not. The police are right, I couldn't kill either of the women. Emotionally, it wouldn't have concerned me, and I wouldn't have had any guilt, but I don't want to spend time in prison when others would kill for me if I wanted.'

'A confession?' Clare asked.

'The best defence any person could ever have, total honesty. I care for little in my life, except for my father and Todd. I'll defend both of them at any cost, but I'll not murder, not if there's a chance of being caught, and Inspector Tremayne is old-school, a dog with a bone. He'll never give up, and Sergeant Yarwood is no slouch. They will find out who the murderers are, but it's not Todd or me.'

'Your conversation with Charlotte?'

'I offered her money to leave the farm, never to contact Todd.'

'What did she say?'

'She wouldn't go.'

'Why?'

'Because she had fallen in love.'

'With Todd?'

'She told me that she had found a good man and she was going to move in with him. A man who treated her well; a man who understood.'

'Wally Plumpton,' Clare said.

'Not a very impressive man from all accounts,' Emily said.

'The money?'

'I offered her fifty thousand pounds.'

'She accepted?'

'For Plumpton, to help him out.'

'Todd?'

'She felt nothing for him. To her, he was using her, and she admitted to her easy way with men. Couldn't help herself, she said, but with Plumpton, she'd take counselling, medicine to suppress her overactive hormones.'

'Is that it?'

'I walked away, told her I would contact her in a couple of days after she had told Todd that the romance was off.'

'The woman was pregnant. It wasn't Plumpton's.'

'She knew whose it was, and she was sure that Plumpton would accept the baby, adopt it as his own.'

'Todd?'

'It wasn't Todd, that's all I know. I never paid her the money, and I would have, just to be rid of her. The next I hear, she's dead.'

'It's a good story,' Tremayne said. 'Unprovable, either way.'

'The truth often is, Inspector. Todd and I will be staying in Salisbury tonight. If you want to talk further, you can find us there. Next time, I will have legal representation, so give me two hours' notice.'

'You could stay here,' Miranda said.

'I don't think that would be advisable, Mother, do you?' Todd said.

'I suppose not.'

Chapter 18

Emily Walker had been exhausting; a woman of few scruples.

'Todd Hampton's petrified of her,' Clare said to Tremayne as they drove away from the farmhouse. 'He'll be henpecked.'

'She'll not see it that way, but she's a manipulative woman.'

'Capable of murder?'

'And more. She admitted it herself, no compunction either way, but smart enough not to get caught.'

'We rule her out?'

'At this time.'

As they drove through the village, Maria was out in front of the pub, putting up a sign announcing the specials for that evening. She beckoned Tremayne and Clare over.

'The bank's agreed to six months and Wally's son is going to help out. He's a good man, the same as Wally.'

'Your husband?'

'He's all for it, not that he can help much. He can't even boil an egg, but he's happy for me to take over the pub. I'm sure I can make a go of it.'

Clare thought Maria a resilient woman, determined, and, above all, likeable and charismatic, a complete opposite to her husband whom Clare had met and disregarded, a man of few talents and less charm.

According to Emily, Charlotte had wanted Wally, the now-dead publican, a man who would accept her for who she was and would accept the unborn child as his own, even if it wasn't.

Tremayne and Clare sat in the pub, at Maria's insistence. 'On the house,' she said. 'I need you to try out the new menu, and I need Clare to ask her husband to attend in a few weeks to say a few words.'

'I'll make sure of it,' Clare said.

After Maria had gone to the kitchen, promising to return in fifteen minutes with something mouthwatering, Tremayne leant over to Clare. 'Will Clive come?'

'Not until we've solved the murders.'

A ruckus in the kitchen, the sound of screaming, of banging plates. Tremayne was on his feet first, although Clare was first through the kitchen door. On the floor, Maria.

'I got it,' she beamed.

'A rat?'

'Not in my kitchen, never, but there's been a field mouse, not really vermin, who's been sneaking in occasionally. I couldn't kill it, but the food safety standards inspector would have a fit if he saw it.'

Maria stood up, the creature in a saucepan, the lid held in place.

'What do you intend to do with it?' Clare asked.

'I'm not sure. If I put it outside, it'll only come back.'

'We thought that something was amiss,' Tremayne said. 'It sounded as though someone was committing an affray.'

'Ten minutes,' Maria said as she resumed preparing the meal. 'Help yourselves to a drink, will you?'

Tremayne poured himself a half-pint of beer, Clare helped herself to an opened bottle of Chablis and poured a full glass.

'You'd better make that a pint,' Clare said. 'It's been a rough day.'

'And likely to get rougher. What do you make of Campbell and Harriet getting together?' Tremayne said, sipping at his beer, enjoying being away from the village and its intrigues.

'It could be second-hand or third-hand information. The woman behind the counter at the store is a conduit for gossip. It may be untrue.'

'We interview Campbell first,' Clare said.

'I'd agree.'

'Roast sirloin, roast potatoes, Yorkshire pudding, all the trimmings,' Maria said as she put two plates on the table.

'It looks wonderful,' Clare said.

Tremayne acknowledged it by nodding his head. He already had some of the Yorkshire pudding on his fork.

'I thought when your husband came,' Maria said, 'I'd serve this. Would he approve?'

'I'm sure he would. Maria, we need to solve these murders first, just in case…'

'In case I'm involved.'

'In case anyone's involved. Everyone's under suspicion until then.'

'My Joe, not that you'd give much credence to what he says, believes it's Harriet.'

'What do you reckon?' Clare asked.

'He doesn't like her, sees her as a miserable old woman. I don't know why as she's lived here all her life, and the house was given to her. She could have sold it, moved somewhere else. If you're not content in one place, don't stay, that's what I reckon.'

'Are you content, Maria?' Tremayne said, taking a break from his meal. 'Great food, by the way.'

'Thanks. I'm sure it'll be a great success, the pub, once you and Clare have found out who's guilty.'

Maria sat down, her head low, and spoke quietly, even though no one else was in the pub. 'I miss Wally,' she said.

'Were you close to him?' Clare asked.

'He wanted to do better, and with this place going broke, it eventually killed him. He couldn't deal with it. Sure, he was a great publican, the jovial host, but he wasn't cut out for it. With me, we could have made a difference.'

'Joe?' Tremayne asked.

'Joe's dependable, a good man, a good father, and I'd never leave him.'

'But you preferred Wally Plumpton.'

'Dreaming, just dreaming. Don't we all; the grass is greener over the next hill, what could be, that sort of thing.'

'Did Wally know of this?' Clare asked.

'I told him once, just joking, what a good catch he'd be for the right woman.'

'What did he say?'

'He laughed it off, said I was foolish, and who'd want him, a fat man with no fixed abode and no money.'

'How long before he died?'

'Three days. I knew he wasn't covering costs, not all his fault, as pubs are closing all the time nowadays, but he could have done something about it.'

'Were you in love with Wally?'

'I'm not sure you'd call it love, and our relationship was never more than what you know already.'

'Could it have been?'

199

'Not with me, and Wally wasn't interested.'

'Charlotte?'

'She liked him, I know that.'

'Is it possible she could have loved him?' Clare said.

'Who would know? Both were addicts, and they obviously got on well. I used to see them laughing out loud, but if there was any more to it, I don't know. I wouldn't have thought so. Wally was much older than her; his eldest son is almost her age.'

'My step-daughter's not that much younger than me, and my husband is seventeen years older than me.'

'Sorry, I didn't mean to imply anything.'

'No apologies necessary. Now, Wally and Charlotte. What do you know?'

'Sometimes, they'd disappear for an hour or so, and I think she spent the night here occasionally.'

'Think or know?'

'Know. She was sleeping with him, not that she didn't sleep with others, some who should be ashamed of themselves.'

'Names?' Tremayne said. His beer was finished, and he could do with another, but the day wasn't over. He'd not drink any more, not now, but at home, whatever time that was likely to be, he would have a bottle of beer with Jean.

'Ben, up at the farm. Everyone knew about that. And Tony, or she tried, I know that.'

'How?'

'He went around the village telling everyone about it. Not that he was sure as to what he was saying, but it was entertaining.'

'Did everyone see the humour?'

'Harriet Huxtable didn't, but she's a fine one to talk, her and Angus Campbell. I would have thought the man was past it, and the woman is a dried-up old prune.'

'Where did you learn about this?' Clare said.

'Down at the local shop. The woman talks too much, and I don't get involved.'

'But you heard something.'

'I was looking for ingredients, not that she had what I wanted, so I had to go into Salisbury. I'm at the back of the shop. It's not that big and I can hear everything that's said.'

'Which woman?'

'Harriet, who else?'

'This doesn't make sense.'

'Not to you and me, not to anyone. The woman's spent her life being miserable, barely acknowledging anyone, and then she's telling the town crier that she and Angus Campbell were involved.'

'Involved?'

'That's what she said. They couldn't be lovers, not at his age, and I can't imagine she'd be game. A lifetime of devotion to the church, an implacable intent to stay chaste and pure, not to sully herself with the grittier side of life.'

'Have you spoken to anyone else about this?'

'Only to Joe, but he wouldn't say anything. The quiet life is what he likes, minds his own business. You'll not find better.'

Apart from Wally Plumpton, Clare thought, at least according to Maria, who by her own admission had preferred the publican to her husband.

The shopkeeper would be asked later why she had not revealed her source about Harriet and Campbell, although a conduit doesn't always reveal sources or to whom they pass on what they've learnt. The woman behind the counter: all-seeing, all-hearing, but never culpable.

***

When the murder investigation should have been winding to its inevitable conclusion, another twist had been unveiled – Harriet Huxtable's unusual behaviour.

Tremayne and Clare walked through the village, needing to walk off a superb meal; at Clare's insistence more than Tremayne's, who would have preferred a short sleep in the car.

'Who's first?' Clare asked.

Tremayne looked to the houses on their left, typical of a small village, some with thatched roofs, others with slate tiles. The majority of them in good condition, the inevitable one that was sadly neglected, weeds growing where there should have been flowers, a dog barking, a cat sitting on a window sill.

'What secrets lurk behind the curtains?' Tremayne said. 'Is this it, the end of the investigation,' he pondered.

'Are you tired of it?'

'There have been so many over the years; this one's no different.'

Clare could see the weariness in him, even if he'd not admit to it. Tremayne, the indomitable spirit, the one person who would never let an investigation go unsolved, not take time for himself until someone was charged, the case watertight, the evidence overwhelming or a confession freely given.

'Harriet worries me,' Clare said. 'I had hoped she wasn't involved.'

'Don't let sympathy cloud your judgement. If she murdered her mother and Charlotte, we would charge her. Prison won't be a lot different from the life she lives now.'

'A prison of her own choosing, and now she's declaring herself a liberated woman, a woman with a man, no longer "a spinster of the parish", to paraphrase her.'

'Did she say that?'

'To me in the pub that night when they reminisced about Wally Plumpton.'

'Paramour of Charlotte and Maria,' Tremayne said.

'Only of Charlotte, let's not forget.'

'Okay, have it your way, imagined lover of Maria. What was it with Plumpton? He wasn't an impressive man, not to me.'

'You'd not understand,' Clare said. 'Women look further than the physical form, especially if they're getting older, their life is unsettled. Decency, a good heart, someone who'll not let you down are also important.'

'You've got that with Grantley.'

'Wally might not have been the mayor of Salisbury, but he had his values, certainly to Charlotte and Maria.'

'Do we believe that Charlotte intended to be with Wally?'

'We still need the father of the child,' Clare said. 'If she did, and we've no reason to doubt it. A troubled woman, pregnant, in need of a kindred spirit, someone to trust; she wouldn't have done worse than Plumpton.'

'The man comes across as a saint.'

'He was no saint, far from it, but he was viable, and Charlotte knew that, as did Maria.'

'I've still got my money on Maria knowing more than she's letting on, and where did Charlotte get hold of heroin? She didn't have any money, and sex wouldn't have got her much; too much of that around these days for the taking.'

'Campbell?'

'Our friendly neighbourhood gossip at the store; find out what else she knows.'

'Frighten her a little?'

'Gossiping's not a crime, just a damn nuisance, but we can have her for withholding evidence.'

'Has she?' Clare said.

'Not knowingly. But she's not to know that, is she?'

'Not in that store. Mind you don't come out with an armful of groceries.'

'Not a chance,' Tremayne said.

***

It was just after five in the afternoon when Tremayne and Clare entered the small shop, Tremayne's bulk making the place seem even smaller.

Behind the counter, the owner of the establishment was at the cash register. An elderly woman that neither of the police officers had seen before was putting her purchases into a string bag.

With a 'cheerio', the woman left the shop a minute later.

'I don't know her,' Clare said to the shopkeeper.

'Mrs Peyton, she lives in the next village.'

'Why come here?'

'She says that I'm cheaper.'

'Are you?'

'No, but I'm not about to tell her.'

'We've a few questions. It would be best if you close up. This is Inspector Tremayne, by the way.'

'I normally close around this time anyway.'

With that, the woman left her side of the counter and went to the door, turning the sign from 'Open' to 'Closed', before latching the door at the top and the bottom.

'We've got to leave later,' Clare said.

'My feet are aching something dreadful. Come around to the back.'

'How long have you owned this store?' Tremayne asked.

'A long time, sometimes it seems an eternity.'

'You would know everyone in this village, what they get up to, who they're…' Tremayne paused.

'Who's putting their shoes under which bed.'

Clare chuckled at the woman's adroit reference to unbecoming behaviour in the village. It sounded quaint to her, old-fashioned. So much better than saying who was screwing who, which is what most people would have said.

The three sat at an old Formica-topped table, a plastic tablecloth as a cover. On the table, a teapot replete with a tea cosy and three cups.

'Your name is Shirley Jenkins,' Tremayne said. 'Is that correct?'

'Everyone calls me Shirley, no need to be formal.'

'Your husband?'

'He was a bad lot, left me with the shop and not much else.'

'Children?'

'A daughter, your sergeant's age. I don't see her often, what with her airs and graces, not that she has any right to them. You'd think she'd married into royalty instead of a chartered accountant.'

'Shirley, you appear to be a cheerful woman,' Clare said, 'in spite of what you've just said.'

'I don't see any reason to complain, not too often, and only then about my feet. You can't imagine how many hours I'm standing each day.'

'You could sell the shop,' Tremayne said.

'Retire, give up my sanity? Never.'

Tremayne understood. It was the same for him. The need to be focussed, to have an occupation, the ability to make a difference, even if the woman was selling products that could be purchased a lot cheaper in any supermarket. To her, it was her life, as was policing to him.

'You serve what some would say was a vital function of village life,' Clare said.

'I'm the only shop here. There was another one, but it closed down years ago.'

'That's not what I'm referring to, Shirley. You're not only the shop's owner; you know all that's going on.'

'Are you calling me an interfering busybody? Is that how you see me?'

'Please, Shirley,' Tremayne said. 'We're not accusing you of anything.'

'I don't hold with being malicious.'

'Harriet Huxtable?' Tremayne said.

'Who told you about her and Angus Campbell?' Clare asked.

'She did; pleased as punch. The first time I can remember her smiling.'

'And you felt that it was free for you to tell others?'

'If she hadn't wanted me to, why come in here?'

'A valid point,' Tremayne conceded. 'Why do you think she said what was obviously untrue?'

'I never thought about it. You've got to admit that it's funny, Harriet and Angus.'

Tremayne did, but he wanted the woman to talk, not to enjoy a laugh.

'You weren't willing to tell me your source last time. Why was that?' Clare asked.

'You never asked.'

Clare realised the woman was correct.

'What else don't we know?' she asked.

'The young woman and Plumpton, you know about that?'

'We do. What else?'

'Harriet is Bess's daughter?'

'Where did you find that out?' Tremayne reacted with alarm. Privileged information in the hands of the one person who would promote it.

'Don't deny that it's true. Bess told me years ago.'

'How many years?'

'I can't remember, a few years after she arrived here.'

'If she told you, why doesn't anyone else know?'

'Because I never told anyone. She wanted me to, to make her daughter see how foolish she was in ignoring her own mother.'

'She could have told the village.'

'That wasn't Bess's style. All she wanted was a daughter's love, but she never got it. I can sympathise with her now, as I understand what she meant.'

'Your daughter?' Clare said.

'A stuck-up cow. I apologise for my bluntness. I know you should never criticise your children, never stop loving them, but that's what she is.'

'Why didn't you tell the village about Bess and Harriet?'

'I couldn't, not something that sad. And besides, I remember Harriet when she had been a lot younger, a friend even, always happy, and then one day, a wall descended. Talking about people, who's sleeping with who, does no harm, and if it does, it serves them right. But Harriet and Bess, I couldn't. I'm telling you now because one of them is dead and the other is acting very peculiar. I mourn one; worry about the other.'

'So far, you've not told us anything new,' Clare said. 'We knew Charlotte was spending time with Wally Plumpton.'

'And others, not Angus though. The man's in his eighties, and unless he's taking medication, he wouldn't be up to it.'

'We'd agree with you on that,' Clare said. 'What else does this village keep close to its chest?'

'I like the woman, but the truth will come out soon enough.'

'Who?' Tremayne said.

'I've not told anyone, none of my business, but I saw it with my own eyes.'

'You must tell us, Shirley,' Clare said. 'We can't protect people just because we like them. There's a murderer amongst us, someone who could come into your store. You could be alone with that person or persons, and if they thought you were a threat, you could be number three.'

'I walked past the place one night, no reason, just a stroll. It was five or six months ago, and the weather was mild. I saw the woman enter, put her arms around the man.'

'Who?' Tremayne reiterated.

'The next morning, it was early, and I was out walking. It helps my feet to get some movement into them, and I saw her come out. She gave the man a passionate kiss, the sort of kiss that lovers have after they've spent the night together.'

'Who?' Clare, this time.

'Maria spent the night with Wally Plumpton. I've told no one, and I've never mentioned it to her. I don't know why I'm telling you now, as Wally committed suicide and she's making a go of the pub. I wish her well.'

'We might come back,' Tremayne said, 'but for now, we'll bid you goodnight. And if you have any more that would interest us, please contact us. Remember, there is a murderer in this village, possibly two, and they have killed for less than idle gossip.'

'I'll remember,' Shirley Jenkins said.

Clare was disappointed with Maria.

Chapter 19

Shirley Jenkins, a woman who knew all that happened in the village, and had profited from it, had never revealed the two most important items of news to others.

'It's puzzling,' Tremayne said as he and Clare walked back to their car.

'Why keep what Bess Carmichael said secret? Do you think that she did it for a reason?'

'It could be that the woman has a shred of decency in her.'

'Maria?'

'As I've told you before, Yarwood, never discount anyone as a suspect.'

'I've learnt that lesson well enough over the years. If she saw Maria and Plumpton that morning, so could someone else.'

'Which means?'

'What would Maria and Plumpton have done to conceal the truth?'

'Maria said she'd never leave her husband, but if he knew?'

'Or suspected. He didn't kill Plumpton, and he hasn't harmed Maria, but the man's not a total dullard; he could have reacted in other ways.'

'Nipped the gossip at the source.'

'Which means?'

'Charlotte may have seen them, although if she'd been sleeping with Plumpton, aiming to move in with him, she would have known without seeing Maria with him.'

'A woman's intuition?'

'Charlotte would have known, leave it at that.'

'What's the conjecture?'

'Joe wouldn't harm Maria, and he knows she won't leave him. Plumpton commits suicide, but he wouldn't have said anything, and from what we know, he was keen on Charlotte. Maria's husband wants a quiet life, not to be the butt of jokes.'

'If Charlotte knew, said something to him, protecting her relationship with Plumpton, he could have reacted.'

'Badly, if he has. We need to talk to him.'

'Maria first,' Clare said.

As they walked, the Reverend Walton passed by on the other side of the street. 'How's the investigation going?' he shouted across.

'A moment of your time,' Tremayne said as he and Clare crossed over to the vicar's side.

'Gossip, there's a lot in this village?' Tremayne said after the three had exchanged greetings, spoken about the weather, the parlous state of English politics. Skirting around the issue, Tremayne would call it.

'No more than elsewhere,' Walton said.

'We continue to receive additional knowledge about this village and the people in it,' Clare said. 'What's true and what's not, we'd like to know.'

'Malicious or harmless?'

'According to Shirley Jenkins, it's mostly harmless.'

'Are you referring to Harriet's recent behaviour?'

'In part. Any truth to it?'

'I've no idea. In all the years that she's been looking after the church, I can't say I know her.'

'No conversations?'

'She'd talk about the church, about the previous Sunday's sermon. Although never the truth, not about the sermon. I know I'm dry, and I drone on, but she always found a positive slant, a message given.'

'Any lightheartedness about her?'

'Not with me. I tried a few times to break through, to ask her about herself, her parents, her time in the village.'

'Her response?'

'She'd answer, but no substance, nothing I hadn't already known, and then she's in the shop telling the world about her amorous adventure. As a matter of fact, I was off to see her now, ask her if she needs help.'

'Do you think she does?'

'I expected her in the church today, but she never came. It'd be the first time in five or six years where she's missed a day, and that was only for a couple of days.'

'Who looked after her?'

'My wife, no one else wanted to.'

'Uncharitable?'

'Harriet would allow my wife, no one else, and they knew it..'

'We'll go with you,' Tremayne said. 'We've a few questions for her.'

On the other side of the road, Maria stood. Clare smiled at her, although it was no longer the smile of a friend, more that of a police officer who needed to ask her some direct and pertinent questions.

'Inspector, I'll go and talk to Maria. You can go with Reverend Walton and check on Harriet,' Clare said. She had wanted to see Harriet, but the pub beckoned.

***

'Good meal earlier?' Maria asked.

'Does your husband know about you and Wally Plumpton?' Clare said, not asking if the rumour was true.

Maria sensed by Clare's tone that she knew.

'Joe was away for a few days, and the children were spending the night with friends. How did you find out?'

'Why, Maria? After all, you told us earlier that you'd never leave Joe.'

'I wouldn't, but it was a moment of weakness. I know I shouldn't have, and Wally was hardly Mr Universe, but he treated me well, and we let ourselves go, just the once.'

'Regrets?'

'Would they serve any purpose?'

'I was disappointed when I heard it.'

'Who else knows?'

'Inspector Tremayne.'

'Who told you?'

'Is it important?' Clare said. 'You've confirmed that it is true. Now, the question is how this impacts on our enquiries.'

'Should it? We were discreet, and neither of us spoke about it to anyone, not even to each other after that night. Wally wanted Charlotte, although if I'd been free, he would have taken me, but I wasn't about to destroy my family.'

'Maria, sit down. We've got to talk this through.'

The woman complied.

'You want to know why I spent the night with Wally?' she said.

'I think we know why.'

'Joe, sometimes he can be boring.'

'Sometimes?'

'I don't want to talk badly about him.'

'Does he know?'

'Not from me.'

'You've done your wifely duty?'

'I have. And Joe's not one for gossip, so it's doubtful that anyone would have told him. Who was it, by the way?'

'One person saw you, and she kept it to herself.'

'Shirley Jenkins?'

'Why her?'

'I saw her that morning. I didn't think she was looking, and why she thought I'd spent the night, I'd not know.'

'She said that your farewell with Wally was not that of two friends. She recognised the signs. She'd also seen you the previous evening when you had been at the pub.'

'Who else has she told?'

'No one.'

'Do you believe her?'

'There are other secrets in the village, more serious than an unfaithful wife. She's kept them to herself, so on balance I'd say she kept your and Wally's assignation secret. Be thankful for that.'

'Should I thank her?'

'I would suggest you say nothing, not until we've wrapped up the current investigation.'

'What do you want from me?' Maria said.

'The truth.'

'It was just the once.'

'It brings another complexity as to who murdered the two women.'

'It wasn't Wally or me.'

'I'll reserve judgement on you for now,' Clare said. 'What if Charlotte had seen you and Wally? What if she knew? If, as we believe, she intended to be with him, how would she react towards you?'

'She never spoke to me about it.'

'If not you, then how about Joe? She was a desperate woman, with another man's unborn child, and she needed stability in her life, if not for her, for her child. Would she have told your husband, hoping that he would deal with you? She wouldn't have mentioned it to Wally, knowing that he would be forced into a conflict as to whether to deny you or support her, or he could have been in a quandary, not sure what to say or do. And we know that Wally had trouble with stress.'

'Joe wouldn't have said anything to me, even if she had. That's Joe's way, to let everything blow over.'

'Let's assume Charlotte's told Joe; he won't tell you, and she can see you and Wally, if not cohabiting, at least very cosy. What would she do? What would Joe do?'

'I don't know about Charlotte.'

'Don't tell me Joe would let it blow over, not if Charlotte intends to go public, to protect her child, to ensure Wally is there for her.'

'But that would destroy any chance with Wally.'

'Charlotte wasn't a stable woman. Who knows what goes through the mind of a desperate woman. Joe could have been forced to take desperate measures.'

'I'll not think badly of him, not Joe.'

'We know that Charlotte was with Bess in her caravan. What if she was looking for allies, told her your secret. Both women had problems, disappointments in their lives.'

'Bess was a lonely old woman, nothing more. She wouldn't have caused trouble.'

'We have to question your husband. He has to know the truth,' Clare said.

'Not Joe.'

'If the women hadn't been murdered, then it would have remained your secret. As it is, we have no option.'

'I need to be the one. Would you be there when I tell him?'

'It has to be soon. In the meantime, we'll continue with our investigations. If it can be avoided, then I'll try to keep him out of it,' Clare said.

'Thank you, my friend.'

'Don't assume that, not any more. I only hope that I don't have to arrest you or your husband, but rest assured, if I must, I will.'

***

No matter how much Reverend Walton hammered on the front and rear doors of Harriet Huxtable's cottage, there was no answer, only barking from the dog. In the end, Tremayne, tiring of the man's attempts, put his shoulder close to the lock on the rear door and pushed hard. The door opened, the lock broken, but the two men were in the house.

'We'd better go carefully here, just in case,' Tremayne said. 'I'll go on alone.'

'If she's hurt?'

'That, Reverend Walton, is the least of our concerns.'

'Murdered?'

'Two's enough for this village. I don't want another one.'

'None of us do.'

Tremayne took a pair of nitrile gloves out of his pocket and put them on. Walton waited as he moved through the kitchen, spotless as the rest of the house, and out into the small hallway. He did not speak, only kept his eyes focussed, looking for the tell-tale signs of an intruder, of violence.

As he climbed the stairs to the two bedrooms upstairs, a faint moaning. Tremayne quickened his pace and opened the door to the room at the front of the house. On the bed, the fully-clothed woman.

It wasn't murder, Tremayne was relieved to see. He moved closer to the woman, smelt the air, her breath.

'You can come up,' Tremayne shouted to the vicar.

'Is she alright?'

'Black coffee and plenty of it would be a help.'

Walton came up the stairs, took one look at the woman and retreated back down, just in time to find Clare at the back door.

'She's drunk, paralytic by the looks of it,' Walton said.

'She's not a drinker,' Clare said.

'The occasional sherry. At least she's alive, we can be thankful for that.'

Clare wasn't so sure; the woman had become the standing joke in the village. 'Have you heard about Harriet Huxtable and Angus Campbell? Who'd have believed it, at their ages' and 'It's farcical, but then she was always off her rocker, living in her house on her own, an old maid, and the Colonel, such a nice man' were two of the conversations that Clare imagined would be rife in the village.

After an hour and half a dozen cups of black coffee, Harriet Huxtable was able to sit in a chair, the two men downstairs, Clare ministering to her. She'd managed to put her in the shower, cleaning off the vomit that had stuck to her and her clothes.

'I don't know why,' Harriet said.

'You've been overdoing it, attempting to deal with tragedy, pretending that you didn't care,' Clare said.

Harriet picked up the ham and cheese sandwich that had been prepared for her, took one bite and rushed off to the bathroom again. Clare waited for her return, aware that the woman needed complete rest and professional care.

On her return, her teeth freshly brushed, her hair combed, Clare said, 'You need complete rest.'

'I can't. There's the church, and then there's the–'

'I'll make it official if I have to. What you told Shirley Jenkins, a pack of lies?'

'I did spend the night at his house.'

'We'll talk to Campbell after here.'

'Nothing happened.'

'Why did you tell the town gossip that it did?'

'Maybe I wanted them to see me differently, maybe I wanted to be liked, not to be ridiculed.'

'Harriet, you've spent your life angry and sullen. Why change now?'

'My mother died, not that anyone knows, or they didn't. Angus Campbell said that you told him.'

'He's a perceptive man. How did you know that he knew?'

'He phoned me up, asked me to come and see him. I was intrigued, in that we had barely exchanged a word in twenty years.'

'He told you?'

'He and my mother had spent time together years ago. He skirted around my mother and me, and how he

218

had come to know. He said you had revealed certain facts to him.'

'We had to tell him that Bess had a daughter in the village; necessary for him to know when we were questioning him, especially as it had been him that had seen you and her at the caravan, Charlotte inside.'

'I didn't know she was there.'

'We'll accept that for now. Angus Campbell realised that you were the daughter, the way the two of you avoided eye contact, the food you left out for her at Christmas. It seems all very childish, don't you think?'

'Now I do, but there's not much I can do about it. I suppose that's the reason I went a little crazy, made up that story for Shirley Jenkins. Me and the Colonel, it's ludicrous.'

'It's not,' Clare said. 'Stretching the imagination, more like it.'

'What should I do? Pray? Continue in the village as if nothing's happened?'

'One week's complete rest. I'd say you've had a traumatic shock and that your behaviour is the result, a mental breakdown. A doctor needs to check you out, prescribe medicine for you, and sedatives to sleep.'

'The church?'

'You're not to go near it.'

'Why was my mother killed?'

'We don't know, not yet. We're not sure that it was because of the two of them being at Bess's caravan, not any more.'

'You have another possibility?'

'Several, and we need to work through them. As for you, Harriet Huxtable, I've just messaged a friend. She's a qualified home care nurse. She'll be here in a couple of hours. And please take it easy.'

'I'll try.'

Clare knew she would, but not for long, but her friend, used to difficult people, would keep the woman under control, at least long enough for her and Tremayne to wrap up the investigation, and for the ridicule that Harriet had caused to abate.

Clare stayed chatting with the woman for the remainder of the day. The nurse made herself comfortable and a doctor who'd arrived later in the day had given Harriet a sedative and a lecture on the need to rest. Tremayne had said that his sergeant was too soft-hearted, but she knew that he could be too, not that he'd ever show it.

***

The next day, at ten in the morning, Clare knocked on the door of Maria and Joe's house. It was remarkably small for a family of four, but it was homely and loved. Maria opened the door.

'Joe's here,' Maria said. 'I've not told him anything. I'm very nervous as to what he'll say.'

'One step at a time,' Clare said as she climbed over a small dog that was sniffing around her ankles.

Inside, Joe sat at the kitchen table. He stood as Clare entered and shook her hand.

'Maria said it was important,' he said. 'I've taken the morning off, but I'm rostered on for this afternoon. This won't take long, will it?'

'I don't expect so,' Clare said.

Maria put her arm in Joe's and they sat down together at the table. Clare watched them interacting, a typical married couple.

'Maria said it was about Wally,' Joe said.

'What do you know about Wally?'

'Not a lot. We were friendly, and I know he was keen on Maria, but he was supposedly messing around with the woman up at Hampton's.'

'Supposedly, or you know?'

'I don't hold with gossip, Maria told you that?'

'She did. She said it served no purpose prying into other people's dirty linen, or words to that effect. Did you know either Charlotte Merton or Bess Carmichael?'

'I'd say hello to the young woman, but I never spoke to her.'

'At the pub, did you ever see her there, talk to her more?'

'Where's this going? Sometimes she'd be up there when I'd gone up to see Maria or have a pint. I could have spoken to her about the weather, how was she, but then you do that with everyone, don't you? Courtesy costs nothing. No reason to go around with a miserable face all day.'

'No reason at all,' Clare agreed.

The subject which needed to be broached was proving difficult.

'Your wife spent a lot of time at the pub when Wally Plumpton was alive,' Clare said, gently easing into what had to be said.

'It was her job, brought in some extra money, enough for the small luxuries, the special treats for the children.'

'And now she's taking over the pub?'

'As long as the family doesn't suffer, that's up to her.'

'That's what you care about, more than anything else, isn't it, Joe?'

'Where's this heading?'

221

'The truth,' Clare said. 'Two women have been murdered. One who probably saw your wife as a rival.'

'Why? What's Maria done?'

Maria held Joe's hand tight. 'You were away with your job, the children were at friends for the night,' she said, her face drawn, her eyes downcast.

Joe sat rooted to the spot. 'Are you telling me that you and Plumpton spent the night together?'

'I'm sorry, Joe. I was weak, and we both regretted it the next day.'

Clare could see the emotion welling in the stoic and usually unemotional Joe.

'Sergeant, you've destroyed our life,' he said, looking at Clare. 'The truth sometimes should not be told.'

'It's the truth that I must have, not to cause harm, or to sever a man from his wife, but to solve two heinous crimes. You must understand that?'

'What do I care for either of the women. It's Maria and our children I care for.'

'I'm so sorry, Joe,' Maria said again. Her husband had removed her arm from his.

'The one time?'

'Just once.'

'I'll not divorce you. This matter won't be discussed again.'

'I'll make it up to you,' Maria said.

'Not today, you won't. Sergeant, do you want me for any more?'

'Regardless of how you must feel, I must ask further questions.'

'Carry on.'

'Did you know about your wife and Plumpton?'

'I did not.'

'Charlotte Merton and Plumpton?'

'Maria would have told me that the two of them were friendly.'

'I'll accept that as meaning that they were sleeping together,' Clare said. 'Charlotte was pregnant, and it wasn't Plumpton's child.'

'I'd not know anything about that.'

'I wasn't asking if you were the father, and judging by your reaction to your wife's confession, you're not a man to stray.'

'That's what men do, but I haven't, never wanted to. I've always had Maria, and she was enough for me, but…I don't want to talk about it, not now.'

'That's understandable,' Clare said. 'But here's the dilemma. Charlotte is pregnant, she's desperate for a father for her child, even if he's not the biological father. She's found Plumpton, and whether it was love or a fondness that she felt the man, we'll never know. However, there's a fly in the ointment: Maria. The man's emotions are torn between a woman he can't have or Charlotte, who is his if he wants, but she comes with baggage. The man couldn't handle stress, and she represented that with a capital S.'

'Maria?'

'Charlotte was a confused woman, probable split personality. If she's cogent, she can see that she can't remove Maria, and she can't murder her, as the repercussions are obvious. But she realises another possibility.'

'What's that?' Joe asked.

'She could have told you about Maria and Plumpton. Charlotte can't tell Maria, but she could tell you.'

'I didn't know, not until you told me.'

'You're remarkably calm under the circumstances,' Clare said.

'To you, I am; not to me.'

'Very well. Let's presume that Charlotte tells you, assuming that you'll deal with Maria.'

'If you want.'

'But you're not a man to chastise your wife, to lay down the heavy hand, to go up and confront Plumpton. You've a laid-back personality, willing to let life pass you by, as long as your family is near you.'

'There are plenty out there chasing after money and promotion, developing ulcers, breaking up marriages. I was never one for that.'

'I'm glad of that,' Maria said, looking over at Clare. 'I told you he was a good man.'

No response from Joe, although he had edged marginally closer to his wife.

'Charlotte gives you time, but you do nothing,' Clare said. 'She confronts you again; you make it clear you won't deal with Maria, not remove her from the pub. She gets angry, threatens to tell the village, knowing that if she tells Shirley Jenkins in her shop, it's as good as a radio broadcast. You're desperate, not sure what to do. You do some research, find out how to inject the woman, a drug addict, although she's not taking the drug all the time. You've got contacts, not that they know what's going on. You get hold of a syringe, and out there near the farm, you kill her. It's possible, you'd agree.'

'Joe would never do that, not my Joe,' Maria said.

'It's not the only motive we have, and it still doesn't explain where Bess comes into it. As I said, we need to investigate every possibility, no matter how remote.'

'And you are here today,' Joe said, 'to create tension between a man and his wife? The truth of what she had done could have died with him, but you couldn't leave well alone.'

'I did my duty. Now, will you do yours? Will you admit to the truth?'

'I've told you all that I know. I didn't know about Maria in Plumpton's bed. Why would I have killed anyone?'

'You're a man who will do anything for his family, even put his life at risk. I'm sorry that I had to come here today.'

Joe got up from the table. 'I've got a job to do.' He kissed his wife on the cheek as he left the room. Clare wasn't sure if it was a conditioned response or deliberate.

Whatever the truth, Joe was a resolute man; decent to a fault, but a murderer? That was something else to consider.

Chapter 20

Angus Campbell did not appreciate Tremayne being in his house, giving him a lecture on interfering in a murder investigation.

'You were aware of the sensitivity, yet you call Harriet Huxtable over to your house. What for? To gloat?' Tremayne said.

Campbell stood in front of Tremayne, maintaining his military bearing, taking the dressing down, not enjoying it.

'It was my duty,' he said.

'Your duty was to keep quiet and let us do our job. And now we've got the woman under doctor's orders to stay calm, to get some rest, although how long she'll do that is anyone's guess.'

Clare knew the answer, even if Tremayne had said that no one knew – not very long. Even now, one day later, Clare's friend, the home care nurse, was struggling to keep the woman calm: she was fretting over the church, the damage she had done by her drunkenness, bragging at the shop.

'I felt that I owed her something. After all, I had seen Bess and Harriet together. If I had said something, done something, back then, Bess could still be alive, and if I'd known, then I could have helped to reconcile the two. I'd been close to Bess once, and her daughter and I had common ground.'

'The situation is complex,' Clare said. 'We can't rule you out as a suspect, nor Harriet. Why did you invite her over? The truth.'

'This village is not always the idyll that you believe it to be,' Campbell said. He had sat down, as had Tremayne, the two men at an impasse.

Clare could see that Tremayne had a right to be upset with Campbell, especially after the man had said that the secret he had guessed at Bemerton Road, about Harriet's mother, was meant to be sacrosanct, yet he had chosen to confront Harriet Huxtable with it.

'We know what this place is, the same as all of them. Incestuous pits of intrigue, backstabbing and people who can't mind their own business.'

Campbell got up from his seat and walked over to a set of drawers. He unlocked one of the drawers and opened it. He took out a large brown envelope.

'You'd better have these,' he said as he gave it to Clare.

Clare put her hand in the unsealed envelope and withdrew a collection of photos.

'Bess gave them to me years ago,' Campbell said.

'What are they?' Tremayne asked, realising that his treatment of the man may have been harsh.

'One is of a small child in a garden. The photo is old and out of focus,' Clare said.

'It's Bess, a happier time.'

'Why give it to you?' Tremayne asked.

'I can't remember any particular reason. I had shown her some of my photos one day, and then a week later she presented me with that envelope. "Here, these are yours", she said. "I've no use for them, not now." That was the last day that we spent time together.'

'Why would she do that?' Clare asked as she looked at the other photos in the envelope.

'We all know now, but at the time it made no sense. All I know is, after that day Bess changed.'

'And you never suspected the reason?'

'Trauma, a pang of guilt over something, that's all. I wasn't in a position to know, but it must have been the time when Bess realised that her daughter was out of her reach. There was always a sadness about Bess; it was deep and unfathomable, but I've seen it before, men in battle, nothing to live for, exposing themselves to unnecessary danger.'

'Bravery?'

'Foolishness, Tremayne. A person needs a reason to live; that way, they think their actions through, even if only momentarily and subconsciously. The foolhardy only endanger others.'

'Do you believe that Bess had spent all those years in that caravan waiting for death?' Clare said.

'Harriet, acting out of character, getting drunk, making herself a laughing stock. Troubled women, the two of them, so much in common, so much that kept them apart.'

'So, you invite Harriet to your house, to talk about old times, her mother, is that it?' Tremayne said.

'I wasn't sure, but after what I learnt from you, I felt I should do something.'

'Did you tell her you knew about her and Bess?'

'I never looked in that envelope, not until I returned home that night from the police station. I'd forgotten that it was there.'

'You saw, didn't you?' Clare said, another photo in her hand.

'What is it?' Tremayne asked.

'There's a picture of a young woman, a baby in her arms. On the back, written in pencil, a date and a name.'

'Harriet?'

'It's Bess and child. The date is one day after Harriet's birth date.'

'You'd not seen this before, Campbell?' Tremayne said.

'Never. I had to give the photos to Harriet, a photo of her as a baby with Bess. It seemed the decent thing to do.'

'You should have given them to us, let us deal with it,' Clare said.

'It was important for me to do it. It was personal, long before the murders. A photo of Harriet and her mother, the only one there is.'

'Her reaction wasn't as expected?'

'I didn't tell her that I had looked. I gave her the envelope, she opened it, looked through them and then started to cry.'

'She told the woman at the shop that she'd stayed the night here, the two of you romantically involved.'

'Bess couldn't deal with the reality of her daughter not wanting to acknowledge her; Harriet couldn't deal with the proof, not only a piece of paper but now a photo.'

'But she stayed the night,' Tremayne said.

'She started to talk, nothing new that I didn't already know, about her time in the village, how she had mistreated her mother, how she wanted to make amends but couldn't.

'We hadn't spoken much in the past, hardly ever, but for three hours, she kept talking. I gave her a sherry to drink. She drank one glass then two. Eventually, she had exhausted what she had wanted to say, and she fell asleep on the couch. I put a blanket over her and left her there. The next morning when I came down, six in the morning on the dot, she was gone.'

'I owe you an apology,' Tremayne said.

'You don't. I realised that the envelope could be evidence and that I should have given it to you first. She never took the photos when she left. I'm not sure if she forgot or if it was intentional. The only thing I know is that the next day she was a changed person, and not for the better. It's strange how people react when confronted with an unpleasant reality. A cheerful person becomes morose; an embittered and disappointed woman became foolish, a childlike behaviour.'

'That's one for the psychoanalysts,' Tremayne said.

'Harriet?' Campbell asked.

'Sedated, I hope,' Clare said.

***

A phone call, a quick drive to Hampton's farm, no chance of grabbing a bite to eat for the two police officers after they left Angus Campbell. Clare had the envelope in the car with her; whether it would be evidence or not was unclear.

At the farm, Jacob Grayson was standing in the centre of the farmyard. On his side of the confrontation were two heavies, one of whom was known to Tremayne. Facing the three who were intent on precipitating action were Eustace Hampton and his wife, Ben and Gavin Fitzwilliams. Margaret Reece and John and Eva Yardley were nowhere to be seen.

'I'm serving notice,' Grayson said on Tremayne's approach.

'Hampton, is there an issue?' Tremayne asked.

'We need longer. There's so much work to do, and I'm trying to get the money together.'

'It's not the money, it's my family's farm. I want it back, and I'm paying plenty for the privilege. You've not done much with it; let's see what I can do,' Grayson said.

Clare knew what Grayson's plans were, the same as the bank's if Maria failed at the pub – to sell the land to developers. The small insular village that Brockenstoke had been was under assault from an opposing force. Clare knew who would win the battle, and even in Stratford sub Castle, where her cottage was empty, new houses were being constructed. She didn't like it, but pockets full of money would always override the wishes of people who didn't want change.

The Hamptons and their vision of self-sufficiency and simplicity were doomed, and Grayson had the law behind him.

'You promised us longer,' Hampton protested, a murmuring of agreement from his side of the standoff.

On the other side, Grayson stood his ground, his fists clenched, a look of determination. Neil Abbott, a pub brawler and part-time bouncer in Salisbury, and one of Grayson's heavies moved forward, only to be met by Ben's hand on his shoulder.

'Back off, Abbott,' Ben said. 'Or you'll feel my fist in your face.'

It wasn't a contest. Ben, always affable at the farm, a gentle giant with a criminal record, was six inches taller than Abbott, who had bulk, but not muscles toughened by hard physical work.

'Gentlemen,' Tremayne said, 'this calls for time out. Let me remind you all that violence won't solve anything here.'

Turning to Grayson, Tremayne said, 'You've got the necessary paperwork?'

'I have.'

'Then why Abbott and the other man? The people at the farm have never shown aggression.'

'Ben has. The man has got a record for GBH, or don't you know?'

'As the senior investigating officer, I know about everyone, even you.'

'What does that mean?'

'I know you're a grovelling toad of a man, and you don't care about the farm, not one iota.'

'You can't speak to me like that,' Grayson protested.

'I can. However, Hampton, the man has a legal claim on this place,' Tremayne said as he looked over at Eustace.

'We need time,' Miranda Hampton said. 'We've got the children to worry about.'

'Mr Grayson cares little for them, as for most things, other than lining his pocket. Now, let me address Mr Grayson. This is still a crime scene, and if I have to, I'll make sure it remains so for the next six months.'

'You can't do that,' Grayson protested weakly.

'I'll do what's necessary. You can either walk away from here in the next five minutes, or I'll have uniforms here to secure the place. It's your choice. Give Hampton and the others time, let us wrap up the murder enquiry, and you can move in here unencumbered, plant your vegetables, milk the cows, feed the chickens, or sell it to the highest bidder.'

'But…'

'There are no buts,' Tremayne said, 'and the next time you want to come here flexing your muscle, let me know beforehand.'

'This is prejudice,' Grayson said.

'It's the law, take it or leave it.'

A rousing cheer from Hampton's side as Grayson got into his car with the heavies and drove away.

'You did us well,' Hampton said.

'Don't misjudge me,' Tremayne said. 'Someone here knows more than they're telling us. Grayson may be an unpleasant weasel of a man, but he's no dummy. I can't hold him off indefinitely, and I didn't threaten him for your benefit.'

Clare smiled imperceptibly. Tremayne, the tough, uncaring man that he portrayed, had enjoyed dealing with Grayson, and she knew he was gratified that he had done some good for Hampton and his people.

'Ben, a word in your ear,' Tremayne said, taking the man by the arm. 'Yarwood, seeing that we're the good guys here today, see if you can make them see sense. Try to get it into their thick skulls that Grayson will be back, and they're leaving sooner rather than later, and we need a murderer. One of them will do.'

Hampton smiled, as did the women, although Clare knew that the man's comments, for their ears more than hers, came with a bite to them.

Ben and Tremayne strolled over to the stream, a place that the police officer gravitated to every time at the farm. He didn't understand Hampton, never would, and the farm and its people irritated him.

'What is it, Inspector?' Ben asked.

'You were ready to give him a punch, weren't you?' Tremayne said.

'I couldn't let them get away with what they wanted to do. Eustace doesn't want to deal with reality, and Fitzwilliam's frightened of his own shadow.'

'Are you the father of Charlotte's unborn child?'

'I wouldn't know. I could be, I suppose. Is it important?'

'Not as important as it was. If we believe that the child was the reason she died, the truth doesn't matter, only what a person believes.'

'Can't you find out who is the father?'

'We can check the DNA of the father, match it against the fetus.'

'I've done time. You must have my fingerprints.'

'A swab from inside your cheek, are you agreeable?'

'I didn't kill her.'

'Not Charlotte, not with your calloused hands. It would have required some finesse, and you, Ben, don't have that.'

'The temper's still there. I could have hit him.'

'The hard physical work, that keeps it under control?'

'Anger management, counselling, is fine for some, but I came from a rough household, a father who was strong on discipline, light on love. He toughened me up, made me slap him down in the end.'

'You'll agree to us checking?'

'If it was mine, I'll be sad that it and the mother are dead.'

'Charlotte told someone that she knew who the father was, but she may have just said that. You don't hold with Hampton's views, do you; not that strongly anyway?'

'I don't understand half, sorry, a quarter, of what he's saying. It all sounds fine, but he uses words that impress some, but I don't need to pretend. I wasn't a good student at school, always wagging off, finding something better to do.'

'Such as?'

'When I was young, fishing, playing games, stealing occasionally. Nothing too serious, a bar of chocolate at the supermarket. Never caught, too quick for them to catch me.'

'When you were older?'

'Smoking cigarettes, and then chasing girls. Caught a few.'

'But here, you don't seem to be interested in women,' Tremayne said. The two of them sat on the bench by the stream.

'The truth?'

'It's always best.'

'When you're young, you're full of bravado, showing off, pretending to be the great stud.'

'You weren't?'

'Sure, I could catch them, do what was necessary, but I was never that much interested. It's not that I'm gay; it's just that I'm not much bothered.'

'Charlotte?'

'She's there, and she's not taking no for an answer. I managed with her, and that was fine. I did like her and children would have been nice, but I wouldn't have killed for her, not for any woman?'

'And you're not homosexual?'

'Prison would have been a breeze if I had been, but no. I hit a few in there who tried it on.'

'Grayson will be back. What will you do after here?'

'I'm not sure. I'd stay here if I could, but I don't think that far ahead, one day at a time for me.'

'If you're the father, will you want vengeance against whoever?'

'I might be angry, but my temper flares and five minutes afterwards I'm calm again. Could it be Fitzwilliam?'

'We can't be sure.'

'Todd Hampton?'

'It's not him, we know that.'

'And Eustace, he'd not play up, not with Charlotte.'

'What does that mean?'

'Nothing. I'm just talking.'

'What do you know?'

'Nothing, not really. Eustace was easy with words; he'd have the men fawning over him; the women, they would have been putty in his hands, so smooth he is, smart.'

'You were capable in your youth, an easy way with words.'

'My success, not that it lasted for long, was that I was taller than most everyone else, athletic, and young women are looking for what I had. Older women look for someone smart and charismatic, and Eustace has got both of them in plenty.'

'Are you suggesting that he had another woman?'

'In prison, you learn to keep your mouth shut; not let anyone get one up on you. That's my philosophy, a word Eustace likes to use.'

'I need a name, Ben. This is murder, not prison, and it's definitely not Eustace Hampton's fairytale world.'

'Margaret Reece, have a word with her. She's stuck-up, always with her daughters. Ask her about that time when her daughters weren't here, and the farm was empty, apart from me, Eustace and her. Now, I'm not saying anything, and Eustace could be innocent, but she was sitting awfully close to him, trying to get him to kiss her. What would the others think if they knew that Eustace had a bit on the side?'

Tremayne thought it unlikely. Miranda Hampton was attractive, looking good for her age; Margaret Reece was plain with a faraway look.

And, even if it was true, there seemed to be no connection to the two women's deaths, other than blackmail.

He discounted what Ben had told him, but it would still need to be checked. He'd let Clare deal with it. As for him, he needed food and a drink. He'd go and see what his sergeant was up to, see if she was interested and whether she'd enter the pub where Maria was, a woman who had disappointed her.

No one disappointed him, as he had no illusions. Everyone had secrets, everyone did things that they regret, but most were never found out, not unless it was a murder investigation. And then, the secrets would tumble, the truth would be unveiled, and people would be shamed.

Chapter 21

Clare found Margaret Reece, a woman she had never found easy to speak to, at the rear of the farmhouse.

'If you've got some time,' Clare said.

'There's a lot to do, and then I've got to pick up the girls.'

'You need to answer one question.'

'What is it?' the woman said as she continued to peg clothes on a clothesline.

'Not here. We need somewhere to talk this through.'

'You said one question.'

'Margaret, were you having an affair with Eustace Hampton?'

'*What?*'

'If you were, it could be important.'

'I refute your accusation. I never would, not with Eustace.'

'I need you to tell me the truth, painful as it may be,' Clare said.

For another two minutes, the woman continued to take the clothes out of the basket on the ground and to hang them on the line, making sure to peg them correctly. Her movements were robotic. Clare could see that her mind was going through the implications, thinking of what to say, whether to be totally honest, or whether to make excuses, to deny, to lay the guilt on someone else.

'Away from here,' the woman said as she picked up the clothes basket and put it in a small shed near the farmhouse. 'I haven't done anything.'

Once they were fifty yards from the farmhouse, not far from the stream that Tremayne knew well, the two women stopped. Margaret Reece looked down at the ground and then up at Clare.

'He's a great man,' she said.

'Eustace?'

'A man to be proud of, an easy man to love.'

'Do you?'

'We all do.'

'An affair?'

'We found solace here after my husband died.'

'That's not the question I asked. Are you or were you having an affair with Eustace?'

'No.'

'But you would have? You were seen close to him, trying to kiss him. Are you going to deny this?'

'I don't know who told you this, but yes, that's true. I'm not that old, sometimes my daughters are not enough. You're a woman, you'd understand.'

'Understand, of course.'

'It was only the once, a moment of weakness. Nothing happened, and I felt foolish afterwards. I even told Miranda, so you can see that it's not a great secret, only something that I'd prefer to forget, and they've never spoken about it.'

'If Eustace had responded?'

'I hope that I would have realised that it was wrong and backed off.'

'Hope or know?'

'Sergeant, I'm not comfortable talking about this,' Margaret said.

'You're a proud woman, your daughters do you credit,' Clare said.

'We are very close.'

'The person who told us was certain that the two of you were lovers. And if that's true, there's a motive for murder.'

'It's not, but continue. My conscience is clean.'

'So is the murderer's, no doubt. If you and Eustace were involved, then neither he nor you would want that known. Eustace is an attractive man to women, but he says he's devoted to Miranda. He's eccentric. He's a man with a liberated view of the world.'

'Liberated or otherwise, nothing happened.'

'I'll be honest,' Clare said. 'When Inspector Tremayne and I first came here, that day when Charlotte Merton's body was lying in the ditch, the four girls, two of them your daughters, not far away, acting as though her death meant nothing, we thought we were dealing with a cult, strange happenings, the children involved in rituals, abused by the men.'

'Nothing is farther from the truth. I had attended one of Eustace's speeches, heard him speak about this place and how he strived for a calmer world, a world without injustice, love for each other.'

'Idealistic, but never achievable,' Clare said.

'It's been good for us three, but it's coming to an end.'

'Once we've solved the murders, probably before, Jacob Grayson will have you all evicted. What will you do then?'

'We'll go back home. We're ready now.'

'And Eustace?'

'I doubt if we'll see him again. As you said, idealistic, Eustace intellectualising his vision, detached from the reality of an imperfect world.'

'What if Eustace was involved with Charlotte?' Clare asked.

'I don't think he would be.'

'Let's assume he is. What would Miranda's reaction have been?'

'Her past would have given her the means to kill.'

'The drug-taking?'

'Her history is well known.'

'Do you think her capable?'

'She's devoted to Eustace, but he wouldn't have been with Charlotte, I know that.'

'Why? Because he was with you, as well as Miranda. A woman can always tell.'

'It's been three years since my husband died, and I've engrossed myself in my daughters' lives, but they're growing up, and they'll not want me hanging around all the time.

'Even now, I can sense the change in them, and that's fine. That's how it should be, but I don't want to be on my own, not into old age. Foolishly, I made that play for Eustace, but he rejected me, and quite rightly too.'

'Are you staying until the final day?'

'We will, not because we have to, but it's been good here for the girls.'

'Not for you?'

'Probably not. I don't agree with Eustace's views on a lot of things. The man's got his head in the clouds, but then, that serves him well. He makes a good living lecturing about his vision, although it's tainted by commercial reality. However, nothing has happened here at the farm. We all came with problems in our lives; most of us will leave better for our time here.'

'Tell me about Charlotte,' Clare said.

Margaret Reece, a woman who usually kept to herself or with her daughters, was being frank and open.

'A troubled life, bad men, bad drugs, but she was still pleasant to be around.'

'Did you like her?'

'She would have been a bad influence on the girls with her casual approach to men.'

'Who had she been with at the farm?'

'Ben, although he's admitted to that.'

'Anyone else?'

'Gavin Fitzwilliam used to look at her.'

'A leering, mentally-undress-you look?'

'Not only Charlotte. Mind you, considering her life, she was the sort of woman that men would lust after.'

'Before this conversation,' Clare said, 'I had you down as a prude, but you're not, are you?'

'I never was. I do what is necessary for my daughters, not for me.'

'Another few years, you'll be free again.'

'You're never free of your children, no matter how old they are. But I intend to find myself another man. I can't see anything wrong with that.'

'Not at all. If you've been lying to me, it will go badly for you.'

'Fitzwilliam, you never answered the question,' Margaret said.

'There wasn't a question for me to answer, but I'll tell you the truth. He did have sex with Charlotte. Are you surprised?'

'Belinda knew.'

'Yet she stayed at the farm.'

'Maybe her time wasn't right to leave.'

'Her husband? Is it his time to go now?'

'I doubt it. Don't ask me about him and me,' Margaret said. 'I've better taste than that.'

Clare had to concede to the woman. Gavin Fitzwilliam, by his own admission, was a probable white-collar criminal, a lecher according to Margaret Reece, a dead man if the Italian family he had cheated ever found out where he was.

***

Joe Connelly sat at his kitchen table; Maria standing close to the kitchen sink.

Tremayne had received the phone call not long after he had finished talking with Ben, and Clare was still over at the farmhouse with Margaret Reece.

'I thought I could handle it,' Connelly said.

'Do you want to press charges?' Tremayne said, looking over at Maria, her face bruised, a black eye on its way.

'Not against Joe. He was right to be upset, any man would be,' Maria said.

'Has this happened before?

'Never,' the husband and wife said, almost in unison.

'I thought we were happy, the four of us,' Joe said.

'We are,' Maria said. 'I was wrong. It'll never happen again.'

'I appreciate you calling me, Joe,' Tremayne said.

'I came in late yesterday, the afternoon shift. Maria was waiting for me, but I'd had a few drinks, more than the usual.'

A lot more, Tremayne could see that clearly in the man's face.

'It had been welling up in me at work. I shouldn't have been driving, not in a fit state, but we were short-staffed, so I did what was right, almost had an accident, that upset I was.'

'No man wants to be told their wife is sleeping with another man,' Tremayne said.

'Just the once,' Maria said. 'Joe knows how sorry I am.'

'We'll be fine,' Joe said. 'In time.'

'Why phone me then?'

'I need to work, and Maria's got a pub. You'd see soon enough for yourselves, and I wanted the air cleared. If wife-beating is an indictable crime, then I plead guilty, Maria knows that.'

Tremayne sat back. 'A cup of tea would go down well,' he said.

'The charge?'

'It's up to Maria, but I don't think she'll want to take it further,' Tremayne said.

'You needed to know, but, no, I want Joe here with the children and me. That's his place, not a draughty prison cell.'

'They're not draughty, not these days, and Joe would have been bailed on his own surety. I'll not pursue the matter, no reason to. Although I'm sure I could come up with a few questions for you both.'

Maria came over and placed three mugs on the table. She exchanged a smile with her husband, touched her swollen cheek.

'Sorry about that,' Joe said.

'Let's not talk about it,' Maria replied.

Tremayne had dealt with domestic disputes before. The usual response the day after was for the anger to remain, and for one of the partners, sometimes both, to demand police action, time in prison for the guilty party. But with Joe and Maria Connelly, there was an undefinable melding of two souls; one had strayed, the other had acted under extreme provocation and out of character and had resorted to violence.

Tremayne's concern was not the violence, unacceptable for any reason, but Joe. He was a man who did not indulge in gossip, but that did not exclude him from the possibility of having a keen eye, observing the villagers closely, seeing things that lay under the surface.

'Joe, what do you know about this village?' Tremayne asked.

'It's quiet, good for the children.'

'Our investigations have uncovered hidden secrets, adulterous relationships, promiscuity, an unborn child without a father, a mother and daughter who never spoke. Is that the village that you know?'

'I see what I want to see. It's been good for us; it's been good for the children. What other people do with their lives is not my concern as long as it doesn't affect us.'

'Admirable sentiment,' Tremayne said. He had to admit to a grudging respect for the unambitious Joe, a man who let life drift along, not becoming involved; a man whose wife, previously devoted to him, still was, had erred.

'That's my Joe,' Maria said. 'He always believes the best of everyone.'

'I'll tell you what I reckon,' Tremayne said. 'Joe knows more than he lets on. While everyone sees the obvious, listening to the innuendo, he keeps a close watch. I reckon he could tell the police secrets that this village has kept hidden, even from the gossips. Secrets that could blow our murder investigation wide open. Isn't that true, Joe?'

'I don't know what you want from me. Sure, I observe, but only to protect my family. If people are misbehaving, that's up to them. I'll not interfere, not even tell Maria.'

'I need to know. I need those secrets.'

'You might want them, but I don't see why I should tell you if they're not important. All I'll do is upset people's lives, and they haven't harmed you or me.'

'Can you be the judge of that?'

'No, but if I tell you about some of them, I'm no better than that woman at the shop, that Shirley Jenkins.'

'You don't like her?'

'I don't like or hate anyone. There are some I'd prefer not to talk to, but that's disinterest, and if the woman wants to peddle gossip that's up to her and those who listen to her. I've heard what they're saying about Harriet Huxtable. I'll grant you that she's not sociable and not a person to have a chat with, but she's nothing to my family, to no one in the village. Yet they're all laughing at her.'

'That's a strong emotion from you, Joe.'

'You asked, so I'm telling you.'

'What do you know about Harriet?'

'I just told you. She keeps to herself, never complained or indulged in gossip. If she's not friendly, which she isn't, that's her business, no one else's. And before you mention it, I know about Bess Carmichael.'

'How?'

'Do you know her secret?'

'If I said I didn't?' Tremayne said.

'I'd be reluctant to tell you.'

'But that's not the situation here. We know from Harriet, and Bess had told one other person in this village years ago.'

'Who?'

'That's not important, not at this time.'

'Maria doesn't know,' Joe said.

'I'll not tell anyone,' she said.

'Maria, my sergeant believes in you, regardless of your past actions,' Tremayne said. 'Can I?'

'You can.'

'Joe, tell us what you know.'

'It was a few years back. I'm out for a walk, and Bess is coming the other way. We would often chat, not about anything in particular, but that day, she wants to sit down and tell me something.'

'Why?'

'I couldn't be sure; sometimes people like to talk about their lives, and Bess felt the need to tell someone.'

'Any reason?'

'She said it was significant. I assumed an anniversary, something like that. It was clear if you spoke to her for any length of time that she was educated, and her voice was clear. She could have had money, but I couldn't be sure. People speculated about her past, but, no doubt, got it wrong most of the time.'

'You?'

'I thought nothing; the woman caused us no harm, minded her own business. That was all I needed to know. Anyway, she tells me about a daughter who was taken from her at birth.'

'The full story?'

'How would I know? I know what she told me. Harriet might have told you something different.'

'Carry on,' Tremayne said.

Maria was once again holding her husband's hand.

'She told me that the daughter had been born when she was very young, still a schoolgirl.'

'The father?'

'She never told me. She said that Harriet was her daughter and that Harriet had found her and then rejected her.'

'Your reaction?'

'Bess wasn't looking for sympathy, just an ear to unburden herself.'

'And you were a safe ear.'

'I never knew,' Maria said.

'Bess told me that she understood how difficult it was for Harriet,' Joe said. 'She had accepted that they could never reconcile, too much history, too long apart, and that the love a daughter should feel for a mother didn't exist. Inspector, is that the full story?'

'It is,' Tremayne said. He saw no reason to elaborate and to tell the Connellys that Harriet had been the result of an incestuous relationship. He saw no need to tell Joe that the gossipmonger, Shirley Jenkins, knew the story also, and she had chosen to keep it to herself. Two people, nothing in common, yet they had shared a secret.

'Is there any more?' Tremayne continued.

'Harriet would occasionally show a gesture of kindness towards her mother, the occasional food left around the back of the house, but they never acknowledged each other, not openly.'

'Angus Campbell?'

'He keeps alert. You should ask him about the village. He's here more than me, and he could probably tell you a thing or two.'

'We've spoken to him on several occasions. He's been helpful, the same as you, but why do we have to pry it out of you and the others? It's like getting blood from a stone.'

'Is this relevant? Bess is dead, so is the young woman. Neither Maria and I are responsible.'

'There's more to come from you, but for now I'll leave you and Maria to deal with your problems.'

'Not now. I've got to go to work, and Maria and me, we'll survive.'

'For the children?'

'For love,' Maria said. 'I erred once, I won't again.'

Tremayne got up from the table, looked over at Joe. 'Are you telling me that you never suspected that your wife and Plumpton spent the night together?'

'Never,' Joe Connelly replied.

Tremayne didn't believe him.

Chapter 22

Betty Iles, frail and diminutive, inconspicuous most of the time, sat on her own in the farmhouse. In her hands, two knitting needles, and to one side of her a box of tissues; she was sniffling, the effects of a cold, which was the woman's most significant feature.

Margaret Reece had been reluctant to speak, yet had opened up afterwards, shown that under the façade beat the heart of a passionate woman. Clare could not believe the same of Betty.

'Why did you come back?' she said as she sat next to the woman.

'I enjoy the peace and quiet.'

'I've just been speaking to Margaret.'

'I could see you both outside, not that I talk to her much.'

'Why not?'

'No reason, not really. She's got her daughters, and as for me, I'm on my own.'

'Do you regret it?'

'When I was younger. I did have someone, but he married another, left me on the shelf, discarded goods, used once and then rejected.'

'Does that mean what I think it does?'

'Sometimes I like to think back to then,' Betty said, an unexpected smile on her face.

'You left here, but you returned. Why?'

'I was content here, but with Charlotte and the Carmichael woman, I felt that it was time to go.'

'Your sister?'

'I wasn't sure if I should have. We didn't get on, never have, not since…'

Betty Iles paused, picked up a tissue and blew her nose.

'Since when?'

'She had always liked him, and then she married him, not that it did any of them any good. He was a sensitive man, suited to me, not my sister. You've not met her. She's domineering, always wanting to be in charge, but George was a whimsical person, happy to have his head in a book, and he liked to play music.'

'An artistic temperament,' Clare said.

'He could play any instrument; you should have heard him.'

'Why did he marry your sister if he was with you?'

'Even when we were young, it was her that told me what to do, and George, he was weak, easily led. She wanted him, not because she loved him, only that he was mine.'

'It's a sad story,' Clare said.

'It was a long time ago. Not that either of us knew that he was to die so young, only twenty-nine. One day, he's as fit as a fiddle, although he's not happy, as my sister's giving him a rough time, telling him to shape up, get a real job, instead of scratching by on a musician's wage. They don't get much, you know that.'

'How did he die?'

'He crashed his motorcycle, crushed under a truck. He should have stayed with me. As long as we had had enough to live, that would have done, but my sister, she's more like Margaret Reece than me, wouldn't let him alone. And now what does she have?'

'Nothing?'

'She's got plenty of money, found herself another man after six months, married him within ten; no children, though. She was beautiful.'

'You would have been,' Clare said.

'I was homely, pleasant to look at, but I was always frail. Men liked women with full figures back then; I suppose they still do. I was waif-like, not that it worried me, not that it worried George.'

'The second husband?'

'He lasted five years, and then he was gone.'

'Gone?'

'Dead. He gave my sister the money and the life she wanted, but the man was a workaholic, the hours he worked wore him out, even though he was only forty-five.'

'Did you like him?'

'I only met him once. He was a fleshy man, larger than life, and he had wandering hands, especially when she wasn't looking. I know that.'

'He tried it on?'

'It was at their house. They'd been married for two years, and I hadn't been able to face her, not since George's funeral. In the end, I did, and she's in the other room, and he's there close to me. "She kept you hidden", he said. "How about a kiss for your brother-in-law."'

'Your sister's reaction?'

'If she ever knew, and I'm not sure she did, she would have laughed it off, mercenary as she was.'

'You didn't kiss him?'

'Only George. I still think about him, say a prayer for him every night.'

'There are some here who don't behave as well as they should,' Clare said.

The room was empty, apart from the two of them. Outside, the temperature was cold, but inside the house it was, as always, too warm for Clare. She took off her jacket and placed it beside her.

'Charlotte Merton had her problems,' Clare said.

'I didn't speak to her often, although she was agreeable.'

'Did she tell you anything of interest?'

'Not me. I think she found me a little odd. I suppose I am. I never wanted much in life. It struck me that she was looking for somewhere, the same as I was.'

'Someone as well?'

'She probably was, but not me, not since George.'

'We know a lot about Charlotte, yet nobody to charge with her murder.'

'I can't believe anyone here killed her, although Gavin, he's not to be trusted.'

'An impression or proof?'

'I tidy up around the place, do what I can. I was in his office, not that I was looking for anything in particular, but his laptop was open and he was outside.'

'You could see him?'

'He was on the phone, and he wasn't happy, talking loudly with someone. I don't know who it was. As I was saying, I wasn't snooping.'

'He's under investigation for fraud,' Clare said. 'And that's highly confidential. Please don't tell anyone that I told you.'

'That's good. I'll tell no one, and besides, who's listening?'

'Are you saying no one here would care?'

'That's Eustace's philosophy. You come here absolved, a clean slate. No one is to judge or be judged.'

'Fraud, but what about more serious crimes?'

'Crimes of passion, abuse of children, not them. He wouldn't have accepted that, but fraud, violence, prostitution, which would apply to Charlotte, he'd accept. And Miranda used to be busy in that area.'

'Not prostitution, not that we know of.'

'I remember the magazines, her picture on the front, her lifestyle. Towards the end, it wasn't the front page, it was inside, not that I bought those magazines, although Gavin Fitzwilliam would have. The man's a pervert, similar to my sister's second husband.'

'What did you see on Fitzwilliam's laptop?'

'I didn't have long. A false name, a bank account in the Cayman Islands, the transfer of a great deal of money.'

'How much?'

'Over two million pounds.'

'His money?'

'He'd used an anagram of his name. He'd not be the first.'

'Why? It seems obvious that someone would pick up on that.'

'Hide the deceit in plain view, have a joke at someone else's expense.'

'Does he believe in Eustace's vision?' Clare asked.

'He's amoral, interested only in self and his family.'

'A murderer?'

'Of Charlotte?'

'Of either of the two women.'

Betty looked down at her knitting, picked up a dropped stitch. She then put the knitting down on her lap, took hold of Clare's arm.

'Why do you think I came back?'

'You told everyone that you couldn't live with your sister.'

'I had no intention of ever doing so.'

'But you did, for a week or so.'

'My sister is dead.'

Out of the mouths of babes, or in this case, out of the mouth of a frail and constantly unwell woman, what was to be revealed, Clare wondered.

'I killed her,' Betty said.

'Who?'

'My sister. Did you think I meant Charlotte?'

'We've no information that your sister is dead.'

'That's because you've not checked.'

'Why are you telling me?'

'George and my sister, the hate I felt for her, the love I felt for him, and they both disappointed me, left me a lonely person, unable to move on. It was delicious, watching her die.'

'Why tell me this? You know I'll check.'

'I wondered when you'd get around to me. I hadn't intended to tell you, only to leave here when this place closes, and to move into her house.'

'What will we find if we look for her?'

'In the cellar, that's where you'll find the answer.'

'Are you confessing to murder?'

'You see, Eustace made it clear when we came here that he'd not countenance crimes of passion, nor of child abuse, of murder, but he took one look at me, and never asked.'

'If he had?'

'I hadn't killed anyone back then.'

Clare felt a chill, a malevolence in the woman. Suddenly, the room which had been too hot for her felt cold. She put her jacket back on.

'Why are you doing this?' Clare asked. 'If what you're saying is true, and nobody knows, then why tell me?'

'It makes no difference, not now. All my life I had harboured that anger, but now I feel nothing. No sorrow for my sister, no love for George, no interest in whether Eustace and the others stay. There is no more that you and anyone can do to me that will affect me. As long as I have my knitting, then I will wait my time, and George will be there waiting for me.'

'You believe that? At the end of the rainbow, he'll be there?'

'It'll be no rainbow; it'll be hell. He will be punished for leaving me; I'll be punished for killing my sister.'

Clare moved away and phoned Tremayne. The necessary checks would be done. In the meantime, Betty had no intention of moving, and if, as she said, she had killed her sister, then she would not be denied her knitting, not even in prison.

***

Clare remained at the farm and would do so until Betty Iles' sister's house had been checked by the local police. Tremayne had given them the address, advised them that it was a possible homicide and to take the necessary precautions on entering the property.

He could see a long night ahead and not much sleep for either him or his sergeant. He wouldn't admit, not openly, that he was feeling exhausted, and that he was hungry and thirsty.

He didn't want to visit the pub for a meal, not after spending time with Joe and Maria Connelly, the visit to their house fresh in his mind.

However, hunger was hunger, and it was Shirley Jenkins' shop that he gravitated to. Inside, the nurse that Clare had arranged for Harriet Huxtable was buying a few items. Tremayne spoke to her for a few minutes, asked after her charge, who was coming along nicely, according to the nurse.

The ever-watchful Shirley Jenkins looked on, ears pricked, nose twitching, mouth ready to spout out what she heard to those who came into her establishment, suitably embellished with her necessary exaggerations.

'Over here,' Tremayne said to the nurse, drawing her away from the shop counter.

The shopkeeper, miffed at the snub, busied herself tidying up behind the counter.

'Highly strung, over-emotional, but she'll improve in time,' the nurse said.

'Yarwood updated you?'

'Enough for me to do my job. Nothing about the murders, although Harriet has been talking; too much for me really, but that's what I'm there for.'

The nurse left the shop; Tremayne could tell that his sergeant had chosen well.

A voice from behind the counter. 'Anything I can get for you, Inspector?'

'Anything to eat?'

'I've meat pies that can be heated in a microwave.'

'I'll take two. Heat them for me.'

'Not eating at the pub today?'

'No time,' Tremayne said, not wanting to add to the gossip in the village.

'How's Harriet?'

'No better, thanks to you.'

'You can't say that to me.'

The shop was quiet; it was just Tremayne and Shirley Jenkins in there. Tremayne walked over to the front door and reversed the 'Open' sign, indicating to those on the outside of the shop that it was closed.

'I'm still open,' an angry voice said.

'Five minutes while you heat those pies for me.'

'I can't say no, can I?'

'Off the record, you're a meddling busybody,' Tremayne said. 'I don't hold with your sort.'

'Are you sure you want to insult me, Inspector? Surely you're not allowed to.'

'It's been a tough investigation, and each time my sergeant and I start asking questions, more comes out. You kept quiet about Bess Carmichael and her daughter, and you knew about Plumpton and Maria Connelly, so somewhere inside of you there is an essence of decency.'

'Harmless, that's what it is; it's what the villagers want from me.'

'Two out of three, so far. What's the next big secret in this village?'

'I don't know what you mean.'

'Life works like that, in threes, or don't you believe that?' Tremayne said, acutely aware that Clare had spoken to a frail woman, obtained a confession to murder. He was convinced the shopkeeper still had hitherto unknown knowledge. He wasn't leaving until he had more from her. If his sergeant could find out more, so could he.

'Your pies are ready,' the woman said.

'Put them in a bag, I'll eat them later. Now, let's get back to what else you know. Bess Carmichael opened up to you, and you knew about Plumpton and his indiscretion.'

'Indiscretion? Joe Connelly's wife?'

'Okay, the man was pushing his luck with her, but that's not why I'm here. The murder count is up to three, not that you'll know that, not yet.'

'Who?'

'Not in this village, and not yet confirmed. You can read about it in the newspaper.'

'I've got an iPad, tells me all I want to know.'

'If the third murder is confirmed, it'll be the first arrest, but it doesn't solve the murders of the other two women.'

'I can't help you. If you don't mind, I've got a business to run.'

Tremayne turned and headed to the door, ready to turn the 'Closed' sign around and to walk out of the shop. He paused, looked back at the woman.

'Your husband walked out on you. Why?'

'Is that any of your business?'

'It could be relevant.'

'He was a bastard, through and through. I was glad when he left.'

'But why did he leave? After all, you've got a steady business here, not a lot of money, but there's a house at the rear, enough for a comfortable existence.'

'If you must know, he was away a lot, and I was here on my own, apart from my daughter. She was growing up fast, a chip off the old block, his block. She was trouble even when she was young, and then when puberty hit, she was putting it about something dreadful; the village bike some called her.'

'You didn't gossip about her?'

'My own daughter? I can't say I liked her, not that a mother should ever say that, but it's the truth. I would cringe when I heard her name mentioned in the village. There are a few here who know her well enough.'

'Names?'

'It's not relevant. She left when she was nineteen, screwed around, made a fool of herself. In her mid-twenties, she calmed down, found herself a steady man and married him.'

'You said you didn't see her, not often?'

'Not at all. Not for a few years. She's still her father, a nasty piece of work. I prefer not to talk about her.'

'Who did your daughter go around with?'

'You mean, who did she lay on her back for.'

'Yes.'

'Joe Connelly was one of them. The others have left the area.'

'Maria?'

'She wasn't married to him back then. She was a friend of my daughter, but they weren't that close, not after they started to grow up. Maria didn't play around, not much anyway. There was a boyfriend in her teens, but he's long gone.'

'Nothing against Maria?'

'Apart from Plumpton, no. We're all allowed to make one mistake,' Shirley Jenkins said. 'Even me.'

'What's your mistake?'

'Not long after Wally Plumpton's wife left, he and I got drunk over a bottle of vodka.'

'You slept with him?'

'He was a few years older than me, but we managed. He was lonely, and I was on my own. One thing led to another. He woke up the next day with a dreadful hangover, not that I was there, not sure if he ever remembered.'

'He never mentioned it?'

'Never, nor do I. Now, Inspector, if you don't mind, you've got your secret, and I need to make money.'

'It would make for good gossip,' Tremayne said, almost wanting to laugh, but did not.

'I'd appreciate it if you kept it to yourself.'

Tremayne opened the door and left. He glanced in the bag, looked at the two sad-looking pies, and then at the pub. Regardless, he would go there, buy a couple of pies and leave; hopefully, avoid any conversation with Maria.

He had had enough of the Connellys for that day, and down at the farm, his sergeant was waiting for an answer on Betty Iles' sister. He would get a pie for her as well.

Chapter 23

Proof had been received that Ben was not the father of Charlotte's unborn child; the field of potential fathers was narrowing, but another development, a detour from the primary investigation, had been confirmed. Betty Iles had murdered her sister.

At Bemerton Road Police Station, the woman seemed even smaller than she had at the farmhouse. Her confession had been typed out and duly signed, and she had meekly entered the cell at the station. Clare had walked there with her.

The knitting needles, sharp objects as had been explained to Betty, were not permitted in the cell, although Clare clarified that subject to whichever prison she was sent to, and once it was clear she was not suicidal, unlikely to self-harm, then they would be returned to her.

A brief nod from the woman as she sat down on the bed in the cell. She faced forward, motionless, no visible emotion.

Clare stood for several minutes outside the cell, observing her. In the end, she walked away, shaking her head. She'll never leave prison, not alive, she thought.

Tremayne, upstairs in his office, was not moved by Betty Iles and what she had done. To him, if the woman could commit one murder, she could commit two. Yet, when she had been questioned, she had said that it wasn't her, but she knew who had killed Charlotte.

Frustratingly, that was all she would say. She would answer when addressed, follow instructions given, listen when charged, acknowledge that she understood. Apart from that, nothing.

'They'll subject her to extensive psychiatric tests,' Tremayne said.

'You think she's involved in the other murders?' Clare said.

'It would be easier for us if she were, but I don't believe she is.'

'According to those who discovered the sister's body, it was a frenzied attack with a carving knife.'

'Probably the other two murders formed the idea in her mind. Betty Iles had spent years dwelling on what her sister had done, and then she sees what happened at the farm, and the murderer's thumbing his nose at us.'

Clare could understand Tremayne's frustration. There were sufficient motives, enough people with dubious histories, secrets buried deep. It was up to her to snap them both out of the inertia.

'If you've got your doubts about Joe Connelly, Campbell spends more time in the village, and he's more astute, more alert,' Clare said.

'Connelly's not the smartest man, I'll give you that,' Tremayne said.

They found Campbell at his house. As usual, immaculately dressed. Clare imagined that the man's pyjamas were pressed and creased and that he looked in the mirror before retiring to ensure he'd pass muster.

'Tremayne, Sergeant Yarwood, an unexpected pleasure,' Campbell said. 'I was about to go out, care to join me?'

'Not now,' Tremayne said. 'A few questions. You've heard the news, no doubt?'

'I can't say I knew the woman, although not many did.'

263

'Who did?'

'Shirley Jenkins said she'd go into the shop occasionally, buy a few items for herself.'

'Who? Betty Iles?'

'The woman you arrested.'

'How do you know?'

'Eustace was in the village. I saw him outside the pub, not that he was going in for a drink.'

'Why not?'

'The place was closed. It seems that you and your sergeant gave her and her husband a hard time.'

'We gave him a hard time, not her. She's an open book, but Joe Connelly, I'm not so sure,' Tremayne said. 'The man sees all, says nothing. Too good to be true.'

'Honest, salt of the earth, is Connelly.'

'Cannon fodder?' Clare asked.

'Not a term the British Army uses, and we definitely don't send troops into battle to be slaughtered.'

'How would you see him?' Tremayne asked.

'Dependable, a man you could trust. Not a leader, but he'd follow orders, do his duty. Not everyone's a hero.'

'You were once,' Clare said, having seen the man's military record.

'I did my bit, could have got myself shot saving others, but it's not something I thought about at the time. They were pinned down, I acted instinctively. I didn't warrant a medal, although I wear it proudly when I can.'

'Connelly knew about Bess and Harriet, can you believe that?'

'Bess never told me. Why would she tell him?'

'According to him, she told him a long time ago. He kept it to himself, never told his wife.'

'Maria wouldn't have repeated it, not her. The soul of discretion, always was, even when she was younger. Not that I was here a lot of the time, you understand.'

'Defending Queen and country,' Clare said.

'Most of the time, I was in England, getting those under my command ready for action.'

'Were they, when they were needed?'

'They were. They acquitted themselves honourably.'

'Tell us about Shirley Jenkins' daughter,' Tremayne asked.

'There's not much to tell. I haven't seen her for a long time, but she was wild. Joe could tell you more about her than me.'

'According to the mother, she was promiscuous,' Clare said.

'She had a reputation. She was about Maria Connelly's age. Maria was a sensible young woman. Her parents, dead now, were decent, hardworking. Her mother worked in a shop in Salisbury, and the father bought and sold farm equipment out of a small yard, a few miles from here. Not a lot of money, but they got by. Is Shirley Jenkins' daughter important?' Campbell said. He needed some exercise, a walk through the village to get circulation into his stiff limbs.

'We don't think so. We just needed to see what else you know, or whether your memory is selective,' Tremayne said, following Campbell in sitting down. Clare remained standing.

'That sounds like an insult,' Campbell said.

'It's not, but Connelly tells us about Bess and Harriet, Shirley Jenkins tells us about her daughter.'

'I don't understand where this is heading.'

'Campbell, you're a smarter man than either of them; you've been trained to observe, to evaluate people. You must know more than you've told us so far. Are you protecting somebody, or is it the village? Are you saving the village from us?'

'Maria and Shirley Jenkins' daughter fought over Joe. Is that what you want?'

'That's for us to judge. What's the full story?'

'You should ask the three of them.'

'We will, but first, we'll get it from you.'

'I don't know why, but Maria hankered after Joe, even when they were young. She's got something about her, but he drifts along, taking life as it comes. Joe was a typical young man, playing the field, egged on by his friends and the occasional beer. Maria was a stay-at-home young woman, comfortable with her parents and her studies.'

'What about Shirley's daughter?'

'Natalie Jenkins was a fireball, keen for the boys. Joe was one of her conquests, although I can't think of anyone else in the village, not now. Most have moved away; some come back occasionally, but it's rare.

'Natalie was easy with her favours, but Joe knew that Maria wanted him, but he's still young, sowing his wild oats. It was later, when the two women had left school, that Maria staked her claim. Joe's calmer then, and the two of them are together all the time, holding hands, that sort of thing, not much more probably, not because Joe wouldn't be keen, but, as I said, he's a decent man, so he's willing to wait. They're engaged, the banns announced at the church, a wedding soon.'

'Natalie?' Clare said.

'Natalie's upset, not because of Joe, but because of Maria. Natalie was popular when she was younger, but she's growing up, her father's features more pronounced. The proportions are distorting, the hair is spiking, and her face is hardening, less feminine. Don't get me wrong, she's still agreeable to look at, but Maria's much easier on the eye, a real beauty, and she's pleasant to talk to, always courteous. Natalie, and if you've met the mother, you'd know, is not. She's harsh, swearing a lot, and people start to avoid her.'

'The fight?' Tremayne said.

'It's just before the wedding. Joe's at the pub with his friends, a few too many drinks, not sure where he is or what he's doing by the end of the evening.'

'Natalie?'

'I'm coming to it. It's late, and Joe's made a fool of himself with the alcohol, but he wouldn't be the first one. He comes out of the pub, and there's Natalie. She's drunk as well, desperate for Joe. They used to call her the village bike.'

'We know.'

'Joe staggers away, barely able to stand. Natalie grabs him, wrestles him to the ground, attempts to get him to make love to her.'

'Joe?'

'He's got no idea what's going on, that drunk he was.'

'How do you know all this?'

'It wasn't far from here. I could hear the commotion. I see the two of them on the grass, Joe underneath trying to extricate himself. I grab hold of Natalie, yank her up. She's furious. I'm ignoring her, making sure that Joe gets home. The next minute, there's Maria, and she's cottoned on to what's happened. She lunges out at Maria, puts a fist into her chest, and then it's the two of them on the ground.'

'What did you do?'

'What could I do? I've got Joe barely able to stand, Maria and Natalie on the ground. Thankfully, after a couple of minutes of the two of them going at each other, Shirley arrives, grabs her daughter and drags her away.'

'And Maria?'

'She took charge of Joe, once she'd calmed down, and walked him back to his house.'

'What did you understand from that event?' Clare asked.

'Natalie left the village the next day. Joe, an innocent party, probably doesn't remember much of it, and Maria, if provoked, is capable of violence.'

'Capable of murder?' Tremayne asked.

'It was the one time, extreme provocation.'

***

The arrival of Emily Walker at the farm came as a surprise. The woman was hopping mad by the time Tremayne and Clare arrived.

'Your son tells me he loved that drug-addicted tart,' she said, not taking any notice of the two police officers, taking no note of the others looking at her. 'After all I've done for him.'

Eustace Hampton came over nearer to Tremayne, whispered in his ear. 'She hasn't let up, and I phoned you ten minutes ago.'

Tremayne could see that the even-tempered Hampton was getting tired of the woman ranting.

'Miss Walker, if you don't mind,' Clare said, taking advantage of a break when Emily took a breath.

'This is nothing to do with the police,' the woman said. Her face was red, and she was shaking.

'Anything to do with the farm is,' Clare reminded her. 'Two murders, it's ours to control, not yours. Now, if you don't mind.'

'It's him,' Emily said, pointing over at the hapless Todd. 'After what I've done for him, and he tells me he wants to end it with me. I could have made something of him, but he's weak, the same as his father, the same as the rest of them here. Nobodys they are, hiding away from the world. What do the police have on them? That's what I want to know.'

Tremayne moved to the centre of the room, looked the woman straight in the eye. 'Miss Walker, if you wish to persist, you'll find yourself at the police station. You've certainly got the anger for violence. Are we wrong? Did you murder Charlotte Merton?'

'A useless lump of lard, that's what he is. You'd be angry.'

'Anger will solve nothing, not here, and definitely not today. Todd may have loved Charlotte; he may have even killed her after she made it clear that she wanted someone else.'

'Who? Who'd have wanted her? A washed-up fornicator.'

'I liked her,' Miranda Hampton said. 'And if you don't want Todd, there are other women who would be pleased to be with him.'

'I never said I didn't want him.'

'*Sit down*,' Tremayne said firmly to Emily. The woman did as she was told. 'Now, let's get this clear. You've driven down here with Todd, and then you walk in and start shouting. Did this start in the car on the way down, or is this an affectation? Your father's an aggressive bully, are you too?'

'I adore my father. What has Todd's father done for him? Made him a whimpering fool, no backbone.'

'Miss Walker,' Tremayne continued, 'you are the most cantankerous and obnoxious woman that it's my misfortune to have met.'

'You can't say that to me. My father…'

'Your father isn't here, and you're an adult. If you want to wage your battles, do it somewhere else and not in my presence. Now, we'll go over this again. Todd felt affection for Charlotte. That's known, even by you before today, so let's not rehash it. Why did you kill her?'

'I didn't. You'll not pin that on me.'

'I might. Your mouth is leading us to that conclusion, and it wasn't Todd or his parents who killed her,' Tremayne said. Clare could see him raising the tempo, looking for a weakness. There was no reason to discount any of the three Hamptons, not at this time. He was applying the pressure to someone verging on hysterical, although Clare was sure it was feigned.

'Todd, what do you have to say?' Clare asked. 'You've been quiet up till now.'

'I did care for Charlotte, but Emily's got it wrong. I need a strong hand to keep me pointed in the right direction, I need her. I told her, but she wasn't listening.'

Emily moved over to Todd and kissed him on the cheek.

To Tremayne, it was as if a dog had just soiled the white carpet, had its nose rubbed in it, had been forgiven. Todd Hampton was to be the woman's pet, yet he looked pleased about it.

Betty Iles was clearly mental, but Emily Walker was off the planet. It reaffirmed Tremayne's opinion of

270

the farm's occupants. He couldn't wait to get out of the place, deal with a few villains who, compared to what he could see in front of him, were normal.

Miranda, quiet until now, moved forward and slapped Emily hard. So much so that she reeled back, grabbing an armrest to steady herself.

'You bitch,' Miranda said. 'If I didn't know better, I'd say you killed the women.'

'Do you know better?' Clare asked.

Miranda didn't answer Clare's question; she just walked through the door at the rear and out into the garden. Tremayne was delighted; the people were showing their true colours, the underlying personal traits suppressed by Eustace's vision.

Clare left the room, heading to where Miranda Hampton was standing. Tremayne left her to it. She'd push the woman, find out what 'If I didn't know better, I'd say you killed the women' meant. Whether it was anger, a weak attempt to quieten Emily, which wouldn't have worked, or whether she knew more, whether she knew who the killers were, had to be known.

Tremayne took a seat. The others could stand, but he was in control now, and those remaining would talk.

Emily sat on a couch, Todd's arm around her. 'It's been a long day,' he said. 'It'll get better, you'll see.' The lapdog had spoken, and if Charlotte had been a better woman than her history indicated, then Todd Hampton wouldn't have been the man for her. A matched pair, Emily Walker and Todd Hampton, Tremayne thought, and the best of luck, as Todd would need it in bucketfuls.

Chapter 24

'Our Todd, controlled by her. It doesn't bear thinking about,' Miranda said.

Clare could only agree. Yet, in the heat of the moment, the previously placid and agreeable woman had lashed out, made an implication that Emily hadn't killed Charlotte.

Was that based on fact or anger, Clare needed to know.

'If Emily didn't kill Charlotte,' Clare said, 'and you seemed pretty certain back there, who did?'

'It would do us all a favour if she had, but she wouldn't, not her; too clever for her own good, and look at how she treats Todd. It's sickening to watch.'

'He accepts it.'

'What can he do?'

'Does she have a hold on him? Did he kill Charlotte? Your holding out isn't going to achieve anything.'

'It will give us another day or two. Isn't that important?'

It was, Clare thought, but she was tired of the investigation, as was Tremayne. Village life, so seductive, had lost its shine. And the village of Brockenstoke had proven itself to be a den of intrigue, inequity, of malevolent and disparate people making out there was harmony when there wasn't.

'It will destroy Eustace,' Miranda said.

'What will?'

'I killed Charlotte.'

Clare took hold of the woman by the arm and walked her around the house. They sat in Clare's car, the heater warming them.

'Now, Miranda, are you confessing to the murder?'

'I am.'

It was a confession, the breakthrough they had been looking for, but it would need more than Miranda's statement.

'Does anyone else know?'

'Bess did.'

'And you killed her?'

'I'd do anything to protect my family, even kill.'

'None of this makes any sense,' Clare said. 'How would killing Charlotte have done anything for any of you? It's illogical, and you know it.'

'Eustace wouldn't have been able to resist her, I always knew that.'

'You killed her for him?'

'I had to, don't you see?'

'Unless you're out of your mind, and a lot are around here, then what you're saying is nonsense.'

'Eustace is weak, though not as much as our son. He could have been controlled, but that wasn't what I wanted. I'd known enough men in my time, some good, most bad, but Eustace was different. He was perfect, and we raised Todd the best we could, but we failed him.

'I wasn't going to let Eustace make a fool of himself again, the same as that time at the university, his student, her death, the scandal. He couldn't endure that again, and I could see that Eustace would have been tempted, and Charlotte was always going to come to an unfortunate end.'

273

'How did you know this? She wanted Wally Plumpton. She would have been happy with him.'

'You'd not understand.'

'Try me,' Clare said.

'I was Charlotte once. I sold myself when my career dried up, when I couldn't keep the weight off or the face fresh and unblemished. I knew the effect of drugs, the need to take them to deal with the shame, the attempt to stop, unable to due to too many regrets.'

'But you came back.'

'Because of Eustace, but Charlotte would have destroyed him. I had to kill her.'

'Miranda, it's a convincing story, only there's one problem with it.'

'What's that?'

'Charlotte was injected. With the angle of insertion, she wouldn't have done it herself. The murderer would have had to have been at the farm during a two-hour window.'

'Yes, I realise that.'

'Miranda, we can prove that you were not at the farm at that time. We've got witnesses' – Clare did not – 'which means you're protecting someone else. It's either Eustace or Todd, which one is it?'

'I was at the farm. I saw her outside. That's when I did it.'

'The needle?'

'I threw it away.'

'You did not. The truth, *now*.'

Miranda looked out of the car window, at the farmhouse, around the yard, before looking back at Clare.

'It has to be one of them, doesn't it?'

Clare had pushed the woman, not willing to take the easy option and to arrest her. The truth was more important, even though other less scrupulous police officers would have taken the opportunity to wrap up one of the murders, to receive the accolades. But that wasn't her style, nor Tremayne's.

'Nobody saw the woman die, and we couldn't identify any shoe prints, not after the rain and the mud, and the four girls peering down at her. We can't prove that any of you were responsible, not conclusively. You could have been convicted if your story had been more convincing,' Clare said. 'Lying to protect your family is one thing, covering up a murder is another. Where's the proof?'

'Eustace is the father of her child. I never wanted to tell anyone that, not even you.'

'He's not. We obtained a DNA sample from your son. Tests were conducted, which proved that neither he nor his father could have fathered the child.'

'Your tests aren't correct.'

'They're admissible as evidence.'

'They're incorrect,' Miranda reaffirmed.

'How?'

'I saw Eustace with Charlotte once.'

'Where?'

'They were in one of the rooms, behind a closed door. I know what they were doing.'

'You confronted your husband with this?'

'I never have, never wanted to. Our life is too perfect, I didn't want it to end.'

'He's still not the father.'

'Your results are invalid because Eustace is not Todd's father,' Miranda said, not looking directly at Clare.

Clare realised that a previously confirmed premise had been shattered. The dates of Eustace and Miranda's marriage, and Todd's birth nine months later, had pointed conclusively to Todd being Eustace's child. But now, the mother was contradicting that fact.

'Does Eustace know?'

'Never, and he mustn't. It was just before we married, a man I had loved once, not a good man. I was still susceptible, even though I had Eustace. This man, he was charming, an easy talker. Before I knew it, he and I were in bed.'

'You're certain it's his?'

'Can't you see it?'

Clare thought of the two, father and son. The father, tall; the son, shorter and rounder, a fat man as he aged. She wouldn't need DNA checks to confirm what Miranda had said. Todd had his mother's face, but nothing of Eustace.

'The truth will come out,' Clare said.

'If it hadn't been for Charlotte's death, nobody would have ever known.'

'I need to talk to Inspector Tremayne. This changes the situation.'

'Don't tell Eustace or Todd, not today,' Miranda said.

'I can't make promises, but I'll try,' Clare said as she left the car. Inside, Miranda sat; the face that had once graced the front covers of magazines no longer showed any of the glamour that it once had.

***

Tremayne noticed Clare enter through the back door, acknowledging her by a momentary glance; one nod of her head to tell him that she had something to say to him.

In the room, Todd sat with Emily, not so close as before, but holding hands. Eustace sat close to the open fire, prodding it occasionally, the flames shooting up before dying down.

'Where's Miranda?' Eustace said.

'She'll be here shortly,' Clare replied. She could only imagine the man's reaction when he found out the truth.

'I believe we should wrap this up for now,' Tremayne said to the assembled group. 'We'll talk to you all individually later today or tomorrow. Miss Walker, Todd, please remain in the area. We've still more questions.'

'We will,' Todd said. He looked at Emily, who smiled in return, squeezed his hand.

Clare couldn't be sure of Emily's reaction when her boyfriend was revealed to be illegitimate, the son of an unknown man, the son of…

She didn't want to think that, Emily and Todd perhaps sharing a common parent. Miranda had revealed that she had known Emily's father years before meeting Eustace. One incestuous child in the village was enough. Another one was too disturbing to contemplate.

Emily and Todd walked out of the front door, she leading, him following. As they left, Miranda gave her son a warm hug and held Emily's hand. 'You look after him, whatever,' she said.

Tremayne looked puzzled, as did Eustace. Clare observed all, said nothing. The odds were firming on one of the Hamptons being a murderer, but the proof was still circumstantial. She and Tremayne would need to work overtime to bring the investigation to a conclusion.

'If you don't mind,' Miranda said, looking over at Clare and then at Tremayne, 'it's been an emotional time. My husband and I would like some time to ourselves.'

Outside the house. 'You need a pint,' Clare said.

'Maria?'

'As long as she doesn't want to talk, we'll be okay.'

In the pub, Maria smiled as they entered. Clare returned the smile, but no words were spoken, the emotion of the previous days still fresh in the minds of the two women. Clare could see the heavier than usual makeup to cover the bruising on Maria's face.

Tremayne, not concerned by the previous day, nor the encounter with the aggressive Emily, called to her from where he sat. 'A pint of beer, a glass of wine, and a couple of meals,' he said.

'It's a nice day,' Maria replied. Small talk on her part, Clare thought.

Tremayne downed half of the pint in one gulp. 'I'm going to need this, aren't I?' he said.

'You'll need two, and I'm having another glass of wine after I've finished this one.' She took a drink, not half the glass but more than she usually would.

'Miranda Hampton?'

'Todd is not Eustace's son, which means—'

'Eustace could be the father of Charlotte's child,' Tremayne interjected.

'Miranda told me bluntly that she killed Charlotte, but I couldn't believe it.'

'She could have if she thought that her husband was playing around on her.'

'I pushed her for the facts as to how she had killed the woman. Not that we have too many clues as to who it could be, other than the mysterious father.'

'Who could be Eustace. Are we sure that he was fooling around with her?'

'Miranda is convinced. She heard the two of them together once.'

'I was willing to believe his denial,' Tremayne said.

'It's what his wife believes.'

'You just said that she confessed, and then you destroyed it. You're talking in riddles.'

'She confessed to protect Eustace. She thinks he did it.'

'Another day and we'll crack these murders wide open.'

'You said that the other week and we're still here,' Clare said as she got up and walked over to the bar. The meals were ready, and she didn't want Tremayne and her to be disturbed.

'We're fine,' Maria said.

'Joe?'

'He's at work. Next week, he's taking a couple of days off; we're going to the coast, a break from the village.'

'The pub?'

'Wally's son is going to look after it for me. He's a good cook, so you'll be able to eat in here.'

'Maria,' Clare said as she picked up the plates, 'do you have any contact with Natalie Jenkins? You were friends at school.'

'Not for a long time. Why are you asking?'

'It's just that Joe had a fling with her, and you and she fought over him.'

'If I saw her in the village, I might have a chat with her, nothing more. We were all young and foolish once, some still are.'

'I suppose so. Joe, have you ever suspected him?'

'Not my Joe.'

'You place a great deal of faith in that man,' Clare said. 'He placed trust in you, but you let him down.'

'Two wrongs don't make a right. We've been over this, haven't we? Isn't it time to leave well alone?'

Clare picked up the two plates and walked back to the table. 'I was just thinking,' she said to Tremayne.

'About what?'

'Joe. Too good to be true.'

Tremayne held up a glass, pointed to Clare's. Maria nodded; she'd be bringing another beer and a glass of wine to the table. The man mulled over what Clare had just said, commenced eating his meal.

'There you are,' Marie said as she placed the drinks on the table and left.

'That Todd's in for a rough time,' Tremayne finally said.

'Weren't you listening?' Clare said.

'About Joe, I was. It needs thinking through. And if what you've been told about Todd is true, it's another angle to consider.'

'And we've got Todd, enamoured of Charlotte.'

'Enamoured?' Tremayne said.

'Infatuation, hardly love. Emily's a tyrant, she'll give Todd hell, but she's more his type.'

'Granted, but where's this leading?'

'We need to prove who is the father. Tell Eustace we need a sample from him, get it checked.'

'And Joe?'

'He'll need to give one as well.'

'Yarwood, how do you intend to do that? Ask him nicely, "Were you screwing Charlotte Merton, even after you gave us that nonsense about only wanting Maria? Are you as bad as your wife?" He's hardly likely to go for it.'

'He beat his wife. We could take him in.'

'Abhorrent as it was, it's not sufficient to force the man to agree. If we coerce him, spin him a tale, then what if it's proved? If he's the murderer?'

'I don't want it to be right.'

'Crunch time, is that what you want? It could get rough.'

'Eustace and Todd might find out the truth,' Clare said.

'Emily's reaction will be interesting,' Tremayne said as he finished his second pint of beer. Clare, usually not a heavy drinker, downed her glass of wine. When she stood up, she had to admit to feeling some effect from the alcohol.

Chapter 25

Jacob Grayson's return to the farmhouse in possession of an eviction order presented a complication that Tremayne didn't want.'

The day was drawing to a close, and even after going over the facts again, neither Tremayne nor Clare could see flaws in the testimonies provided.

Grayson was sitting down when the two police officers arrived. The atmosphere was cordial, and he and Eustace were seated.

'Hampton's ready to move out,' Grayson said as he stood up and shook Tremayne by the hand.

'I need two days,' Tremayne said, realising that a delay in acceding to Grayson and the paperwork that he carried would only mean more forms for him to fill out, and an explanation to his superintendent as to why a straightforward murder investigation had dragged on for so long, and why he needed more time. Reasons such as 'it's complex' and 'soon' weren't going to wash. The man would be pushing, and then the inevitable question as to his inspector's age and health would be brought up, and another round of medicals and tests of stamina and physical strength would follow, which he wouldn't pass.

'Have you told the others?' Clare asked Hampton.

'If we're in agreement,' Eustace said.

It was unlikely that Todd's parentage could remain a secret indefinitely, even if none of the three was on trial.

The farm had once been a place of serenity, but it was soon to change.

'Two days, agreed,' Grayson said. 'You know who killed the two women?' He had a broad smile on his face; it did nothing to change his appearance, weaselly and conniving.

'If you've got a few minutes?' Tremayne said.

'Here?'

'Outside, a few questions.'

The two men walked away from the farmhouse, and towards the stream which had by default become Tremayne's preferred place to conduct questioning.

'Inspector, what do you want?'

'A murderer, possibly two.'

'Don't look at me.'

'Grayson, I'll be honest with you,' Tremayne said. 'You're streetwise, a bit of a rogue. I don't mean that you've broken the law, but you're not averse to taking advantage when a man's down.'

'You don't like Hampton any more than I do. Are you suggesting that I should be sorry for him?'

'Not at all, but he's got his head in the stars, whereas you're like me, ferreting around in the dirt. You see more than the others. What I want from you are insights.'

'Fitzwilliam's not all he seems, and as for that Betty Iles, I missed that,' Grayson said.

'So did we. It must have been what happened here that tipped her over the top. Not that it'll make any difference to her; she has no relatives, and a quiet bed and somewhere to sit are all she needs.'

'It should suit us all, but men such as us are driven. You, Tremayne, have never been much interested in money, enough to get by, but you're the same as me in many ways.'

'I hope I'm not,' Tremayne said.

'Aggressive, determined, willing to push the envelope. I've banged a few heads in my time, although nowadays I pay others to do the banging.'

Tremayne saw no reason to debate semantics with the man; he knew that he had an underlying ethic of decency, whereas Grayson did not.

'We're not sure if Charlotte Merton's pregnancy is the motive for her death, or whether it's jealousy on someone's part.'

'I wouldn't know, but why ask me? You've spoken to Fitzwilliam and Ben, they had both been with her.'

'Neither is the father of the child, nor is Todd,' Tremayne said, confident that Grayson would not know that Todd's DNA should have precluded the father too.

'I met his girlfriend once.'

'The charming Emily?'

'I liked her, tough like her father.'

'A contradiction in terms.'

'Her father, a regular hard-case.'

'You've met him?'

'Not personally, but the man's notorious, never gives in until he's got what he wants. Todd's girlfriend is just the same, no idea why she wants to take on a hopeless case. The man's bright enough, but he's got his mother's vagueness, not that it's a problem with her, and as for his father, head up his arse.'

'Why would she be with him?'

'Who knows why we choose who we do? I've had a few over the years, but I prefer to be on my own most of the time. Todd's weak like his mother; Emily's tough. She sees Todd as ripe for moulding.'

'She intends to control him, firmly if he doesn't toe the line.'

'You know what I'd do if a woman, anyone, tried to control me?'

'You wouldn't allow it, but you were willing to listen to Eustace.'

'It was more a holiday for me. I could stay in my previous home, enjoying the peace. Cheap, as well. A few baubles to the upkeep, better than a holiday overseas.'

'You always intended to take the farm back?'

'I'll be straight with you, Tremayne. It wasn't at the forefront of my mind, but I'm here. I can see that Hampton's not got a clue about money, so I did a few checks. Found out that the bank was pressing, and if he didn't get the money outstanding, they would act.'

'You made him an offer?'

'I could see that the money that was needed wasn't that much, and I made sure Hampton would be paid a suitable amount for his share of the place.'

'You screwed him?'

'The man was desperate to stay, although he could have sold it, got himself out of trouble. Anyway, that's past history, two days and he's out.'

'You won't be moving in, will you?'

'I might put a tenant in for a few months, long enough to get the planning permission approved, and then I'll bulldoze the buildings, put up seven or eight four-bedroom houses, make myself plenty.'

'The nostalgia for the place, your father's attempt to make a go of it?'

'He'd not care. Tougher times back then, but he hated the place as much as I did. He didn't have options, I do.'

'Could you be the father?'

'Charlotte! No way, not my scene. Miranda's more my age, but not Charlotte, young enough to be my daughter, not that she would be, no children.'

'Incapable?'

'Smart.'

'Eustace and Charlotte?'

'Unlikely,' Grayson said.

'There are some that believe they were involved.'

'It's always possible, and I wasn't here to police the place. If his rambling on at the evening sessions could have got her into bed, then good luck to him, but I don't think that was the man's want. Not that I'd know, but I'd say that he was devoted to his wife; classy woman in her youth, still looking good.'

Clare walked over, which confused Tremayne as she would typically have messaged, though he wouldn't have looked at his phone. 'You'd better come back,' she said.

***

'I wasn't getting much from him,' Tremayne confided to Clare as the two of them walked back to the farmhouse, Grayson walking behind them, engrossed in a phone conversation, with words such as 'profit', 'return on investment' and 'how soon before you can start' overheard by Clare, although Grayson didn't interest her, not anymore.

'It's Maria,' Clare said. 'Joe came home drunk, hit her again.'

'Charge him this time, get a DNA sample.'

'She's frightened, not sure what to do.'

'It's domestic abuse. Where is she now?'

'At the pub.'

'You've been there?'

'Campbell's with her. She phoned him, a steady hand in an emergency.'

'Joe?'

'We need to find him.'

'We let it pass once, not this time, even if Maria objects.'

Clare phoned for a patrol car; they could find Joe Connelly. After that, Tremayne and Clare drove to the pub. Maria was sitting down in the bar, her face swollen more than before, her arm in a temporary sling.

'I did the best I could,' Campbell said. 'Not something I expected, Maria and Joe.'

Clare moved over to Maria, put her arm around her. 'It'll be alright,' she said, not that she believed what she was saying. To her, Joe had crossed over from angry and disappointed to dangerous and to be handled with care.

'I thought we were okay, but Joe can't accept it, not from me. It's not as if…'

'If what? He's not so innocent, is that what you're trying to say?'

'I didn't mean it like that.'

She did, Clare knew. The previously unimpeachable Joe had a dark side to him, carefully hidden, known only to Maria.

'We can't let this pass, not this time.'

'Please don't, not now, not seeing that our life is better, what with the pub.'

Tremayne listened without interfering, leaving it to his sergeant, who was much better in situations that required compassion and a soft touch.

Tremayne had seen it before. Joe Connelly, no longer to be the primary earner in his household, about to be usurped by his wife, who with the pub would make more money than him; and not only that, she had committed an unforgivable sin. The man probably wasn't fully conscious of why he was as angry as he was.

'He called me some terrible words,' Maria said.

Campbell stood close by, not saying a word.

Tremayne pulled him off to one side. 'Are you surprised, really?'

'I knew of some of it.'

'Such as?'

'Maria at the pub, clearly enjoying Plumpton's company. Can't blame her really, but Maria's not the sort to stray.'

'And if she has?'

'Nobody's perfect. Had she?'

'Once, Angus,' Maria said, the conversation between Tremayne and Campbell not as secret as it should have been.'

'I'll not think the worse of you,' Campbell said. 'Joe's not perfect, either, is he?'

'I think you'd better level with us, Maria,' Clare said. 'And you too, Angus.'

'Joe met up with Charlotte once or twice. Not that I knew about it, not until tonight,' Maria said. 'He was angry, trying to upset me. I'm not sure why. He had every right to be upset about Wally, but that was once, and we'd talked it through, willing to let bygones be bygones. But then, he's dwelt on it, maybe heard the others at the bus company talking about their wives, how they cheated, were cheated on, and he gets riled up, starts drinking.'

'Campbell, your take on this?' Tremayne said.

'Not a lot to say. Plumpton wasn't a bad man, and if Maria made a fool of herself, and we all do from time to time, then so be it. As to Joe, that's not a side I've seen before, but I had my suspicions about him.'

'How?'

'My regular walks around the village, up the hill. I observed, saw him talking to the young woman on a few occasions.'

'Charlotte?'

'I wasn't close, so no idea what they used to talk about, but they obviously got on well.'

'There must be more than that.'

'There were four at the caravan that day I saw Harriet outside with Bess.'

'Charlotte wasn't on her own?'

'Joe was inside with her. I didn't see what they were up to, so I can't be certain.'

'Maria, are you surprised?' Clare said.

'The caravan, I am. Joe was a stickler for cleanliness, always washing his hands, two showers a day.'

'I meant Charlotte.'

'I suspected once,' Maria said.

'Campbell, why the caravan? Why would Bess Carmichael have approved of the two of them inside?' Tremayne asked.

'Bess, who knows?'

'Hazard a guess.'

'She liked Charlotte, wanted to help, remembering how Harriet had treated her. I'd say she thought she was keeping a watch on the woman, allowing her to take Joe in there.'

'Others?'

'Not that I know. I saw Charlotte leave, and then a little later, Joe. He went one way; she went the other,' Campbell said.

'Was Bess supplying drugs?'

'She could have been, but why? And more importantly, how did she get hold of them?'

The four of them waited in silence. There was no more to be said, not for the present. Clare sat with Maria, comforted her as best she could. The physical scars would vanish with time; the emotional ones wouldn't.

Tremayne walked out of the pub after five minutes, the inactivity getting to him. He was joined by Campbell, who was glad to be in the fresh air.

'Joe?' Campbell said.

'It's not looking good for him. It's often that way, the people you least expect.'

'You've been a police officer for a good few years, you must be used to it.'

'I cease to be amazed. We've got Betty Iles locked up, and you'd think that butter wouldn't melt in her mouth.'

A patrol car drew up outside the pub, Joe Connelly in the rear seat.

Tremayne leant in the passenger door and looked at the man. 'You've got some answering to do,' he said.

'Maria, the children?' Joe said, his hands cuffed behind him.

'We'll make sure they're fine. As for you, it's a night in the cells. We've got additional information that places you close to where the murders were committed.'

'What information? I didn't kill them, not me.'

'Then who?'

'I don't know.'

'That's the trouble, isn't it? You don't know a lot when we're asking questions, but you see a lot.'

The patrol car drove out of the car park, Maria momentarily appearing at the pub door, looking over at her husband; him looking away.

***

Joe Connelly sat in the interview room; his wife was outside, Angus Campbell with her. In a show of unity, the Connellys' neighbours on either side were looking after their children.

Maria was fraught, wanting to protest that Joe was a good man and that his family needed him. Tremayne knew it had passed that stage now. It was in the hands of the police, and regardless of the outcome, not favourable from what he could see, Joe Connelly wouldn't be spending time with his family anytime soon.

'Mr Connelly, you assaulted your wife for the second time,' Tremayne said.

'I was wrong. Maria will forgive me; I'll make it up to her.'

'Whether she does is not the issue, and you know it. You'll be charged for your crime. And we'll need a swab from inside your cheek.'

'What for? What if I don't agree?'

'Your refusal will be noted, but we'll have the swab, DNA check, to prove if you're the father of Charlotte Merton's child.'

'How could I be?'

'Mr Connelly, your denial does you no credit,' Clare said. 'We know about you and her; we know about the caravan. Why there?'

Connelly blustered, unable to speak coherently. He drank some water.

'You make it sound cheap,' he finally spluttered out.

'A caravan, Charlotte, a devoted wife at home; it was,' Clare said.

Tremayne was concerned that his sergeant was getting personal; he'd let it go for now, see where it led.

'It was only the once. Maria was busy at the pub, coming home tired, and the eldest wasn't well for a few weeks.'

'It's not a defence.'

'No, it's just a reason. Charlotte was there, so was the caravan. She said that Bess wouldn't mind, not that she did when she turned up, and then there's Harriet Huxtable outside. I was panicking, but Charlotte saw the humour in the situation, made light of it, listened as the mother and daughter spoke.'

'You knew already that Bess was Harriet's mother.'

'I did, but Charlotte didn't, not that it stopped her.'

'She got a kick out of screwing you in the caravan while the two women were outside?'

'She was high, just had a hit.'

'Heroin?'

'Yes, not that I knew where she had got it from, but Charlotte's insatiable. I didn't stand a chance.'

'A weak defence,' Clare said. 'You were stronger than her. You could have stopped it.'

'Not with Harriet outside. She'd tell Maria, I knew she would, unable to resist.'

'You allowed yourself to be seduced by Charlotte rather than be seen by Harriet?'

'I know how it looks, but Bess knew, and she wasn't going to tell anyone,' Joe said.

'The fatal flaw in your defence,' Clare said. 'What were you doing in the caravan in the first place. According to Maria, you're a man who likes to be clean, and that caravan is anything but.'

'We could see Harriet coming. We went in at the last minute.'

'Connelly, it's a pack of lies,' Tremayne said. 'We know you were in the caravan before Harriet arrived. Agreed that you could have used it to stay out of sight, but it doesn't explain what you were doing with Charlotte in the first place. The caravan's out of the way, and if you tell us you were taking a stroll, you'd be insulting our intelligence.'

Clare felt sad for Maria. She knew this was going to end badly.

A technician came into the interview room, took a swab from inside Connelly's left cheek. 'Twenty-four hours,' he said, pre-empting Tremayne's question.

'You've got twelve,' Tremayne's reply.

'You'd better have a chat with our boss. She'll not be too keen on your demands.'

'She knows me of old.'

'She said you'd want it quicker than we can deliver. She said, "Tell Tremayne we can't perform miracles, and what he wants is beyond even us."'

Clare enjoyed the technician's riposte, but it was the interview room, and Connelly was being grilled. She suppressed her smirk and looked at the man.

'Your answer, Joe. How long had you been spending time with Charlotte?'

'Just the once, that's the truth. Never looked at another woman, not since I've been with Maria. I know it looks bad, but—'

'It is.' Clare interrupted him, knowing that he was going to continue talking ad infinitum, hoping that his indiscretion would remain just that. 'Even if it is the once, you're in that caravan. You have sex with the woman,

Harriet's outside, Bess is standing guard; no idea why, but there it is.'

'Bess never held much with what society said was right and wrong; something to do with her troubled youth, I suppose.'

'You'll be held over,' Tremayne said. 'It would have been the magistrate in the morning, but it's more serious than that now.'

'Maria and me, we'll be right,' Connelly said.

'Explain this to me,' Clare said. 'You get angry with her for spending a night with Plumpton, but then you believe that what you've done is acceptable.'

'I was wrong, the same as her, but we made a sacred oath to each other, in sickness and in health, for richer or poorer.'

'For someone who's never been in the church, you've become religious all of a sudden. Is it because you're jealous of your wife, a dynamic person, while you, Joe Connelly, work a nine-to-five job, not wanting any more, worried that your wife will see through you, find someone else, another Plumpton?'

'Okay, I'm jealous, and I don't want to leave her, not because of Charlotte, nor because of Plumpton. What she saw in the man, I'll not know.'

'What did you see in Charlotte, a bit on the side? Your workmates egging you on, always talking about their conquests, you feeling out of it.'

'I want the life we had. Not much money, but we were happy. And then it changed when Charlotte died, and then Plumpton's death affected Maria, not that she'd show it, not to you, not to anyone, but I'm there at night, and I can see her over her side of the bed, crying. It wasn't for me, was it?'

'Wasn't it?' Clare said. 'Shouldn't she be upset that you hit her?'

'It was before that. Sometimes, she would talk in her sleep, mention his name.'

'You felt rejected, in need of reassurance,' Tremayne said. 'That's why you spent time with Charlotte.'

'She didn't care for me, I know that. She was looking for someone steady, someone available. Plumpton was the man she wanted. He wasn't anything to look at, but he could draw women to him like bears to a honey pot.'

'You have Maria; she must have seen something in you,' Clare said.

'Solid, dependable, easy to live with, that was me. It wouldn't have been so bad if she had been attracted to someone worthwhile, but Plumpton wasn't.'

'It seems to me,' Tremayne said, tiring of the man's conversation, 'that you could have killed Charlotte, knowing that Plumpton would have felt the hurt.'

'That's illogical.'

'Is it? Think it through. You couldn't harm your wife, but you can get to him through Charlotte.'

Clare was struggling with Tremayne's logic, although she realised that he was sounding out probable scenarios, no matter how absurd.

'You were aware that Plumpton was under pressure from the bank,' Tremayne continued. 'Maria could have told you, and you knew the man's fragile condition, his drug abuse when he was younger. You wanted the man to suffer, to pay him back for what he had done to you. But you, Joe, weren't a man to complain, to confront your wife with the truth, which could only mean one thing…'

Clare spoke up. 'Joe, you knew about your wife and Plumpton. You knew they had spent the night together.'

'It wasn't the only time,' Connelly conceded. 'And yes, I knew. The man had a distinctive odour about him; you must have noticed it close up. Something to do with the dampness in the pub, the beer barrels in the cellar. Most people wouldn't notice, but I've got a keen sense of smell, always have. I kept it to myself, even though it hurt.'

'Why hit her after she told you?'

'It was out in the open. You two knew; God knows who else. We're private people, and if Shirley Jenkins got hold of it, we'd be the laughing stock of the village. I couldn't allow it.'

'So, you're in that caravan with Charlotte, and she's keen on Plumpton; Bess is standing guard, but she's not likely to talk. Or is she? That's it, Joe, isn't it? You were worried that Charlotte with another man, with Plumpton, would talk, especially if she's spaced out on drugs. That's why you killed her.'

A silence fell over the room. A pin dropping would have made a noise, before Joe calmly said, 'We had a perfect life, the four of us. I couldn't let her destroy it, not at any cost. Don't you see?'

'It's murder, Joe, plain and simple.'

'It's my child, isn't it?'

'We'll know soon enough,' Tremayne said. 'In the meantime, we need a signed statement from you.'

'You're destroying our family, you know that, don't you?'

'Maria would have forgiven you,' Clare said. 'However, we can't forgive murder. The law holds, and you will be going to prison for a long time.'

'One day, I'll be free, and Maria and the children can come and visit me.'

They could, but whether Maria could forgive the man for murder remained to be seen. Somehow, Clare thought she wouldn't.

Chapter 26

DNA tests proved that Joe Connelly wasn't the father of the unborn child. Even so, it made little difference, as he had given a full confession.

A legal aid lawyer sat beside him as he signed it, advising him that the evidence was tenuous, and the onus of proof rested with the prosecution.

Tremayne had to admit that, to his credit, Joe had accepted the blame, and no amount of pressure from the lawyer – not very competent, Tremayne thought – would stop him signing.

'I had to, you must know that,' Joe continued to say as he was led to the cells.

Maria had been so devastated that she had returned to the village, not asking to see him, not that night.

Clare drove Maria back to the village, staying with her until late, a doctor administering a sedative. Angus Campbell agreed to remain downstairs in the house. The children stayed with the neighbours, although they had seen their mother briefly, asked about their father.

'He'll be back with us soon,' Maria said, not telling them the truth, not that they would have understood. Clare was concerned as to what would become of them. They would suffer the most, tainted by a father who had murdered, the brunt of the school playground teasing.

Finally, at one in the morning, Clare made it back to Bemerton Road.

'I can't say I'm pleased with today,' Tremayne said when he noticed her.

'Have you eaten?'

'Jean came in earlier, brought me dinner. I'm fine for now, although I could do with a rest.'

Clare didn't mention he had been asleep on his chair when she had walked into Homicide.

'What now?' she said.

'The superintendent's been in, congratulated us on a job well done.'

'It doesn't feel like that to me,' Clare said.

'Maria?'

'Sedated. The full impact will hit tomorrow.'

'What about the pub?'

'Closed tonight. The village will be alive tomorrow with the news.'

'Only Campbell knows,' Tremayne said. 'He'll not say anything.'

Clare knew that Tremayne was attempting to put an optimistic slant on the day's events: the Connellys' children not at school, Maria not visible, the pub not open, and Shirley Jenkins, her radar attuned to the change in the air.

'If Campbell had told us about Joe in the caravan, it would have saved us a lot of time,' Clare said.

'I was thinking about that just before you came in.'

'Is that why your eyes were closed? Think better when then are?'

'It's too late, Yarwood, for your attempt at humour.'

Fifteen minutes later, the two left the police station. Tremayne went back to Jean in Wilton; Clare back to Clive in the cathedral close.

***

Logic would suggest that Joe had murdered Bess Carmichael, but the man was adamant that he had not.

A conviction against Joe for Charlotte's murder would be based on a confession, not on proof. He had told Tremayne after his lawyer had left and the confession was secured that he had thrown the syringe away. He also told Tremayne where he had discarded it: a hedgerow not far from the village.

Tremayne had phoned Jim Hughes, the senior CSI, the man commenting on the unearthly hour and if it could wait until the morning. Tremayne took no notice, informing him that he'd have six uniforms out in the area at seven in the morning, suitably kitted up to mount a search, and for Hughes to have six of his team. Joe Connelly would be at the site to point out exactly where to look.

Jim Hughes spent another thirty minutes after Tremayne had hung up organising his people, much to the chagrin of his wife who rolled over and attempted to go back to sleep, but in the end put on the light and picked up a book.

The respective teams assembled in the pub car park at the agreed time, Tremayne arriving ten minutes late, claiming it was the traffic. Clare, who had slept well, knew it was not, and she had arrived early, before anyone else, although Shirley Jenkins was there, as was Angus Campbell.

'He won't tell me anything,' Shirley Jenkins said, looking over at Campbell.

'It's not any of your business, is it?' Clare said. She was not in a mood for the woman. It was not a day for levity and idle chit-chat.

'I heard there was trouble down at the Connellys.'

'If you've no more to add, other than gossip, I would suggest you go back to your shop. I don't want to get official with you, Mrs Jenkins, but this is police business.'

Shirley Jenkins walked off, cursing under her breath.

'You told her off,' Campbell said.

'You'll be next,' Clare said. 'Wasting our time, not telling us about Joe Connelly and the caravan. What else is there?'

'I knew what Maria's reaction would be. She didn't need to know. It was my decision, and I'll stand by it.'

Clare could sympathise with the man's sentiment, not with his decision.

Joe Connelly arrived in the back of a patrol car. Not far away, Eustace and Miranda Hampton.

Clare walked over to them. 'I thought you had enough problems of your own without being here.'

'Grayson's at the house,' Eustace said.

'Your plans?'

'We'll be fine, all of us.'

Clare wasn't about to tell them, but one of them wouldn't be. The Fraud squad, on advice from Tremayne, intended to arrest Gavin Fitzwilliam that morning. And, at Tremayne's instigation, they were to conduct enquiries into Jacob Grayson, to conduct an audit, to look for irregularities, criminal activity.

The farm was Grayson's, but Tremayne had never liked the man; the least he could do was to make his life uncomfortable.

'We made an arrest,' Clare said.

'The father?'

'Not of the child. That still remains a mystery.'

'Maybe it'll never be known,' Miranda said. 'Charlotte could have been with other men.'

She could have been with Eustace, Clare thought, and which his wife had confirmed, but it had not been admitted by the man; not yet, not proven.

Maria walked down the road from the other direction. Clare left the Hamptons and walked over to her.

'What are you doing?' Clare asked.

'Someone's got to open the pub,' Maria said.

'Not today, you need to take it easy; time heals everything.'

'I saw Joe. How is he?'

'He's not the father.'

'He still killed the woman to protect me. I was the guilty one; I fell for another man, but Joe, dear Joe, hadn't been able to resist her, and it's come to this. Still, that's life, it could be worse.'

Clare couldn't see how it could be, not unless Joe had killed both women. There was nothing she could do with Maria, other than watch her walk over to the pub, casting a sideways glance at her husband. Him mouthing, *I love you*; Maria not responding. It was all very tragic, Clare thought.

Tremayne had finished his briefing on the day's activities, the teams getting back into their vehicles and heading off, Connelly in the lead car.

'I see the Jenkins woman wasn't long getting here,' Tremayne said as Clare joined him.

'She's still in the dark; hopefully, it'll stay that way for a bit longer.'

On Joe's advice, the lead car pulled to one side of the narrow road outside the village and stopped, the other vehicles stopping as well. A couple of uniforms set up bollards in the road and stood to direct any traffic around them.

Connelly, free of the handcuffs, led a group of four across the field adjoining the road, stopping at a hedgerow and pointing. 'In there.'

The four were joined by two more, with one of Jim Hughes' crime scene investigators in overall control, directing them how to search, where to look, and whatever they did, not to tread on it.

Another group fanned out from the hedgerow, looking for further proof.

The syringe, especially if it had Connelly's fingerprints still on it, would be vital evidence, but it had rained solidly for a week, and animal contamination was a possibility. To Jim Hughes, it was like looking for a needle in a haystack, even though Connelly had been precise.

'Under pressure, the mind plays tricks,' Hughes said. 'It could be where he said, or in another field, under another hedgerow. We could be here for some time.'

Tremayne knew Hughes wouldn't let him down.

A voice from across the field. 'We've found it.'

Hughes left Tremayne and Clare and walked over. He bent down; the syringe was clearly visible after the undergrowth had been cleared away. A crime scene photographer was taking photos. Some of the team were looking in the immediate vicinity, while two others were standing by, hands in pockets, looking as though they could do with a cigarette.

The search had taken less than twenty minutes. Connelly had been exact, but then that was the man: uncomplicated, decent. His first mistake, not resisting Charlotte Merton, the second mistake, not confronting Maria earlier on, before she had slept with Plumpton; the third mistake, killing the woman. One mistake too many, and for which he would pay severely.

The patrol car delivered Connelly back to Bemerton Road. Jim Hughes took the syringe, enclosed in an evidence bag, to Forensics. Tremayne intended to give them a couple of hours before he phoned, knowing he would be rebuked, aware that his call would ensure a speedier result.

Tremayne was feeling good with himself; Clare was not. It was, as it often is, the innocent who suffer, long after the perpetrator has been incarcerated and accepted his fate. It was Maria and her children that she felt sad for.

Back at the pub, Maria made a token effort to put on a brave face, even managing sandwiches for Tremayne and Clare, not once asking questions as to what had happened or how Joe was. The woman, Clare could see, needed to rest, but having got to know her, she knew that she would not agree. And maybe she was right.

Clare thought back to when Harry had died, and the time away from the police station, back with her parents, her mother trying to help, but failing miserably. And then, two months later, she was in front of Tremayne's desk, reporting for duty. The man had been the best therapy, not once attempting to console her or to treat her gently, but throwing her into the deep end, another murder investigation, and he had worked her hard, and she admired him more than anyone else, apart from her husband, Clive, whom she loved.

***

It seemed in the days after Joe's arrest that most people had forgotten one fact: there had been two murders.

At Bemerton Road Police Station, the paperwork regarding Connelly was well in hand, and even though they weren't clear, Connelly's fingerprints on the syringe were admissible as evidence.

In the village, the pub stayed open, Plumpton's son and former wife helping out; Maria was there most days, the children at home or next door with neighbours.

Clare had been in on a couple of occasions, sensed the atmosphere, not the bonhomie that Maria had intended to cultivate.

The friendship that had once existed between Clare and Maria was strained; it would never return. It should have made Clare sad, or sadder than she was, but for her and Tremayne, Bess Carmichael's death still had to be solved.

At the farm, not the focus for a couple of days, a stillness had settled over the place. Clare had driven by, called in briefly to find that Margaret Reece and her daughters, Sally and Bronwyn, had left, a forwarding address supplied.

That news didn't concern Clare, as the three had only ever been regarded as minor players on the periphery.

The Fraud squad had made their move, and Gavin Fitzwilliam was under arrest for money laundering, but his partner, Dominic, was nowhere to be found. The one upshot of Fitzwilliam's arrest had been that his wife and two daughters had visited him.

Tremayne felt that he and Clare needed to get a different perspective on Bess Carmichael's death; they had agreed to meet just outside the village and to visit the caravan.

Tremayne pulled over, parked his car, and got into Clare's. 'No point in getting both of them dirty,' he said.

'We could have used yours,' Clare's reply.

No direct answer from Tremayne, just 'What do you fancy in the two-thirty at Goodwood?'

He was feeling better, and if he started talking about horse racing, asking her opinion on a subject she had no knowledge of and even less interest in, it meant he was confident the last murder would be solved.

'Give me a pin, and I'll close my eyes. Pin the tail on the donkey, or in your case, the three-legged knacker's yard special.'

'Yarwood, get serious. Picking a winner is a precise art, all to do with the track, the weight the horse is carrying, the odds for a win.'

'I'll take your word for it. What's the plan?'

'What we discussed. We visit the caravan, not sure what we'll find there, but try and reason out what has happened, find a murderer. We'll accept that Connelly's not responsible,' Tremayne said. 'Although Bess knew about him and Charlotte. She must have been suspicious when she died.'

'Or protective of Joe.'

The condition of the caravan had been woeful when Bess had lived in it, but now Tremayne and Clare could see that it had deteriorated immeasurably. Even though crime scene tape was still secured to the outside of it, and the door had had a solid lock installed, the door was hanging off its hinges.'

'Local children,' Tremayne said.

'It's probable unless someone was looking for something.'

Clare opened the door to the caravan – an overpowering smell of rotting food pervaded the air. She closed the door quickly and walked away.

'I wouldn't go in there if I were you,' she said.

'Not the most romantic place, is it?'

Clare realised that regardless of what she had just said, she had to enter the caravan. This time, she held a handkerchief over her nose and mouth.

At the rear of the small caravan, a bed with a filthy blanket on top. In the centre of the caravan, a makeshift kitchen with a metal sink and a gas stove which hadn't been used for years. All in all, it was a pitiful sight, a sad life for a woman who had endured much in her eighty-plus years.

Tremayne stayed outside and walked around the area, placing Harriet where she had stood facing her mother, the window that Charlotte and Connelly would have seen them from, and more importantly thinking about what they had heard – according to Connelly, not much, just mother and daughter attempting to communicate, a fragmented conversation.

Something wasn't right, Tremayne could feel it. He took his phone out of his pocket and called Campbell. 'I need you up at the caravan,' he said. He then called for a patrol car to pick up the man and bring him to the site.

'What is it?' Clare said when she rejoined Tremayne.

'It's Campbell's word as to what went on here.'

'And Joe's.'

'Joe makes sense, Campbell doesn't.'

The weather was warmer than on previous days, and the two police officers walked down the track that led to the farm, returning when the patrol car could be seen approaching.

Campbell, dressed in a suit, wearing a coat over the top, came over to them.

'What is it?' he said.

Tremayne went through Campbell's earlier testimony, placing boxes where the two women had stood talking.

'Is that right? Where I've placed them?' Tremayne said.

'I'd say so,' Campbell's reply.

Clare wasn't sure where Tremayne was heading, but she was watching and listening.

'Campbell, I don't like this. You said you were up the hill, yet you could clearly see the two women.'

'I did, but I couldn't hear them.'

'I'll grant you that, but look up the hill, what can you see?'

'Nothing.'

'And if you were there and Joe Connelly had come out of the caravan, he would have walked back to the village down the track.'

'I would have said that.'

'We've just walked down there, and if you come out of the caravan, the door can't be viewed from up the hill, and there's a lean-to of sorts, as well as a tree.'

'Where's this heading?' Campbell asked.

'What I'm saying is, you couldn't have seen Joe, not from where you were standing.'

'It's what I saw.'

'Your version of it, not mine. Either you didn't see Joe, or you were somewhere close. And if you were, why? What reason would you have had to be near the caravan?'

Clare looked at Campbell, attempted to see subtle changes.

'After Harriet left, I came down here, but I didn't speak to Bess,' Campbell admitted.

'It's like pulling hen's teeth,' Tremayne said, 'getting the truth out of you.'

'I don't like your tone,' Campbell indignantly replied.

'Your opinion of me or of what I say does not concern me. You've constantly failed to tell us the truth, feeding us dribs and drabs when we've pushed. You withheld the fact that Joe was in the caravan. If we had known that before, we could have arrested him earlier, possibly prevented Bess Carmichael's murder. Have you considered this?'

'Nothing would have prevented that.'

Campbell sat down on the caravan's metal step. He pulled his coat tightly around him.

'I was up the hill,' he said. 'I could see Bess and Harriet. They were talking, not that I could hear, but they were animated, Harriet flaying her arms, not raising her voice. If she had, I might have picked up some of it.'

'You decided to come down.'

'I always kept a watch out for Bess over the years. If Harriet was angry with her, I wasn't sure what would happen. It was my duty to be on hand if needed.'

'Why didn't you tell us before?'

'Each time I do, another person is arrested.'

'Do you have a problem with that?'

'I came closer, not that either of the women could see me. Bess was saying that she was going to tell the village that her daughter lived among them, to tell everyone who the father was, her own grandfather.'

'Bess had lived with that secret for years, never told anyone, apart from Shirley Jenkins and Joe Connelly. Why would she do that now?' Tremayne said.

'She wasn't going to live for much longer. Maybe she felt it was time to tell, or her memory was going.

309

Whatever it was, she needed to feel loved before she died; she needed her family with her.'

'Her only family,' Clare said.

'That doesn't explain why Harriet was at the caravan,' Tremayne said.

'You'd need to ask her that. I can only tell you what I saw.'

'Charlotte and Joe?'

'They left a few minutes after Harriet, and Joe walked down the track. You were correct there.'

'Is there any more? Or do we need to use thumbscrews?' Tremayne said.

'No more. You'll never understand why I protected Joe and Harriet.'

'We never will.'

Clare agreed with her senior, and the woman who diligently cleaned the church and ensured the prayer books were in place for the Sunday services was due for another visit from the police.

Chapter 27

Tremayne felt there was a probable case against Angus Campbell for withholding evidence, but he'd not pursue the matter. The man had provided the information that had led to Joe Connelly's confession, and now he had produced another vital piece of information: the fact that Harriet was concerned that the secret that had been concealed for so many years was about to be revealed.

Clare checked with the home care nurse, to be told that Harriet was much improved and determined to get back to her chores at the church. The nurse, however, was not pleased to be told that her patient was to be subjected to another round of questioning.

Regardless of her concerns, that was about to happen.

It was just after four in the afternoon when Tremayne and Clare knocked on Harriet's door. In the time that they had left the caravan and arrived at the house, they had called in at the pub, Wally Plumpton's son behind the bar, his former wife in the kitchen.

The two were cordial, but the meal, although it looked fine, did not taste the same as when prepared by Maria. Clare conceded that without her, the pub would fail soon enough. And from what Maria had said earlier in the day when Joe had passed by the pub on his way to Bemerton Road, she was unlikely to continue; the fire that she once felt had been extinguished by Joe's actions, instigated by her weakness.

In the village, Shirley Jenkins was holding court, and the takings were up.

Angus Campbell had wanted to come to the pub with them, but Tremayne had said that he and Clare had police business to discuss, which wasn't true.

Clare thought that Tremayne would want to talk about the case, but he didn't, only to eat his meal without comment, and to drink a lemonade – no alcohol before meeting with Harriet one more time.

All the indicators were pointing to her as her mother's murderer, although Clare hoped she was not. But the motive was strong, in that Harriet had spent years maintaining a distance, until she went to the caravan.

Joe Connelly had made his confession, asked to see his children and Maria, a request that would not be denied once he had been moved from Bemerton Road to prison to await trial.

Whether Maria would allow the children to see their father was unclear, but the family unit, once so strong, was irrevocably broken. A tragedy, but matricide, killing your mother, was worse.

The door opened at Harriet's house, the nurse letting Tremayne and Clare in.

'Harriet's waiting for you,' she said.

'And you?'

'I had hoped to leave tomorrow, but if you go upsetting her, I might have to stay for another three or four days.'

Clare apologised for the inconvenience; Tremayne did not. Typically, he'd be fired up, ready to go on the offensive, but he was calm.

Harriet stood up as the two entered the room. 'You've a few questions for me,' she said. She looked better for the rest, her face was fuller, and she had applied makeup.

'You've been told about Joe Connelly,' Tremayne said when the three were seated.

'I've heard, not that anyone comes here.'

'How?' Clare asked.

'It was on the television that you'd made an arrest, and I can see the road outside, I saw him and his wife.'

'What do you think about it?'

'I should feel sad, shouldn't I?'

'Not necessarily,' Clare said, looking over at the nurse who stood in the background.

A nod from the nurse was all that was necessary. Harriet was mildly sedated, the reason for her vagueness.

'Harriet, you visited your mother at the caravan,' Tremayne said.

'She had sent me a note, pushed it through my letterbox.'

'Do you still have it?'

'It wasn't the first time; I did the same as with the others.'

'You threw it away?'

'I burnt it.'

'In the past, you've always ignored them, so why did you go?'

'Once or twice in the past, I've wanted to go; even left the house and started walking up there, but I never could.'

'The last time you did.'

'She looked older.'

'You went and saw Angus Campbell?' Clare said.

'He's shown you the envelope?'

'We have. It is a picture of you, isn't it? The baby?'

'I should have been pleased to see it, but I couldn't be. So much hatred, too many years.'

'Shirley Jenkins? What was all that about? Going in there bragging about you and Campbell?'

'The doctor may have been correct. Strain, too much work, stress, who knows?'

'We'll accept that,' Tremayne said. 'What we don't understand is what happened at the caravan, not only you but the two inside.'

'It was just my mother and me,' Harriet said.

'Unfortunately, it wasn't,' Clare said. 'The caravan is crucial to our investigation, and you were there when the two murdered women were present.'

'The young woman, was she in the caravan?'

'And one other?'

'Joe Connelly?'

'You knew?'

'No, but it has to be him, doesn't it?'

'Which means that of the four at the caravan, two are dead and one has been arrested; you're the only one free and alive.'

'I believe that you are overtiring Miss Huxtable,' the nurse said.

'I'm fine, for now,' Harriet said. 'I didn't murder my mother, I couldn't have.'

'If she had revealed that you were her daughter, how would you have reacted?'

'Badly, but I couldn't have killed her, not my own mother. It's complicated. I should have loved her, but I couldn't. I didn't hate her either; it was just that she reminded me of what I was, where I had come from.'

'Tell us about the conversation at the caravan that last time,' Clare said.

'I asked her not to say anything; to keep it our secret. I suppose I wasn't very tactful, and I could have handled it better, but I was under strain, knowing that I

314

would be a joke, unable to show my face in the church. What would Reverend Walton have thought, the devil's child?'

'Harriet, you were wrong. The vicar would have said nothing, nor would the village. After a few days of gossip, it would have been forgotten. Did you know that both Joe Connelly and Shirley Jenkins knew you were Bess's daughter? Bess told them a long time ago, and Joe would never have spoken about it, and Shirley Jenkins had decided not to repeat it.'

'There's some good in the woman.'

'Not a lot,' Clare conceded. 'Neither knew about your father, though.'

'Did you see anyone in the caravan?' Tremayne asked. He didn't feel comfortable with the softly-softly approach, but he didn't feel inclined to push it with the clearly still fragile woman.

He had been confident that Harriet Huxtable was the prime suspect for the murder of her mother, but in that house, he wasn't so sure. And, as with Charlotte, where was the proof? Bess's death had required some physical strength, and Harriet, although not a robust woman, could have managed. He'd seen her in the church moving pews to sweep under them, and then climbing the pulpit, dusting as she went, stacking the prayer books, and polishing the cross on the altar. He wanted to believe she was guilty, but his sixth sense had told him that they needed to look elsewhere.

After thirty-five minutes, Tremayne and Clare left the house and walked back over to the pub car park.

***

At the farm, only three of the original twenty-four remained. Eustace and Miranda were in the house, Ben was around the back of the barn. For once, he was sitting, a cigarette in his mouth.

'A smoke?' he said when Tremayne walked around and sat next to him.

'Not for me,' Tremayne replied, although he wanted to. The nicotine patches had helped, so had his wife's encouragement, but the lack of dopamine, released by the receptors in his brain activated by nicotine, still troubled him.

It had been a complex and tiring investigation. Tremayne changed his mind and took a cigarette from Ben's pack and lit up. He sucked in the smoke, coughed, savoured the moment.

He had intended to revisit Angus Campbell, to get the thumbscrews out, as had been suggested, but Clare had talked Tremayne out of it. If Campbell had more to reveal, he'd wait; the farm was more immediate. It was the day that the Hamptons were leaving, and even though they had given an address, a remote part of Cumbria in the north of the country, skirting the border with Scotland, it wasn't somewhere readily accessible for further questioning.

'What do you intend to do?' Tremayne asked Ben.

'I'll go and stay with my brother for a while. After that, who knows.'

'You're not going with Eustace and Miranda?'

'It's just the two of them from now on.'

'They've got a son.'

'And a future daughter-in-law.'

'She's a tough woman.'

'They'll not see him much after she's married him; they know that.'

'Families. You can't choose them, not like your friends.'

'Apart from my brother, and he won't want me around for long, that's all the family I've got.'

'Friends?'

'Plenty of them, but they would want to go to the pub, to drink one too many, and we both know what happens.'

'You cause trouble, put someone in hospital, meet up with Joe Connelly in prison.'

'I'll show you something,' Ben said as he stood up.

The two men walked a few feet past where Bess Carmichael had died.

'It's this,' Ben said as he pointed to a can.

'What's the significance?'

'It was just before you arrived. I found it hidden under a piece of wood. I've been cleaning up around the place, just keeping myself busy, as Grayson intends to knock the place down, build houses for those that have got money.'

'It's grease,' Tremayne said.

'The pulley up the top, where the rope that hoisted Bess Carmichael went through. It had been there all through last winter; it would have been tight and would have squealed like hell.'

'Are you saying someone climbed up there and greased it before murdering Bess?'

'I'm not saying anything. It just strikes me as odd why someone would go to so much trouble. The woman was old, and whoever wanted to murder her could have done it somewhere else, and the farm normally had people around, or at least it did.'

Tremayne phoned Jim Hughes who would have a person out within the hour. The can of grease still had fingermarks smudged on the side.

'Who could have got up there?'

'Not so difficult if you use a ladder. It's usually somewhere or other around the back of the barn.'

'If you're correct, then it's premeditated murder. Tony Frampton?'

'Not Tony. He could have greased the pulley, but he wouldn't have been smart enough to think it through, not beforehand.'

'You didn't kill her?'

'Inspector, don't try that on me. And besides, the grease can. Did your people check the pulley for fingerprints?'

'They would have.'

'My prints will be on the can, so will Tony's. Who else is what's important, isn't it?'

'It is.'

***

Tremayne waited with Ben, Clare having taken the opportunity to meet up with Maria.

'I can't see him, not yet,' Maria said. 'I've told the oldest, not that he understood, not really. The youngest, she thinks he's coming home soon, but he won't.'

'Will you support him?'

'I'll not divorce him if that's what you're asking.'

It wasn't, but she could understand the bitterness against the woman who had arrested her husband.

'Eventually, in the future, when he's served his time?' Clare asked.

'I don't know, but I think he'll be dead to me by then. How the children will react, that's up to them.'

Clare didn't stay long, and she was glad of Tremayne's phone call to get over to the farm.

Around the back of the barn, on her arrival, Jim Hughes was explaining the situation. 'We checked the pulley, no fingerprints, only glove marks.'

'That'd be right,' Ben said. 'You don't want to get the grease on your hands, impossible to wash off unless you use something aggressive, and we'd not have anything like that around here.'

'Hughes, the grease can?' Tremayne said.

'Forensics will check it out. There are fingerprints on the outside, and we've got Ben's and Tony Frampton's. Anyone else, and we'll let you know.'

Tremayne explained the situation to Clare, about how Ben had found the can and the possible murderer.

It would be three to four hours before Forensics got back to them. In the meantime, they would wait at Bemerton Road, the time for further questioning was passed.

An arrest was made in the early hours of the next morning, the man transported in the back of a patrol car from where he lived, a two-hour drive from Salisbury.

Jacob Grayson, presented with the report from Forensics, could only prevaricate. The lawyer that he had engaged, highly skilled and expensive, had tried his best, but the evidence was overwhelming as Grayson's fingerprints were on the can, along with Ben's and Tony's.

In the end, Grayson admitted his guilt.

'She was causing trouble. It was because of Charlotte Merton. For some reason, she wanted to save the woman from herself, no idea why.'

Clare did, as did Tremayne. The rejected mother had found a substitute in Charlotte and had wanted to protect her.

'She confronted you?'

'She said that she had contacts who had researched me, found out irregularities in some of my business dealings. I don't know how, but she was right, not that it matters now. I'll not go to prison for those crimes.'

'You won't, but why murder her?' Tremayne asked.

'She had obtained a copy of the agreement I had with Hampton, found out anomalies in it.'

'But Hampton had the bank demand.'

'That old woman who looked as though she didn't have two pennies to rub together had millions in the bank. She was going to bail out Hampton, and all because of the young woman.'

'But the woman died before you killed Bess Carmichael.'

'She was convinced it was me. She was threatening to go to the police, to tell Hampton. I did what I had to.'

Two weeks later, Clare drove through the village and past the farm. It was deserted, the bank had taken possession, and the village had returned to its old sleepy self.

Harriet Huxtable was walking down towards the church; Shirley Jenkins was outside her shop looking for customers, and in his garden, Angus Campbell.

At the pub, a sign stated that it was closed indefinitely. It would not be opening again. The father of the unborn child would never be known.

The End.

ALSO BY THE AUTHOR

DI Tremayne Thriller Series

Death Unholy – A DI Tremayne Thriller – Book 1

All that remained were the man's two legs and a chair full of greasy and fetid ash. Little did DI Keith Tremayne know that it was the beginning of a journey into the murky world of paganism and its ancient rituals. And it was going to get very dangerous.

'Do you believe in spontaneous human combustion?' Detective Inspector Keith Tremayne asked.

'Not me. I've read about it. Who hasn't?' Sergeant Clare Yarwood answered.

'I haven't,' Tremayne replied, which did not surprise his young sergeant. In the months they had been working together, she had come to realise that he was a man who had little interest in the world. When he had a cigarette in his mouth, a beer in his hand, and a murder to solve he was about the happiest she ever saw him, but even then he could hardly be regarded as one of life's most sociable people. And as for reading? The most he managed was an occasional police report, an early-morning newspaper, turning first to the back pages for the racing results.

Death and the Assassin's Blade – A DI Tremayne Thriller – Book 2

It was meant to be high drama, not murder, but someone's switched the daggers. The man's death took place in plain view of two serving police officers.

He was not meant to die; the daggers were only theatrical props, plastic and harmless. A summer's night, a production of Julius Caesar amongst the ruins of an Anglo-Saxon fort. Detective Inspector Tremayne is there with his sergeant, Clare Yarwood. In the assassination scene, Caesar collapses to the ground. Brutus defends his actions; Mark Antony rebukes him.

They're a disparate group, the amateur actors. One's an estate agent, another an accountant. And then there is the teenage school student, the gay man, the funeral director. And what about the women? They could be involved.

They've each got a secret, but which of those on the stage wanted Gordon Mason, the actor who had portrayed Caesar, dead?

Death and the Lucky Man – A DI Tremayne Thriller – Book 3

Sixty-eight million pounds and dead. Hardly the outcome expected for the luckiest man in England the day his lottery ticket was drawn out of the barrel. But then, Alan Winters' rags-to-riches story had never been conventional, and some had benefited, but others hadn't.

Death at Coombe Farm – A DI Tremayne Thriller – Book 4

A warring family. A disputed inheritance. A recipe for death.

If it hadn't been for the circumstances, Detective Inspector Keith Tremayne would have said the view was outstanding. Up high, overlooking the farmhouse in the valley below, the panoramic vista of Salisbury Plain stretching out beyond. The only problem was that near where he stood with his sergeant, Clare Yarwood, there was a body, and it wasn't a pleasant sight.

Death by a Dead Man's Hand – A DI Tremayne Thriller – Book 5

A flawed heist of forty gold bars from a security van late at night. One of the perpetrators is killed by his brother as they argue over what they have stolen.

Eighteen years later, the murderer, released after serving his sentence for his brother's murder, waits in a church for a man purporting to be the brother he killed. And then he too is killed.

The threads stretch back a long way, and now more people are dying in the search for the missing gold bars.

Detective Inspector Tremayne, his health causing him concern, and Sergeant Clare Yarwood, still seeking romance, are pushed to the limit solving the murder, attempting to prevent any more.

Death in the Village – A DI Tremayne Thriller – Book 6

Nobody liked Gloria Wiggins, a woman who regarded anyone who did not acquiesce to her jaundiced view of the world with disdain. James Baxter, the previous vicar, had been one of those, and her scurrilous outburst in the church one Sunday had hastened his death.

And now, years later, the woman was dead, hanging from a beam in her garage. Detective Inspector Tremayne and Sergeant Clare Yarwood had seen the body, interviewed the woman's acquaintances, and those who had hated her.

Burial Mound – A DI Tremayne Thriller – Book 7

A Bronze-Age burial mound close to Stonehenge. An archaeological excavation. What they were looking for was an ancient body and historical artefacts. They found the ancient body, but then they found a modern-day body too. And then the police became interested.

It's another case for Detective Inspector Tremayne and Sergeant Yarwood. The more recent body was the brother of the mayor of Salisbury.

Everything seems to point to the victim's brother, the mayor, the upright and serious-minded Clive Grantley. Tremayne's sure that it's him, but Clare Yarwood's not so sure.

But is her belief based on evidence or personal hope?

DCI Isaac Cook Thriller Series

Murder is a Tricky Business – A DCI Cook Thriller – Book 1

A television actress is missing, and DCI Isaac Cook, the Senior Investigation Officer of the Murder Investigation Team at Challis Street Police Station in London, is searching for her.

Why has he been taken away from more important crimes to search for the woman? It's not the first time she's gone missing, so why does everyone assume she's been murdered?

There's a secret, that much is certain, but who knows it? The missing woman? The executive producer? His eavesdropping assistant? Or the actor who portrayed her fictional brother in the TV soap opera?

Murder House – A DCI Cook Thriller – Book 2

A corpse in the fireplace of an old house. It's been there for thirty years, but who is it?

It's murder, but who is the victim and what connection does the body have to the previous owners of the house. What is the motive? And why is the body in a fireplace? It was bound to be discovered eventually but was that what the murderer wanted? The main suspects are all old and dying, or already dead.

Isaac Cook and his team have their work cut out, trying to put the pieces together. Those who know are not talking because of an old-fashioned belief that a family's dirty laundry should not be aired in public, and never to a policeman – even if that means the murderer is never brought to justice!

Murder is Only a Number – A DCI Cook Thriller – Book 3

Before she left, she carved a number in blood on his chest. But why the number 2, if this was her first murder?

The woman prowls the streets of London. Her targets are men who have wronged her. Or have they? And why is she keeping count?

DCI Cook and his team finally know who she is, but not before she's murdered four men. The whole team are looking for her, but the woman keeps disappearing in plain sight. The pressure's on to stop her, but she's always one step ahead.

And this time, DCS Goddard can't protect his protégé, Isaac Cook, from the wrath of the new commissioner at the Met.

Murder in Little Venice – A DCI Cook Thriller – Book 4

A dismembered corpse floats in the canal in Little Venice, an upmarket tourist haven in London. Its identity is unknown, but what is its significance?

DCI Isaac Cook is baffled about why it's there. Is it gang-related, or is it something more?

Whatever the reason, it's clearly a warning, and Isaac and his team are sure it's not the last body that they'll have to deal with.

Murder is the Only Option – A DCI Cook Thriller – Book 5

A man thought to be long dead returns to exact revenge against those who had blighted his life. His only concern is to protect his wife and daughter. He will stop at nothing to achieve his aim.

'Big Greg, I never expected to see you around here at this time of night.'

'I've told you enough times.'

'I've no idea what you're talking about,' Robertson replied. He looked up at the man, only to see a metal pole coming down at him. Robertson fell down, cracking his head against a concrete kerb.

Two vagrants, no more than twenty feet away, did not stir and did not even look in the direction of the noise. If they had, they would have seen a dead body, another man walking away.

Murder in Notting Hill – A DCI Cook Thriller – Book 6

One murderer, two bodies, two locations, and the murders have been committed within an hour of each other.

They're separated by a couple of miles, and neither woman has anything in common with the other. One is young and wealthy, the daughter of a famous man; the other is poor, hardworking and unknown.

Isaac Cook and his team at Challis Street Police Station are baffled about why they've been killed. There must be a connection, but what is it?

Murder in Room 346 – A DCI Cook Thriller – Book 7

'Coitus interruptus, that's what it is,' Detective Chief Inspector Isaac Cook said. On the bed, in a downmarket hotel in Bayswater, lay the naked bodies of a man and a woman.

'Bullet in the head's not the way to go,' Larry Hill, Isaac Cook's detective inspector, said. He had not expected such a flippant comment from his senior, not when they were standing near to two people who had, apparently in the final throes of passion, succumbed to what appeared to be a professional assassination.

'You know this will be all over the media within the hour,' Isaac said.

'James Holden, moral crusader, a proponent of the sanctity of the marital bed, man and wife. It's bound to be.'

Murder of a Silent Man – A DCI Cook Thriller – Book 8

A murdered recluse. A property empire. A disinherited family. All the ingredients for murder.

No one gave much credence to the man when he was alive. In fact, most people never knew who he was, although those who had lived in the area for many years recognised the tired-looking and shabbily-dressed man as he shuffled along, regular as clockwork on a Thursday afternoon at seven in the evening to the local off-licence.

It was always the same: a bottle of whisky, premium brand, and a packet of cigarettes. He paid his money over the counter, took hold of his plastic bag containing his purchases, and then walked back down the road with the same rhythmic shuffle. He said not one word to anyone on the street or in the shop.

Murder has no Guilt – A DCI Cook Thriller – Book 9

No one knows who the target was or why, but there are eight dead. The men seem the most likely perpetrators, or could have it been one of the two women, the attractive Gillian Dickenson, or even the celebrity-obsessed Sal Maynard?

There's a gang war brewing, and if there are deaths, it doesn't matter to them as long as it's not their death. But to Detective Chief Inspector Isaac Cook, it's his area of London, and it does matter.

It's dirty and unpredictable. Initially it had been the West Indian gangs, but then a more vicious Romanian gangster had usurped them. And now he's being marginalised by the Russians. And the leader of the most vicious Russian mafia organisation is in London, and he's got money and influence, the ear of those in power.

Murder in Hyde Park – A DCI Cook Thriller – Book 10

An early morning jogger is murdered in Hyde Park. It's the centre of London, but no one saw him enter the park, no one saw him die.

He carries no identification, only a water-logged phone. As the pieces unravel, it's clear that the dead man had a history of deception.

Is the murderer one of those that loved him? Or was it someone with a vengeance?

It's proving difficult for DCI Isaac Cook and his team at Challis Street Homicide to find the guilty person – not that they'll cease to search for the truth, not even after one suspect confesses.

Six Years Too Late – A DCI Cook Thriller – Book 11

Always the same questions for Detective Chief Inspector Isaac Cook — Why was Marcus Matthews in that room? And why did he share a bottle of wine with his killer?

It wasn't as if the man had amounted to much in life, apart from the fact that he was the son-in-law of a notorious gangster, the father of the man's grandchildren. Yet, one thing that Hamish McIntyre, feared in London for his violence, rated above anything else, it was his family, especially Samantha, his daughter; although he had never cared for Marcus, her husband.

And then Marcus disappears, only for his body to be found six years later by a couple of young boys who decide that exploring an abandoned house is preferable to school.

Murder Without Reason – A DCI Cook Thriller – Book 12

DCI Cook faces his greatest challenge. The Islamic State is waging war in England, and they are winning.

Not only does Isaac Cook have to contend with finding the perpetrators, but he is also being forced to commit actions contrary to his mandate as a police officer.

And then there is Anne Argento, the prime minister's deputy. The prime minister has shown himself to be a pacifist and is not up to the task. She needs to take his job if the country is to fight back against the Islamists.

Vane and Martin have provided the solution. Will DCI Cook and Anne Argento be willing to follow it through? Are they able to act for the good of England, knowing that a criminal and murderous action is about to take place? Do they have an option?

Standalone Novels

The Haberman Virus

A remote and isolated village in the Hindu Kush
mountain range in North Eastern Afghanistan is wiped
out by a virus unlike any seen before.

A mysterious visitor clad in a spacesuit checks his
handiwork, a female American doctor succumbs to the
disease, and the woman sent to trap the person
responsible falls in love with him – the man who would
cause the deaths of millions.

Hostage of Islam

Three are to die at the Mission in Nigeria: the pastor and
his wife in a blazing chapel; another gunned down while
trying to defend them from the Islamist fighters.

Kate McDonald, an American, grieving over her
boyfriend's death and Helen Campbell, whose life had
been troubled by drugs and prostitution, are taken by the
attackers.

Kate is sold to a slave trader who intends to sell her
virginity to an Arab Prince. Helen, to ensure their
survival, gives herself to the murderer of her friends.

Malika's Revenge

Malika, a drug-addicted prostitute, waits in a smugglers'
village for the next Afghan tribesman or Tajik gangster to
pay her price, a few scraps of heroin.

Yusup Baroyev, a drug lord, enjoys a lifestyle many would
envy. An Afghan warlord sees the resurgence of the

Taliban. A Russian white-collar criminal portrays himself as a good and honest citizen in Moscow.

All of them are linked to an audacious plan to increase the quantity of heroin shipped out of Afghanistan and into Russia and ultimately the West.

Some will succeed, some will die, some will be rescued from their plight and others will rue the day they became involved.

Prelude to War

Russia and America face each other across the northern border of Afghanistan. World War 3 is about to break out and no one is backing off.

And all because a team of academics in New York postulated how to extract the vast untapped mineral wealth of Afghanistan.

Steve Case is in the middle of it, and his position is looking very precarious. Will the Taliban find him before the Americans get him out? Or is he doomed, as is the rest of the world?

ABOUT THE AUTHOR

Phillip Strang was born in England in the late forties. He was an avid reader of science fiction in his teenage years: Isaac Asimov, Frank Herbert, the masters of the genre. Still an avid reader, the author now mainly reads thrillers.

In his early twenties, the author, with a degree in electronics engineering and a desire to see the world, left England for Sydney, Australia. Now, forty years later, he still resides in Australia, although many intervening years were spent in a myriad of countries, some calm and safe, others no more than war zones.

Made in the USA
Columbia, SC
30 April 2020